CW00506804

A Burden Shared:
The Dundee Murders

Malcolm Archibald

© Malcolm Archibald 2013

The author asserts the moral right to be identified as the author of the work in accordance with the Copyright, Designs and Patents Act, 1988.

All characters appearing in this work are fictitious. Any resemblance to real persons, living or dead, is purely coincidental.

All rights reserved. No part of this publication may be reproduced, stored in a retrieval system or transmitted in any form or by any means, electronic, mechanical, photocopying, recording or otherwise, without the prior permission of

Fledgling Press Ltd,

7 Lennox St., Edinburgh, EH4 1QB

Published by Fledgling Press, 2013

www.fledglingpress.co.uk

Printed and bound by:

Latimer Trend, Plymouth

ISBN: 9781905916597

Following his adventures in *The Darkest Walk*,
Detective Mendick returns in this, the second of
the Mendick Mysteries.

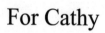

For Cathy

Acknowledgements

I would like to thank Iain Flett and staff of Dundee Archives for their help in searching through the police records, the staff at the Central Library Dundee for their patience while I read through hundreds of Victorian newspapers and Rhona Rodger and Fiona Sinclair of Dundee Museums and Art Galleries for allowing me to sift through the whaling journals in Barrack Street. Also, I would like to thank Clare Cain of Fledgling for her incredible patience in editing this book.

PROLOGUE:
DUNDEE, Autumn 1827

"Get up there, you little dog, and get it swept."

The voice echoed in the choking darkness, distorted by the surrounding brickwork but still containing enough menace to make Jamie shiver. He looked upward to where the flue ascended forever, the sides black and slippery with soot and the exit a tiny circle of light diminished by distance.

"Move you bugger! Or it will be the worse for you."

Aware the threat was genuine Jamie continued the climb, coughed as the soot entered his throat and tried not to sneeze as particles irritated his nostrils. Soot had smoothed the inside of the flue so he had to scramble for hand and footholds. He brushed continuously as he did so, for if the fall of soot lessened his master would take it ill. His master was not a man to cross. His voice boomed up the flue, echoing horribly as it always did, and Jamie inched upward, sweeping, pushing the soot before him with his cap and blinking the soot from his eyes. He did not cry: he had stopped crying years ago. Tears only invited blows.

He had been a climbing boy since his father had died of fever and his mother had signed him onto a seven year apprentice. He knew nothing else but he knew life was a nightmare of misery, pain and work. He hated the restriction; he hated the dark; he hated the rough, bullying voice of his burly master; he hated the smell of soot nearly as much as he hated the smell of drink on his master's breath that was an invariable precursor to unremitting violence. He had been so young when his mother signed the articles of apprenticeship he had all but forgotten his earlier life: his world was restricted to the circumference of a flue, the exhausted slumber of end-of-work and the cringing acceptance of his master's belt.

"Faster you wee bastard! There are two more to go after this one."

There were always more to go. There was always more work, always more sweat and more pain and always the gnawing agony of hunger in his shrivelled belly.

Jamie braced himself with his back against one side of the flue and his feet on the other and brushed into the tiny wedges between the brick. He blinked against the renewed clouds of soot; felt for the tiny hand and footholds and inched up. The circle of daylight seemed to recede even though the desperate darkness beneath him increased. His master delighted in telling him about climbing boys dying up these chimneys; losing their footing and sliding downward, screaming to a crashing death on the grate far below. The lucky died at once; the less lucky survived in mangled agony and lived the remainder of their miserable lives as broken cripples. Other boys had vanished in a maze of flues in some old building or were trapped in a restricted space to die of thirst and terror in the dark.

Jamie gasped as an intense heat beat upon the soles of his feet. He looked down, coughed in the spiralling smoke and knew at once what had happened. His master had placed a pile of straw on the grate and set light to it. The heat was only a taste of what to expect, a warning that the fire would be lit now to urge him to greater endeavour. Never a patient man, the master would brook no excuses. Jamie began to brush even more furiously and shoved his skinny body upward at a greater rate.

He felt his feet slip but clung on with broken nails, he whimpered as the smoking vacuum beneath invited him to fall, but slammed his knees against the brick and moved upward. He gasped as the orange glow beneath him increased and the heat came in waves against his bare feet and legs. He reached up, but too quickly, and his fingers slid on a soot-smoothed shelf so he slithered and had to push flat hands against the brickwork opposite. His brush fell, bouncing once, twice, three times from the walls of the flue, to clatter into the fire below and sent biting sparks against the legs of his Master.

"You clumsy wee bastard! Come down here and get your brush, and take what's coming to you!" The flue hideously deformed the word and intensified the menace and Jamie knew too well what would happen when he returned. He had experienced his Master's rage too often; the whirring belt and the plunging fists and boots until he was reduced to a cringing broken, wreck as his Master leaned over him, panting, with his broad red face dripping with sweat and his mouth open.

Reinforced by a score of memories, the fear overwhelmed him. Jamie looked downward, listened to his Master's repetitive curses and knew what was going to happen, and then he began to claw his way upward. He had no plan and no real idea what he was doing; he only wanted to get as far away as possible from his Master and the agonising brutality that was the inevitable result of dropping the brush. The flue narrowed as he climbed, so the sides were scraping against his shoulders and hips, but still he pushed on. He gasped; sobbed as the rough bricks rubbed him raw, tore away the skin of elbows and knees, rubbing the flesh from shoulders and hips and buttocks as he strove to escape.

"Where the devil are you, Jamie?" The voice thundered through the dark tunnel of the flue, battering against his ears. "Get down here, you little bastard!"

The circle of light was like a beacon, a lighthouse in the turmoil of darkness and fear. Feeling his breath rasp in his throat and the soot clog his nostrils and eyes, Jamie edged himself up, reaching for the tiniest of holds as he strained for escape. He felt the downdraught cooling his face and knew he was within a few yards of freedom, and then he stuck. As he neared the top, the chimney abruptly narrowed so even his underfed body could not wriggle through.

Fresh air tantalised his face but he was trapped. The sweep's cap on his head had pushed the soot ahead of him so now it had constricted even the small space of this flue. For a moment Jamie gave way to frustration as he struggled with the weight of compressed soot above him. He wrestled himself an extra inch and screamed as the sharp bricks scraped skin and flesh from his hips. "I'm not going back," he said, repeating the words like a mantra, "I'm never going back."

He strained, moaning with effort as he pushed hard with his cap. Tears had coursed white lines down his face before he felt the mass above him give. He shifted slightly and a black avalanche of soot descended on his face and cascaded down his naked body. He felt the ripping agony of unyielding brick slashing deep into his skin, but he knew there was hope and pushed himself the final few feet upward.

His Master's voice was far below him, half-heard and wholly unheeded now. All that mattered was easing out of the chimney and escaping along the roof. He could not see beyond that; he thought only of escape. Next week, tomorrow, the next hour; none of that mattered. The panic that drove him recognised only his need to run from the immediate threat; the future was irrelevant.

Jamie's hand waved in the air, and then his arm; he moaned at the agony of torn flesh but hauled himself upward, feeling the bricks shred the skin from his hips and ankles but he was free. He ripped off his cap, threw it back down the flue and allowed the cool air to dry the sweat from his body. He leaned over the chimney, feeling the first surge of triumph he could ever remember experiencing. It was a sensation he savoured, unfamiliar but so welcome that he shouted an incoherent animal cry of victory. He looked around. He had expected to see the familiar sight of a roofscape, but instead he was on top of a tall factory chimney. The chimney stretched downward, thirty, forty, maybe fifty feet of vertical brick with a keen wind already raising goose pimples on his unprotected skin and ruffling the filthy, lice-ridden tangle of his black hair. For a long time Jamie sat on the rim of the chimney, unsure of what to do. He knew he had two choices; he could return the way he came and face his Master, or climb down the outside of the chimney.

When he closed his eyes a vision of his Master returned; the bulging eyes and foul breath, the sagging jowls, the ever-ready fists. The decision was made, he looked down the stalk of the chimney, if he fell he would die; but better a quick death than the constant torment of life. Jamie inhaled the crisp air, turned around, and lowered himself downward. He held onto the rim for a minute, aware that once he released his hold he would be unable to return, and then took a deep breath and felt for the first foothold.

For years he had been used to climbing in enclosed spaces with a hard surface on which he could lean back, but here there was nothing. The space behind him beckoned with sucking tenderness, inviting him to fall, encouraging him with the appeal of freedom, the subtle siren call of nothingness and peace, but he resisted. The chimney was just an inverted flue; a problem to be overcome. He could not think what lay beyond; the next hour was a distant country, tomorrow was unthinkable, only the next handhold mattered, the next inch of red-brick chimney to negotiate, the next level to clamber down.

There was no end to this circular monstrosity, life was reduced to fighting the chill wind that threatened to pluck at him, to fighting the pain in his fingers and toes, to surviving another minute, another second, another breath as he eased down. He knew he was trembling, he knew he could not last another single level of unending brick; he must surrender to the pain and fall into the peace of oblivion. And then there was a different sensation, a roof of sliding blue slate, and he sagged down in disbelief.

He had made it; he had survived and now all he had to do was shin down one of the cast-iron waterspouts to the ground and run as far away as possible from the Master. Run and run and run until the breath rasped in his chest and his throat burned from heaving in air that tasted rich and sweet after the smoke-choked thickness of the flues. He was free, he had survived. Never again would he look upward in fear as the black confines of the chimney dragged him in, never again would he cringe before the rage of his Master; never again would he listen with dread for his Master's dragging footsteps.

He was hungry. The realisation dawned slowly. Hunger was nothing; many master sweeps starved their apprentices so they did not put on weight and remained undersized and scrawny for negotiating the constricted spaces within the flues, but now something was different. Jamie frowned as he explored his novel position until he found an answer. Yes, he was hungry and he could do something about it.

Glancing upward, he judged the time by the sun. Nearly evening and late summer, so there would be fruit in the gardens. He had seen fruit many times on the servant's tables in the houses of the wealthy, and he had even eaten it once or twice, if a kindly cook had taken pity on him, or he had sneaked an apple when nobody was looking. Now he could see an apple tree beyond a high wall, with the fruit hanging heavy on the branches, inviting him to help himself. The concept of theft was as unknown to him as possession and kindness; he had never owned anything and never expected to.

It was the work of a second to climb the wall; another moment saw him scramble along a branch and then he sat astride a bough with his bare legs swinging on either side as he munched into the sweetest apple he had ever tasted.

"Hi! Get out of that!" The challenge was as rough as it was unexpected, and Jamie almost fell from the tree in surprise. He looked down to see a tall man waving a fist at him, but before the man could speak again Jamie had scrambled higher up the tree and was racing along an overhanging branch. It was nothing to reach the edge, balance for a second and drop to the ground ten feet below. He rolled as he landed, picked himself up and continued to chew on the apple as he loped along, relishing this new freedom.

He did not think what to do, he moved instinctively as he explored the town of Dundee. He had lived here all his life but knew it only as a place of work and oppression. Now he could see the opportunities, the shops with displays tempting nimble fingers, the windows not quite closed through which he could squeeze, the gentlemen with silk handkerchiefs and silver watches placed carelessly for any slender hand to slide away with.

Yet Jamie ignored these sweet temptations and wandered down to the docks. He did not know how often he had dreamed of running away to sea, of tasting the freedom of these beautiful vessels that sailed to strange places. He did not know to where they sailed, he only knew there would not be any chimneys there, or masters with hectoring voices and ready fists. Now he heard the call of the seagulls and smelled the strangely exciting aroma of tar and damp canvas and whatever cargoes these vessels carried.

The first vessel was a passenger ferry so no good to him; he did not want to slog back and forth to Fife. The second was a recently returned whaler, reeking of blubber and battered by ice and gales. The third was larger, with three tall masts and the figurehead of a Highland warrior. He sneaked on board, slipped under the first hatch cover he saw and finished his apple.

He felt the sudden cold blast before he realised he had been sleeping, but the face that stared at him was more perplexed than angry, and the hand that lifted him was gentler than his master had ever been.

"Now what do we have here? A young stowaway."

Other men joined the first, hard of face but without the predatory cruelty he had come to recognise so well.

"A naked young stowaway," Jamie's experience with people was limited, but he knew enough to avoid this man, his eyes were too interested.

"What's your name, boy?" The first man pushed the second aside.

"Jamie."

"Jamie what?" The first man asked. "What's your last name?"

Jamie thought for a long time; he did not think he had a last name. He had always been Jamie. He looked up.

"Wee bastard." It was the only name he knew.

"Poor wee bugger," one of the men said. "Look at the colour of him. He's either a runaway climbing boy or a beggar." He bent closer, his scarred face concerned. "You don't know your name, do you?"

Jamie shook his head.

"Well then, I'll give you one. You're a mendicant, I guess, so you can be Jamie Mendicant. No . . . that's too long; not Mendicant, Mendick. That's your name now and forever more." The man straightened up. "Well, James Mendick, you and I and everybody else on this ship are bound for the Indies, so you'd better bid farewell to Dundee and prepare yourself for hard work."

When James Mendick looked over the taffrail he could see the town of his birth and childhood already fading behind a pall of its own smoke. He felt no emotion when the ship dipped her foremast to the incoming waves and slid clear of the Firth of Tay.

CHAPTER ONE
DUNDEE, SCOTLAND 23 March 1849

Fluttering bravely in a fitful easterly wind, the red and white house flag proclaimed that the Dundee, Perth and London Shipping Line steamer was back home in the Tay. Detective Sergeant Mendick of Scotland Yard watched the smuts trail astern, fought the slow sinking sickness in his stomach, struck a Lucifer match and puffed his pipe to life. He stared at the passengers who milled at the rail, listened to their excited chatter and contemplated his immediate future.

He was returning to Dundee, God help him. He was returning to the only place on earth that frightened him. He had experienced the humid heat of India and the alien cultures of China; he had survived tropical typhoons that could raise waves sixty feet high, Baltic ice so thick it imprisoned a whole fleet of ships and the results of battle and siege. None of these had scarred him as Dundee had. Only the death of Emma, his wife had left a deeper impression.

Mendick did not smile as he watched the passengers stare at their surroundings or huddle into their cloaks as if doomed to exile. He felt like an exile himself: exiled to return to the place of his birth. He watched as Dundee loomed up on the north bank of the Tay, a town of slender mill chimneys penetrating an eternal pall of smoke, of mud-coloured tenements and of a harbour crowded with shipping. Above all was the Law, rising

1

over five hundred feet of rock, grass, and woodland to dominate the town.

He remembered his childhood thoughts of the Law as a watchful mother caring for her teeming children. Mendick snorted; he left her by sea, and now he was returning the same way. He would not stay long; he could not stay long, he must leave by the next tide. He had no desire to confront his past; he wanted to forget it, together with the nightmares that sometimes surfaced from his sleep.

Even as he struggled to avoid the plunge into dismal memories, Mendick eyed the crowd, sorting them into their various categories and unconsciously searching for criminals. After the voyage from London he knew they were a heterogeneous bunch: tradesmen and businessmen, a few genuine travellers, a peddler or two, a sprinkling of families and a couple of gentlemen who filled the first class cabins. He grunted as he saw two undoubted pickpockets hovering on the fringes, their half-furtive swagger typical of their type and their youthful faces lean and predatory. Mendick searched his memory and nodded; he knew their names and most of their criminal history.

Seeking one of the benches that lined the upper deck, Mendick sat, placed his cane between his knees, folded his arms and tipped his hat forward over his face as though trying to sleep. It was a trick he had picked up years ago: a man sitting down was far less conspicuous than one standing, and he could observe while being overlooked. The pickpockets were working together, each moving either side of a large but flustered-looking gentleman in a morning coat. Mendick sighed, rose and stepped forward, swinging his cane. As always when

Mendick was working, one or two of the not-quite-respectable guessed what he was and moved away, but the less guilty, or those who had not yet been detected in their crimes, remained static. He raised his voice slightly and allowed the authority to creep through.

"Move aside, there!"

Although the pickpockets had closed with their target, the large man seemed completely unaware he was a gull. While one lithe youth engaged him in conversation the other slithered at his left arm, nimble fingers ready for the quick dip. Mendick lifted the rattan and struck left and right, delivering a stinging cut to the shoulders of each youth.

"Jesus!" The nearest youth gasped at the unexpected pain. He swung around, snarling, but stopped at the sight of Mendick's steady stare.

"Be off with you!" Mendick balanced his cane over his right shoulder and jerked his head in the direction he intended the pickpockets to go.

With a sneering glance at their intended victim, the youths slid along the deck, mouthing unheard obscenities over thin shoulders as they rubbed their injuries.

"Good God!" The intended victim adjusted his spectacles and stared at Mendick through pale, startled eyes, "What on earth was that all about? That young fellow was merely enquiring the correct time, sir!"

"That young fellow, as you call him, was distracting you, sir, so his companion could lift your pocket-book," Mendick told him. "I am Sergeant Mendick from Scotland Yard. Those rascals were Robert Mitchell and Peter Smith – they are old lags, sir, and well known to the police courts . . . don't check your pockets, sir, they will still be watching . . ."

"Good God," the man repeated and immediately produced a fat pocket-book from the depths of his coat. "Well, I am very much obliged to you, Sergeant Mendick, very much." Opening the pocket-book so the whole ship could see the contents, he fished out his card and handed it over. "My name is Leslie, sir, Adam Leslie, and I am a merchant in general goods and crockery."

Mendick glanced at the card:

Adam J. Leslie:
Crockery dealer and general merchant;
Reform Street, Dundee.

He placed it in his inside pocket. "Thank you, Mr Leslie. If either of these young blackguards should come close again, pray do not hesitate to call on me." Mendick prepared to return to his seat, but Leslie clung to his sleeve, flinching as the crowd surged to the rail. Men and women waved greetings to Dundee as if they had been at sea for months rather than days.

"If these boys are pickpockets, should you not arrest them?"

"I cannot arrest them on suspicion that they may commit a crime sir, but I will alert the local police to their presence the moment I step ashore in Dundee."

Leslie pulled at Mendick's sleeve, his eyes wide. "Does Scotland Yard appoint a detective to watch for pickpockets on every London boat? I rarely travel by boat, you understand. My son, my stepson rather, died at sea so I prefer the coach or the railway, but London is so very far away."

Mendick shook his head. "No sir. I am afraid Scotland Yard do not appoint a detective on any boat. I am going

4

to Dundee on quite another matter. I am sorry to hear about your stepson, sir; you have my condolences."

"But sir . . ." Leslie retained his hold of Mendick's sleeve and followed him, his heavy steps thundering on the deck. "You must be off-duty, then. You had no need to help. I really am most grateful to you."

"You have no need to be grateful, sir, I assure you. It is my constant charge to prevent crime and catch criminals wherever and whenever I can." Mendick touched his hand to the brim of his hat, "Now, if you will forgive me sir? I must prepare to disembark. You be heedful of such people in the future." Mendick removed Leslie's hand and sauntered along the deck in the wake of the two pickpockets. It had been a small episode, nothing of importance, but it served as a reminder that he was not the small boy who had left Dundee, but an experienced police officer. If he kept that in his mind he could face Dundee with more equanimity. He straightened his coat, swung his cane through the air and nearly whistled, but that was bad luck on board a ship, so contented himself with poking the weighted end of his cane into the back of Mitchell. "I am watching you, my lad!"

London eased into Dundee docks and Mendick stepped ashore; his feet sounded like the sonorous drumbeat of hell on the quay. He was back in Dundee but not for long. Please God, not for long. As if on order, the rain started.

Dundee police headquarters squatted morosely in West Bell Street, slightly to the north of the town centre. It was not an unlovely building, but to Mendick it still appeared as grim and unprepossessing as the prison next door. He stood outside for a moment, watching the coming and goings of the uniformed police as he tried to get the measure of the place and the people. One officer stopped, doffed his hat and reached out to touch the square pillars that framed the entrance. Raindrops collected on the scar disfiguring the man's face, then ran down from his forehead to drip from his chin. The officer mouthed something, replaced his hat and vanished inside; Mendick tapped his cane on the ground and followed.

The duty officer carefully closed his book and looked up. He saw what seemed like a civilian thrust through the door, remove his hat and stand just inside the entrance. Water eased from his coat onto his glossy boots.

"Here's another one." The duty officer did not try to hide the contempt in his voice. "A so-called gentleman, I wager, enticed into a disorderly house by a girl and relieved of his wallet."

The office Sergeant, grey-haired and running to fat, grunted, "I doubt he's a gentleman, Sturrock. Not with that stance. See those shoulders? Erect as a guardsman, and his left thumb is in line with the seam of his trousers. Ex-ranker in the military or he's a Frenchman."

"He could be an officer," Sturrock guessed. "That would make him a gentleman."

"An officer has private means," the Office Sergeant said, "but no gentleman would entertain a cheap one shilling hat like that. He is no officer and no gentleman. Look at his face, he has seen more life than a man of his age should have."

Sturrock grunted. "If he is ex-military, he should have had more sense than to listen to one of those sirens."

The sergeant grinned. "Few men have sense where women are concerned, son. As soon as a woman shows a hint of ankle, all sense flies out of the window. You'll

6

learn that in time. Now, look at this fellow: about five foot nine, maybe 32, 33, maybe 35 years old? Yes? Now observe the way he's dressed. He's not dressed like a soldier," the sergeant nodded across the room. "That's a fine Chesterfield coat he's wearing so he either stole it or he has aspirations to something better than a mill hand or cab driver; his boots are polished to a glitter, so he has pride in himself, and see the way he carries that cane? A sign of some authority. A corporal at least, I would say."

The sergeant watched, intrigued, as Mendick continued to stand just within the doorway, tapping his cane against the side of his boot as he inspected every inch of the office. "Now you think on, Sturrock," the sergeant said, "and we'll see how right I am."

Mendick stepped to the desk, nodded to Sturrock and addressed the sergeant.

"Good afternoon. I am expected." He reached inside his Chesterfield and produced an official staff, adorned with the Crown and VR. "The name is Mendick, Sergeant Mendick, Criminal Officer of Scotland Yard. I am here to collect a prisoner and take him back to London."

"Ah, Sergeant Mendick," the sergeant glanced at Sturrock. "We have your man all tucked up nice and secure."

Mendick replaced the staff in its inside pocket and tapped his cane on the desk. "No sense wasting time then. Take me to him, Sergeant."

"You surely have time for a mug of tea, Mendick?"

Mendick shook his head. "I have neither time nor desire to linger, Sergeant. I stepped off the DLP steamer London a bare half an hour ago and I have tickets for the DPL ship Perth to London; she leaves on the next tide. Pray take me to the prisoner."

The sergeant glanced at Sturrock. "Definitely a military snap there!" He nodded to Mendick. "Come this way if you please."

The cells smelled exactly the same as police cells did in London or Manchester and probably anywhere else in the world; the same mix of urine, sweat and human misery, and the inhabitants held the same expressions of fear, desperate defiance or hopeless, broken passivity. The last of the night's drunks lay hollow-eyed and supine, waiting for their summons to the Police Court and the inevitable petty fine they could not afford. One man was singing, badly off-key.

"Stop that horrible noise!" The sergeant shouted. He swaggered to the end cell, swinging his keys as the sound of his boots echoed around the short corridor.

"This is your man, Mendick. Jeremy Thatcher. Swindler, coiner and thief."

The cover of the peephole scraped slightly as Mendick opened it and peered into the cell then took a sheet of paper from his inside pocket and compared the description written on it with the man in front of him. He was looking for a man of small stature, shabbily dressed and with the marks of smallpox on his face.

"That's my man," he confirmed. Thatcher huddled on the plank bed, shackles around his ankles and his wrists clamped in handcuffs. One eye was badly bruised and his jaw was swollen. "You have him well secured."

"He has to be," the office sergeant said. "He's tried to escape three times already. This is a devious and spunky man."

Mendick slid the peephole shut. "How did you apprehend him?"

"He tried to pass a false bank note in an Overgate

pub," the sergeant said. "Two of our constables had to rescue him when the locals found out." He grinned, "It was probably the first time he was pleased to see a policeman in his life."

"You did well, catching him," Mendick gave grudging praise. "He's been convicted of forgery and sentenced to 14 years transportation, but he escaped from the courthouse right after the trial." He re-checked the cell. "I've been chasing him ever since, the length and breadth of the country."

"Well, here he is." The sergeant fitted the key into the lock and turned. Mendick pushed open the door.

Thatcher glanced up from the plank bed, met Mendick's eye and looked away quickly. Mendick studied him, tapping his cane against his leg. "I hope you are fit to travel, Thatcher. You're going on a long trip."

Thatcher said nothing; the chains rattled as he shifted his feet.

Mendick rapped the chains with his cane. "Up you get."

Thatcher lifted his manacled hands as if for help, but Mendick left him to it. He watched as Thatcher clattered from the bed and shuffled across the stone-flagged floor. The office Sergeant led the way upstairs, with Mendick making up the rear and the prisoner in between.

"You will have to sign him out," the sergeant said.

"Of course." As Mendick dipped the wooden pen in the inkwell, he was aware of the great front door opening. Two agitated men in civilian clothes stumbled in, but when they nodded to Constable Sturrock Mendick realised they must be off-duty police or Dundee criminal officers. Both men began to talk at once. Mendick ignored them and concentrated on the matter in hand. He wanted to complete his business as quickly as possible and get back home.

There were a number of forms to fill in and sign. Mendick wrote rapidly with the clumsy pen, dipping into the inkwell and blowing the words dry. He checked what he had written, lifted his copies of the release documents and put his hand on Thatcher's shoulder. "Right, lad, you're my prisoner now and it's Van Diemen's Land for you."

Thatcher said nothing and kept his shoulders hunched as he shuffled towards the door. He looked up with his left eye partially closed, and spoke thickly through his damaged mouth.

"Can I have these slackened, please Mr Mendick?" He raised his arms high. They looked so thin Mendick wondered how he had the strength to bear the weight of the chains.

"No. Wait here and keep your mouth closed." As Mendick nodded a farewell to the sergeant, two uniformed policemen crashed in, each holding a struggling man. One constable was hatless, the other bleeding from a cut lip while their prisoners were kicking furiously and shouting. A group of women crowded behind in a flurry of skirts and a volley of screeching abuse as they waved their hands aloft. A waft of stale whisky accompanied each word.

"You damned blackguard!" One woman pointed a furious finger at the hatless policeman, "You let my man go!"

When the constable ignored her, the woman swung her fist, sending him off balance, and pushed him in the chest. The policeman sprawled to the ground and his prisoner lunged for freedom, dived under the outstretched arm of the second constable and yanked open the door of the police office.

"Stop right there!" Mendick reached for the escaping prisoner but two of the women dived in his way, screaming language that would embarrass any hardened marine. He barged into them, lost his hat and momentarily wrestled with a woman whose arms were muscularly defined by long hours of mill labour. In that split-second Thatcher took his chance. He raised his arms to his mouth, pushed a sliver of metal through his teeth, opened the catch of his manacles and let them drop to the floor.

Mendick heard the clatter even through the drunken racket. He clamped the woman in a headlock just as Thatcher transferred the tiny picklock to his hand, bent down, opened the leg irons and pulled them apart.

"Hey you!" One of the worried-looking plain-clothed officers stepped forward, but Thatcher lifted the irons, swung them like a club and caught the man across the mouth. The officer yelled and covered his face as the second criminal officer grabbed at Thatcher's arms. Thatcher ducked low and swung a second time so the heavy manacles caught him around the legs, wrapped around like a bolas and brought him to the ground in a tangle of limbs and chains.

"Enough of that!" Sturrock stepped clear of the desk and came to help, his ginger hair a beacon in the drab room.

"Don't do it, Thatcher!" Mendick released the woman and jumped over the writhing body of the second Criminal Officer, but Thatcher had slipped through the crowd and dodged into the grumbling traffic of Bell

11

Street. Mendick pushed back into the screaming mob obstructing the door of the Police Office and one filthy hand grabbed at the sleeve of his coat while another clutched his throat.

"You near broke my neck," the muscular woman yelled. "Bluebottle bastard!"

Mendick raked his boot down her shin so she squealed and snatched back her hand, shook his sleeve free from the second woman and pushed clear, but two more women leaped at him. He thrust the tip of his cane into the throat of the closest and swung it against the hip of the next to send her yelping away. He looked up in time to see Thatcher disappearing down Constitution Brae, a street that sloped steeply towards the congestion of the town centre. Carts growled over the cobbles as their drivers ignored the drama. Mendick sprinted over the road, bounced off the back of a laden cart, dodged the clattering hooves of a cab-driver's horse and ran around the corner.

"Thatcher! Don't be a fool!"

He could see Thatcher running full pelt for the massed houses of central Dundee. Constitution Brae descended to Barrack Street, opposite which was the walled and gated cemetery of the Howff. Beyond Barrack Street began the heaped buildings, the intricate closes and the narrow wynds of the Overgate, in which any fugitive could vanish for hours or days before the police winkled him out. Mendick glanced right and left, hoping for a glimpse of the friendly blue of a police uniform, but saw only the slow trundle of traffic on the road and a group of masons working around spindly scaffolding. Thatcher was ahead, running as if the devil was at his heels rather than a single detective.

"Stop! Thief!" Mendick roared the old, familiar words, and saw the masons look around. One spotted the small figure of Thatcher, lifted one of the long wooden scaffolding poles and threw it into his path. Thatcher jumped and continued, but the pole bounced, its end rising just enough to clip his right ankle. He gave a shrill yell, hopped for three steps and continued, more slowly than before.

"Got you, my lad", Mendick said, but Thatcher did not hesitate. He ran, limping, up to the outside boundary wall of the Howff graveyard, pulled himself onto the three foot high wall and vaulted the iron railings.

Mendick followed, balanced on top of the railings and watched as Thatcher jinked between the ranked gravestones. The rain was heavier than ever, and the oncoming dusk did not help his visibility, but he could see the lithe body when it emerged from the cover of the grey, lichen-smeared stones.

"Have you caught him yet, Sergeant?" Sturrock puffed up behind him, red-faced with his staff held firmly in his right hand.

"Not yet, Sturrock, but I know where he is. Tell me, how many entrances are there to this graveyard?"

"Four. Two on the northern wall and two on the western." Sturrock came up with the information immediately. He peered between the railings. "I can't see him."

"Only four. Then it won't be difficult for you to watch them while I flush out this thief. You stand up here and shout if you see Thatcher move, and catch him when I chase him out."

"Yes, Sergeant, but I have to watch all four gates?" Sturrock sounded dismayed.

13

"Yes. Don't concern yourself with anything else and don't let him escape." Mendick jumped down and strode in the direction he last saw Thatcher. He made no pretence at hiding, instead announcing his advance by striking each gravestone with his cane. "I can see you, Thatcher. If you give yourself up it will be easier for you."

There was no reply except the hiss and patter of rain on the grass. Mendick strode on, following a gravel path and checking to left and right. At each step he expected to see Thatcher cowering behind a tombstone, but there was no sign of him. Just the ranked stones of the dead, one newly-made grave and one empty, waiting for its occupant.

"Sturrock!" Mendick turned and roared. "Have you seen him?"

"No, Sergeant." Sturrock remained on top of the railings. Mendick swore and began to work his way back through the gravestones, again checking to left and right. He stopped at the newly-dug grave and pushed his cane into the turf; it sunk easily into the damp soil. The empty grave showed promise too; Mendick looked inside. Rain water dripped down the mud of the walls and onto the black canvas tarpaulin six feet down, forming a succession of small, shallow pools but with a distinctive dry bulge in the centre. Mendick glanced up, Sturrock remained exactly where he had left him, balancing on the rails with the rain bouncing from his tall hat and his arms folded across his chest.

"You keep watch, Sturrock!" Mendick shouted and, balancing one hand on the edge of the grave, he vaulted down and landed heavily atop the suspicious bulge.

"No!" The canvas bucked beneath him and Thatcher

14

emerged. His hands scrabbled at the stiff canvas as he launched himself at the mud walls of the grave and scrambled up with hands and feet. Mendick waited until Thatcher had secured a handhold at the lip of the grave, then lifted his cane and landed a smart crack on each hand. Thatcher yelled and tumbled back down. He landed on his back and immediately jumped up, intent on escaping until Mendick pressed hard on his thin shoulders.

"Stay where you are," Mendick said, "and bend over!" As Thatcher glowered at him, Mendick thrust him into a crouch and used him as a stepping stone to climb out of the grave.

"Sturrock!" Mendick shouted, "Come here with your shangies." He pulled his watch from his waistcoat pocket and swore. "Damn you, Thatcher! We've missed our boat. Now I must stay an extra day in Dundee."

Thatcher looked up, rainwater streaming from his face and his eyes bright and defeated. He said nothing.

The voice that sounded behind Mendick had the hard lilt of the Highlands. "You may be in Dundee a good deal longer than one day, Sergeant Mendick."

Mendick turned around and faced the newcomer. Despite the rain he wore no coat above his close-fitting dark suit. His eyes were a cold blue above hectic red cheekbones.

"Indeed, sir?" Mendick kept a firm hold of Thatcher as he turned around. "I am afraid you are mistaken but thank you for your interest." He touched a hand to where his hat should have been, frowned slightly as he remembered its absence and returned his hand to his side.

The man placed his forefinger on Mendick's cane.

15

"That seems a handy tool, Sergeant, lead-tipped I would say?" He held Mendick's eye for a long moment. "Aye, I thought as much. You might have need of that during your stay in Dundee."

"I will be on the first steamer to London, sir, with my prisoner." Mendick said.

"I see I have not explained myself, Sergeant Mendick." The Highlander held Mendick's gaze. "I am Donald Mackay, Superintendent of Dundee Police. Both my Criminal Officers were injured in that riot in the Police Office and I have a most unpleasant murder to solve, so I am keeping you here for the present. I have already prepared the paperwork for your Inspector Field. Now," the blue eyes turned granite hard. "If you have finished playing in the mud, you may come with me and see if your Scotland Yard skills work in my town."

Mendick said nothing as he felt the weight of childhood horrors crushing him once more. Dundee would not allow him to escape.

CHAPTER TWO

What was it about murders that attracted bad weather? Mendick crammed his battered hat further down on his head, cursed as rain splattered onto his face, turned up the collar of his Chesterfield and glowered across the road. Even if the weather had been better, there would be nothing picturesque about the shop in Candle Lane. It was situated in a tenement building beside a foul-smelling fish curer, and opposite the piled timber of a wood merchant, but in the soot-laden rain of a March evening it was as dismal a picture as he could imagine. The sign above the door tried its best to entice customers but the cheap paint had peeled so the reader needed great patience to decipher the words.

Oriental Emporium: all the delights of the East

Mendick grunted. He knew all about the delights of the East: dirt, flies, disease and a thousand nameless horrors under a humid, pitiless sky. There was little Oriental about a seedy shop mouldering in the chill damp of a Dundee evening. The shop was about half way up the lane, with a common close to the right and two storeys of a stone-built tenement pressing down on it, the dark windows glaring onto the dark roadway like the black eyes of a failed pugilist. The door was firmly closed against the predators of the night. Mendick looked up into the steady rain – a broken waterspout spilled its contents into the lane and slates sliced upward to a stack of chimneys.

He pulled his silver watch from his fob and checked the time. Half past eight and he was stuck in this town that he hated beyond all others. It was already dark and the sub-human inhabitants were swarming out from wherever they hid during the day, turning the night hideous with their drunken bawling and assaults. This dockland area of Dundee was just like the back streets of Rotherhithe or Wapping; a festering warren of lanes and dead ends, streets crammed with pawnshops and dingy lodging houses. Candle Lane was a narrow, ancient thoroughfare that pointed towards the town centre as directly as a disembarked sailor heading for a pub.

Mendick looked around, seamen and befeathered women crammed the doorways and spilled onto the road. The women's skirts trailed along the granite cobbles and through the central channel that sluiced away the rainwater mingled with the droppings of passing horses, but their voices shouted raucous invitations and their eyes were bold and devoid of pity. Mendick looked away. He could see the masts and spars of ships just a short step away and he shivered. There were too many memories here, he had to concentrate on the job, solve this murder and get back to London. He could not stay long in Dundee.

"Is that how Scotland Yard operates?" Mackay did not sound impressed. "Up here we tend to look at the murder rather than admiring the scenery."

Mendick grunted. "Take me to the murder, then."

Two uniformed police stood sentinel at the shop entrance. Legs apart, heads erect and each holding the long staff that acted both as their prime method of deterrence and a badge of office, they looked as formal as guardsmen.

Mendick followed Mackay inside.

"There is a shop and a store room with living quarters," Mackay explained, "and both inner and outer doors were locked." Mendick touched the outside door: two panels had been smashed and the heavy iron bolts drawn back. The key was in the lock inside.

"So how did we find the body then?"

The familiar smell of damp, mould and decay wrapped around him, mingled with the throat-catching stench of raw blood and a surprising aroma of cooked meat. Mendick lingered just within the door. Smells could be very revealing sometimes, he had expected to smell spices in an Eastern Emporium, but there was little hint of them in here. The hissing gas jet cast flickering shadows around the interior.

Mendick looked around. The shop was filled with cheap Brummagem trash, with a few knick-knacks that were vaguely oriental and may have been brought back by seamen from the East, or possibly thrown up by an underpaid woman in some garret sweatshop. A shelf on the wall held a row of jars that carried vague labels: Indian Spice, Chinese Spice, Arabian Spice, Best quality Tea, Green Tea and Coffee. A quick inspection found a few pounds of tea or coffee, probably mixed with other less savoury substances while he had no idea what was in the spice jars and had no intention of finding out.

"Our two criminal officers suspected this place of being used to reset stolen goods," Mackay said quietly. "They came in to check and walked straight into a nightmare."

Mendick pointed to the broken exterior door and the interior door where one of the panels had also been obviously kicked in. "We tend to more subtle methods in London."

"Indeed," Mackay's voice was dry. "Well, step subtly through the door and see what you make of it, Mendick. But I warn you, it is not a pretty sight."

Mendick grunted. After his time in the army and his experiences in the rookeries of London he did not expect a small provincial town to have anything to shock him. "It never is, Mr Mackay, but I have seen dead bodies before."

"It's worse than anything you can imagine, Mendick. Take a deep breath first."

Mackay opened the door and Mendick stepped inside. A gas jet pooled faint light and dark shadows over a room obviously used for both living quarters and storage. There was a box bed hard against one wall together with a chest, a small table and a tall stool. Piles of poor quality clothing covered most of the remaining floor space. All this Mendick took in without conscious effort while he focussed on the object that lay on the floor.

He had thought nothing in Dundee could shock him. He had been wrong. On his first night back he was looking at something that made his stomach heave. He should have never returned to this town. He should have said no to Mr Mackay, caught the next packet boat to London and chanced any repercussions. Mendick tapped his cane off the table and stepped closer. During his police career he had seen a score of murders and hundreds of assaults, from Saturday night pub brawls to sordid domestic disputes, but he had seen nothing like this since he left the army, and not often then. Scattered over the floor were bits of a man, or perhaps more than one man; he could not be sure.

The body had been ripped open and the insides

removed. Heart, liver and kidneys, all were there, but so mangled they were almost unrecognisable. The limbs had been hacked from the torso and lay in a bloody heap, while the head had been chopped off and placed on a china plate a few feet away.

The entire mess lay in a wide puddle of blood, crusted and congealed in places, while the intestines had been uncoiled to form a roughly oval frame for the body parts. The scene would have been bad enough in silent daylight, but in this shaded room, with the gas jet providing a sinister, prevalent hiss, the shadows appeared to writhe with agonised memory.

"Oh, my eye." His army experiences had hardened Mendick to most things, but he had not expected to come across such butchery in Britain. "What sort of man could do this?"

"Nobody I want loose on the streets of Dundee," Mackay stood at the doorway, watching. He spoke sombrely, as befitted the scene of a death. "This man was not murdered, Mendick, he was mutilated. He was ripped apart as if by a pack of dogs. It's like a ritual killing."

Mendick nodded. "I have seen something similar, once before, outside Nanking, but this is Dundee not China."

"This was an Oriental Emporium, remember," Mackay said. He lowered his voice. "Some of my men have heard rumours of a Chinaman moving among the criminal class, so maybe there is a Chinese connection."

Mendick glanced at the severed head; the eyes were wide and the lips had been stitched closed. "Do we know the name of this unfortunate fellow?"

"This gentleman was David Thoms, the tenant of

this shop." Mackay looked at the remains without any expression on his face. "We also think he was still alive when they cut him up. Look at his eyes, Mendick, look at the horror in those eyes."

Only then did the full nightmare of the murder strike Mendick. Somebody had entered the shop, stripped Thoms naked and dismembered him. His eyes were wide and staring, still holding the agony of what had been done to him, but with his lips stitched closed, he could not have screamed. His would have been a silent, agonised death.

The arms and legs had been thrown together; a jumble of hairy limbs, smeared with blood. Mendick frowned and lifted the topmost leg. Flesh from the thigh had been sliced off, leaving the bone exposed. "Dear God almighty, how this fellow must have suffered!"

He placed the leg back down as a mark on the right arm caught his attention. "Did you notice this, sir?"

Mackay adjusted the gas jet to increase the light. Thom's hand had been hacked off but the arm was weather-beaten, muscular and hairy with a distinctive tattoo. Mendick peered closer. "It's a bit smudged," he said, "but there are two words. The first is Rose but I can't make out the second." He stood up. "Rose is probably the name of his girl. We can try and find out who she is."

"That's a start," Mackay said. "I wonder how many girls called Rose there are in Dundee."

"Scores, probably," Mendick said.

He inspected the room. The only window was locked and the shutters were bolted from the inside, while the fireplace was much too small to allow access. The embers on the grate were still warm.

22

"You said both the outer and storeroom doors were locked?"

"Both doors were locked and the key was still on the inside of this one. That is why my criminal officers had to make a hole in the door panel."

"Is that door also locked?" Mendick pointed to a door in the far corner of the room.

Mackay glanced and nodded. "Yes, but it's only a cupboard."

"Has anybody checked inside?" Mendick took two steps towards it and stopped as his boot clattered against something. He looked down and frowned. He had kicked over a plate and a mess of cooked meat now joined the shambles on the floorboards, together with Thoms' missing hand. "What's this, sir?" Mendick stooped and prised a linen bag free from Thom's stiff fingers. It jingled when he lifted it.

He looked inside. "It's full of coins, sir." Mendick lifted a handful and allowed them to trickle through his fingers, holding one coin secure. "Silver shillings, sir; they are all shillings. Dozens of them." He shook the bag, watching the sheen of silver as the coins shifted around inside. "I can't see anything special about them though." He examined the coin he held. "Queen Victoria, 1842." He lifted a second coin, "Same again: 1842." He lifted a third. "So is this one, sir . . ."

Mendick lifted another handful and checked them one by one, shaking his head. "They are all dated 1842, sir, every blessed one."

"Pass that over here, Mendick." Mackay ordered. "Silver from a dead man. Now we really have a mystery on our hands."

"Indeed. A man butchered inside a locked room,

a killer who cooked himself a meal and a bag full of shillings, all dated 1842." Mendick forced a smile. "I think we can discount suicide?"

Mackay did not reply. He looked inside the bag, frowning.

"I'll check inside that cupboard." Mendick tested the panelled door to ensure it was locked and then leaned his cane against the wall. He took a small wallet from inside his pocket, opened it and pulled out a small lockpick. "This is a simple lock," he said. "It won't take me a minute."

Mackay watched closely. "Are you sure you have always been on the right side of the law, Mendick?"

"I have been many things, sir," Mendick said, "and I have picked up quite a few tricks along the way." He pushed in the pick and grunted when it met resistance. "The key is still inside the lock, this will be easy." He pulled a pair of longnosed pliers from his wallet. "This is what is known as an 'outsider', if I just insert it in the keyhole, grab the butt end of the key and turn . . ." After a second there was an audible click and he pulled open the door. "Easy as pie."

The cupboard was about four feet deep by three feet wide, with old clothes piled on the floor. A rope ladder dangled from a hole in the ceiling above, a metal spike fastened it to the floorboards.

"Well, that is one mystery solved," Mendick tugged at the ladder which was quite secure. "Whoever he was, he came down here, locked the doors so he would not be disturbed, murdered Thoms and climbed away again, turning the key in the lock behind him."

Mackay pointed to the hole in the ceiling, "Thoms must have been deaf not to have heard someone making that hole."

24

"That is another mystery," Mendick agreed. "Now sir, with your permission, I will go up." The ladder was made of thin but strong rope, with wooden rungs. He tested the first rung as Mackay nodded assent.

Mendick pulled himself up. "You know, sir, an active man could swarm up a rope, or at least a rope with knots for hand and footholds. Why go to all the trouble to make a ladder such as this? That may be significant." He squeezed through the small gap in the ceiling and found himself in the flat above the shop. He had emerged flush against the wall, where the hearth of the fire should have been.

"Can you send up a constable with a bull's eye?" Mendick shouted. "I can't see a blessed thing up here."

The beam of light came first, flicking through the gap in the hole, followed by the tall hat and broad face of Constable Sturrock.

"Evening, Sergeant Mendick. I thought you would be well on your way back to London by now." Sturrock peered around and raised the lantern high. "What are we looking for?"

"Anything, Sturrock. We are looking for anything that is not as it should be." Mendick held out his hand, "Up you come, man. You're no good to anyone half in and half out."

Sturrock was a large man and he had to manoeuvre his shoulders and wriggle his hips through the gap. He stood up, gasping. "That hole must have been made for a blasted dwarf! No normal-sized person could crawl through there."

Mendick nodded. He did not mention Mackay's suspicion of a Chinese connection. "Just you concentrate on your job, Sturrock, and leave the thinking to those of us who have some brains."

25

The upper flat was obviously unoccupied but there were signs of plastering and carpentry work. A hammer, chisel and small saw lay beside the hole and Mendick handed them to Sturrock.

"You look after these," he ordered. "And don't lose them. Examine the windows and doors."

Mendick took the lantern and opened the shutters to allow the flickering light from the gas lamps on Dock Street into the room. He knelt beside the hole, searching for footprints on the dusty floorboards or anything that the burglar may have dropped.

"The windows were all locked and shuttered, Sergeant," Sturrock's boots thumped on the bare wood, "and the door is locked. There is no key and no mark of a forced entry."

Mendick looked up. "So the murderer did not break in, he either had access or he used a false key." He rocked back on his heels and looked around. "He made it easy for himself, Sturrock. He lifted out the hearthstone and just sawed through the plaster, dropped the rope ladder and swarmed down, murdered the unhappy Mr Thoms, cooked himself a meal and came back."

"He was a cold fish then," Sturrock said.

Mendick stood up. "Now we have to follow the trail and catch him." He handed back the lantern.

Sturrock nodded. "Yes, sergeant. What will you do next?"

"I will find out who owns this flat, and whether it was leased to somebody. I want to see the owner and the tenant, and there is obviously work going on in here. I want to speak to the tradesmen."

Mendick paused. What he really wanted was to catch the next packet boat to London with his prisoner, but that was not possible. He had to solve this murder first. It was no longer just a duty; the nature of the killing disgusted him and he had to apprehend the murderer. Dundee had caught him and now held him fast.

CHAPTER THREE

The interior of Bell Street Police Office was solid, unpretentious and cold, despite the false promise of the pale sun that peeped between the tenements opposite. A chill wind blasted through the slightly open window, it rustled the papers on the desk Mendick had been given and caused him to reach for his coat until he noticed Sturrock watching. Instead, he pretended to search in his pockets for his pipe, placed it beside him and looked up as Superintendent Mackay entered the room.

"Yes, sir?"

Mackay motioned for Sturrock to leave his chair and dragged it over beside Mendick. "All right, Mendick, we must discuss these coins." Mackay carried the bag of money Mendick had found at the murder scene. With a brief nod to Sturrock, he placed it on top of Mendick's desk. "I confess that the significance of these coins eludes me, and I implore your assistance. What can they mean, Mendick?"

Mendick sighed. "I have been pondering the same question, sir." Mendick emptied the bag on top of the desk and counted the coins. "There are twenty-nine shillings, and all with the same date: 1842. Some appear hardly used and others are worn. I am not sure if they are genuine or bit-faker's forgeries."

"They are genuine, Mendick." Mackay placed capable hands on the scarred surface. "Considering where and how they were found, I would imagine there is great significance here."

Mendick drew on his pipe. "I am intrigued sir. There are so many mysteries here that the whole thing is just a tangle. The murder was horrific but I cannot see why anybody would leave a bag of silver behind."

"Nor can I, Mendick. Twenty nine shillings is a good week's wages for a skilled artisan." Mackay looked through the coins again and frowned. "The murderer is leaving us a message here, but I'm blessed if I know what it can be." He looked up abruptly. "Now listen Mendick, and you too Sturrock," Mackay waved the constable closer. "What I am about to say must not go beyond these walls until I say so. Understand?"

"Yes, sir," Mendick said, while Sturrock looked suitably solemn.

"There have been rumours for some time of a new force in the Dundee criminal classes." Mackay said. "We became aware of this when some of the more notorious of our thieves left the town. They were scared of a man known only as China Jim." Mackay stopped and repeated the name. "China Jim, and now we have this murder of unparalleled horror within an Oriental emporium." When he looked up his eyes were like chips of granite. "I believe you know China, Mendick?"

Mendick lowered the shilling he had been studying. "Yes, sir. I was with the 26th Foot through the China War."

Mackay nodded. "Is the number twenty-nine of any special significance there? Or is the date 1842 important to China?"

Mendick shook his head. "I have never heard of twenty-nine being important sir, but 1842 may be. That was when the Chinese War ended."

Mackay nodded. "Of course. Perhaps there is a

Chinaman who resents us winning that war and who has come to Dundee to take his revenge?" He tapped his fingers on Mendick's desk and looked up. "What kind of Chinaman would do that sort of thing? What sort of man could do that?" He looked away for a moment and took a deep breath. "I understand they have criminal gangs in China, Mendick?"

"They do, sir," Mendick agreed.

Mackay stopped tapping. "Have you ever heard of the Triads?"

Mendick wondered if Mackay had ever been a gambler, the way he played his cards one at a time, never revealing the full strength of his hand until the final play. He looked up slowly. "Yes, sir, but I do not believe they have any reason to operate outside China."

"Tell me of the Triads, Mendick." Mackay said.

"I am no expert, sir. We did not have much to do with them." Mendick began.

Mackay held Mendick's eyes. "Tell me what you do know of them, Mendick."

Mendick lifted his pipe and began to stuff tobacco in the bowl. He dredged his memory for the little he knew. "There are many different Triad groups sir. They began as secret societies dedicated to getting rid of the present Manchu dynasty that rules China. The Manchus are foreigners, you see, from Manchuria, and many of the Chinese want the old Ming dynasty back." For a second he was back in the humidity of Chusan, with fever decimating the ranks of the 26th and the men muttering of mutiny. He remembered the nerve-wracking patrols outside the town and the terrible fate of the men captured by the Chinese.

"Carry on, Mendick. They began as secret societies,

you said? And what are they now?" Mackay was listening intently, his eyes fixed on Mendick's face.

Mendick pulled himself back to the present and concentrated on the Triads. "Some triads are still politically minded, but many are mere bandits or thieves. Although some are depicted as Oriental Robin Hoods, in reality they just terrorise the countryside. The ones we met had a slogan—*Plunder the rich to relieve the poor*—but I cannot recall much relief given."

Mackay grunted. "Were they pleasant people?" He gave a wry smile, "Would you introduce them to your mother?"

"I never knew her sir, so I cannot say." Mendick refused to venture on that dark walk of his own history. "But the Triads were not pleasant people. There was one occasion when a whole mob of Chinese captured two of our lads. They stoned one to death there and then and gave the other to the Triads. The Triads locked him in a bamboo cage so small his face was pressed against his knees, and took him around the villages so they could torment him. Other Europeans they captured were stripped naked and crucified. When a bunch of pirates boarded the ship Black Joke they murdered the crew except for one man. They cut his ear off and stitched it in his mouth . . ."

Mackay held up a hand. "All right Mendick, that is enough now."

"Yes, sir." Mendick nodded. He tried not to think of that terrible campaign in China, but when the images returned it was hard to shake them away.

"We have an increasing amount of Oriental trade, Mendick, and I am fearful that this China Jim and other such people are now operating in Dundee." Mackay's mouth hinted at a smile. "It was no accident you came up here to pick up Thatcher, Sergeant. I spent quite some time searching the police forces of Britain for a criminal officer with knowledge of China. The accidents to my men just provided the excuse."

"Yes, sir," Mendick did not know what else to say.

Mackay continued. "I am anxious to resolve this abominable affair." He glanced around the dim, cool room. "You may have Constable Sturrock here to assist you and I will send along Constable Deuchars whenever he can be spared from his other duties." He rose from the chair. "If the general populace learn the details of this outrage, Mendick, there will be an outcry. I am depending on you to use your utmost exertions to find this China Jim."

"I will do my best, sir." Mendick looked up as a constable carried in the rope ladder which he dumped unceremoniously on the floor. Another young constable placed a small wooden box on the desk with only slightly more care.

"That is all the evidence from the scene," Mackay turned away, straight-backed and alert as a hungry bird. "I will leave you to it then. Catch me this Chinaman, Mendick."

Mendick watched Mackay leave the room. He stuck his pipe in his mouth and leaned back in his chair, wishing he had never come back to Dundee.

"Get up there, you little dog, and get it swept." The words came out of nowhere, an ugly reminder of his childhood and he shivered. He could almost smell the soot.

Sturrock stomped across to Mendick and lifted the first rungs of the rope ladder. "This is a lovely piece of workmanship," he said. "It was certainly not just cobbled together by an amateur, but I have never heard of a burglar using anything like this before."

"Nor have I," Mendick looked closely. "The rungs are of pine, I think. One side is plain and the other side painted green. It looks as if the maker took the wood from something else, a box perhaps, in order to make it."

Sturrock looked and nodded but said nothing.

"And the rope has been cut from smaller pieces and spliced together, see? It's not new rope, it's discoloured. So that was taken from somewhere else and not bought new for the ladder, either."

Sturrock nodded, "Yes, Sergeant."

"Somebody has gone to a lot of bother to make this," Mendick said. "Look at these knots. That is a round turn and two half hitches: used for tying a boat to a mooring ring or a piling. It is a maritime knot. This ladder was made by a seaman." Mendick looked up. "Do you know of any burglars in Dundee who used to be seamen?"

Sturrock shrugged. "Dundee is a busy port, Sergeant. There are thousands of seamen here and lots of them end up in the police court, mainly for petty stuff."

"I am not interested in drunken brawls or riot," Mendick said. "I want theft or burglary. Check the court records, Sturrock and see what you can find. I don't want a youngster either: an experienced seaman made this ladder."

"Yes, Sergeant." Sturrock took a note.

"Now, let's see what else we have here." Mendick tipped open the box. The saw and chisels rattled onto the desk, along with a single silver shilling. He checked the date. "1842 again," he said, and placed the coin with its brothers inside the bag. "This one must have fallen out when I kicked the plate."

"Do you know what that means, Sergeant?" Sturrock lifted the bag. "You now have thirty shillings."

Mendick nodded. "Thirty pieces of silver, Sturrock. The price paid to Judas Iscariot to betray Christ." He stuffed the pipe back in his mouth and bit hard on the stem. "We may have found a motive. It would appear that Mr Thoms betrayed somebody very badly. If we can find out whom, we may have found this China Jim fellow." Mendick spread the coins over his desk and hoped for inspiration. "That is something else to check, Sturrock. See if Thoms had any Chinese connection apart from his Oriental Emporium."

Sturrock smiled, "Yes, Sergeant."

"Is something amusing you, Constable?" Mendick looked up from the desk. "Tell me what, pray?"

"I was smiling at the thought of a Chinese connection, Sergeant." Sturrock said. "I have never seen a Chinaman in Dundee in my life."

"It's not who you have seen that matters, Sturrock. It's who Thoms saw." Mendick scooped the coins back into the bag. "This case just gets more complex by the minute, what with Chinamen and seamen and bags full of shillings."

Sturrock grinned to him. "It is certainly an intriguing case, Sergeant. I've never seen a murder like this before."

"Really?" Mendick was in no mind to be charitable. "What kind of murders do you usually deal with, Constable?"

Sturrock looked away. "This is my first."

"Well, if you are a very fortunate policeman, this

will also be your last. Murders are always dirty, sordid, unpleasant affairs. The stench of death and despair lingers forever." Mendick stopped himself, "Have you discovered who owns the flat above Thoms's shop?"

"Yes, Sergeant." Sturrock lifted a ragged scrap of paper from the top of the desk he had commandeered. "It's a woman called Johanna Lednock."

"You have her address?"

Sturrock nodded. "Unicorn Cottage, down in the Ferry − that's Broughty Ferry, Sergeant."

"I know Broughty Ferry, constable." Mendick reached for his hat and cane. "All right, Sturrock. Call us a cab and take me to Miss Johanna Lednock." He touched the rope ladder with his foot. "She might be able to explain this beautiful piece of craftsmanship."

An easterly wind whipped the tops off the grey rollers in the Firth of Tay and lifted a haze of spindrift across the exposed sandbanks. Mendick stepped out of the cab, threw the driver the one and sixpence fare and shivered. He had grown used to the comparative warmth of the south and now the climate of eastern Scotland seemed cold and raw to him. He tapped his cane off the door of the cab, "Come back for us in an hour," he ordered, and looked over to Unicorn Cottage.

Set back a garden's length from the edge of the beach, it was built of light sandstone, tall and solid, the roof complete with an impressive cupola and large windows facing the sea.

"What's this woman's name again?" Mendick asked. He watched as a three-masted ship dipped into the swell, rose again and tacked with the wind. The sails descended in a cloud of canvas. God, he wished he was on board her, away from the bitter memories of Dundee.

"Johanna Lednock," Sturrock said.

Mendick pulled the black iron bell and was surprised at the speed with which the door opened. The maid was young and her black uniform clean and neat.

Mendick responded to her quick curtsey with a nod. "I am Sergeant Mendick, at present with the Dundee Police. Could you tell your mistress I would like a word?"

The servant showed them into a light and airy room with tall windows overlooking the Tay and walls covered in pastel oil paintings of scenes and people. Mendick glanced around and walked straight to the fire that sparked in the hearth. "Now that is a welcome sight!"

"Oh, make space for me!" The woman rushed through the door and stood close beside Mendick, holding out both hands to the fire. "It's freezing out there! I do so wish summer would come. I know winter has lovely crisp days but I do dislike the cold so." Green eyes laughed at him. "You must be the sergeant?"

"I am Sergeant Mendick . . ."

"Oh good," the woman, looked at her hand, shrugged and held it out. "I do apologise about the stains but I have been painting you see."

Mendick grasped her hand. "It is a pleasure to make your acquaintance, Miss." He fought to restrain his smile. "You are cold," he said.

"That's why I am pushing you away from the fire," the woman had already eased herself to take most of the heat. "Excuse me," she stopped for a moment to lift a small boy who had followed her into the room. She balanced him on her hip with the ease of long practise. "Now what can I do for you?"

Mendick glanced at Sturrock, who shrugged. "I

am waiting for the mistress of the house, miss . . ." he looked to the boy who was cuddling in to the woman's shoulder. "Am I to understand you are the governess?"

"Good heavens, no! I don't have a governess for my John. I am perfectly capable and more than willing to look after him myself." The woman held his gaze, her eyes were very clear. "I am Johanna Lednock."

"My deepest apologies, Ma'am; I meant no insult—" Mendick began, but Johanna silenced him with a shake of her head.

"How can thinking of me as a governess be in any way an insult?" Johanna waved away Mendick's apology. "Now, Sergeant. Is it that terrible business in my Candle Lane properties you want to ask about?"

"Properties? Do you own both the shop and the flat, Mrs Lednock?" There was no wedding ring on Johanna's finger but the presence of the child was surely proof of marriage.

"Mrs Gordon," Johanna corrected easily. "Lednock is my maiden name although I use it most of the time."

"Is there still a Mr Gordon?" Mendick asked.

"Very much so," Johanna told him. "David is very much alive and kicking. Really Sergeant, I am very surprised you do not know him. He is one of the most successful merchants in Dundee."

Mendick ignored the implied reproof. "Perhaps I should speak to him then? Is he the owner of the properties? Does he deal with the leases and the tenants?"

Johanna allowed the boy to slide to the ground but retained hold of his hand. "No, Sergeant Mendick. I am as capable of looking after my property as I am of looking after my own son." There was no mistaking the steel in her eyes, "Are you determined to insult me today?"

Mendick ducked his head in an apologetic bow. "Indeed not. In London it is a bit unusual for a married lady to own property, obviously Dundee is different. Or you are special in some way." Mendick looked to Sturrock for help, but the constable was admiring the pictures on the wall.

"I can't imagine why you should think that," Johanna's brows began to draw together and there was a tiny curl at the corner of her mouth.

Mendick decided to move on as quickly as possible. "Could you tell me what was being done to the flat above the shop, please?" He signalled for Sturrock to take notes.

"Oh, I have workmen in there making the place habitable for the next tenants." Johanna gave the workmen's names to Sturrock, who scribbled them down.

"We will speak to them," Mendick promised. "Now, Mrs Gordon, I would be obliged if you could tell me everything you know about the night of the murder."

"I know where I was, if that is of any interest to you," Johanna said. "I was at home with John," she indicated the small boy who was busily engaged in unpicking the edge of the hearth rug with his fingernails. Johanna sighed and picked him up again.

"Were you aware of any unusual activity around the flat or the shop in the days previous to the murder?" Mendick felt a pang as he watched Johanna with her son, his daughter would have been about that age, had she lived. He pushed that thought away to concentrate on the matter in hand.

Johanna shook her head. "No more unusual than normal for that part of the world," she said.

Mendick glanced at Sturrock, who was busy with his notebook. "This may sound a strange question, but have you seen a suspicious-looking seaman in Candle Lane? He may have been looking up at the flat?"

"The flat is only a few steps from Dock Street. There are hundreds of seamen passing every day." Johanna's smile brought life to her face. "And may I be permitted to ask you a question, Sergeant? Have you ever seen a seaman who did not look suspicious?"

Mendick could not help his own smile. "I have one final question." Mendick said. "Does the name Rose mean anything to you? Do you know anyone of that name?"

Johanna shook her head. "I don't recall anyone called Rose."

Mendick stood up, "Thank you for your time, Mrs Gordon. I will leave you in peace now." He glanced back as he left to see Johanna watching him with her head tilted to one side and a small smile twitching on her lips. He was still thinking of her as his cab pulled away. A dark brougham coach passed on the opposite side of the road and he noticed the curtain at the coach window move and a woman's face peer out at him. She saw him, pulled her green cloak about her and closed the curtain again. He filed the incident away in his mind but said nothing. When he closed his eyes he saw Johanna's smile.

"How did you get on with the workmen, Sturrock?" Mendick sat back at his desk, shuffled through the fresh pile of papers that had miraculously appeared since he was last there and took out his pipe. He sighed, he had not anticipated so much paperwork when he became a detective, sometimes he missed the simplicity of life on the beat.

"None of them were at the flat on the night of the murder," Sturrock pulled his notebook from his pocket. "I checked on them and their stories seem firm."

Mendick frowned. So was this a case of dead ends and mystery. He began to stuff tobacco into the bowl of his pipe. "Did you learn anything?"

"Only fragments, Sergeant," Sturrock consulted his notes. "I asked if anybody had been sneaking around the flat, and they said there had been a couple of people looking to rent it, a man and a woman, but separately. The workmen sent them to the factor and I had a word with him."

"Did you get names and descriptions?" Mendick put down his pipe and added the information into his own notes.

"Yes, Sergeant," Sturrock read out loud. "They were a Mr Robert Marmion and a Mrs Elizabeth Deacon. I could not find an address for Marmion: the one he gave the factor was false, but Mrs Deacon was genuine. A woman with three daughters, looking for a place to live."

Mendick nodded; "Well done, Sturrock. Did you get a description for Marmion?"

"I tried," Sturrock said, "but the factor could hardly remember him. He said Marmion was just a man with nothing out of the ordinary about him at all."

"That's not much help," Mendick said. "Did you check out the factor as well? He will have access to the flat."

"He is a very respectable gentleman," Sturrock's forehead puckered in confusion.

Mendick nodded. "I have no doubt he is, but I have known the most respectable gentlemen to be blackguards and scoundrels too. Go back and question him; find out where he was the night of the murder and if anybody else has access to the house."

Mendick turned away, but Sturrock turned over a leaf of his notebook. "There was one other thing, Sergeant, that was a bit strange. Two of the workmen said the key to the front door had some white powder on it one day, two weeks ago. They thought it was the same day Marmion came but they were not sure."

"White powder?" Mendick nodded. "It sounds as if the key was pressed into something. That's an old trick: the thief makes an impression in china clay or some such and then makes a false key." He scribbled that down. "It seems obvious that this Marmion fellow was involved in some way or other, Sturrock. Did the workmen give any clue as to what he looked like?"

"Only one remembered him at all," Sturrock said, "and he described him as ordinary, with nothing distinctive to remember."

Mendick nodded. "The same description as the factor gave. Marmion will not be an easy man to find then: a false name and no description. I'll pass the name around but we'll get nowhere." He sighed, "Now let's go through what we have so far. We have your notes from the interview, the statement by the surgeon, the bag of silver, the Rose tattoo and the rope ladder. Let's see the surgeon's report next."

Mendick struggled to read the surgeon's untidy script. "The surgeon thinks the man was eviscerated and the slices of flesh removed before he was killed."

"He was tortured then?" Sturrock's lip curled in disgust. "Maybe he eloped with China Jim's sweetheart, or stole from him. Maybe he stole some money from him."

"And the murderer kindly gave him a thirty shilling reward?" Mendick shook his head. "That bag of silver confuses me. I have never seen the like before."

"Why are the coins all the same date? That cannot be a coincidence." Sturrock re-checked the bag. "Somebody has gone to the trouble of collecting thirty coins all dated 1842 to leave with a dead man."

Mendick nodded. "We agreed that the number of coins suggests it's possible this unfortunate man was murdered for betraying somebody. I think the date is significant. Mr Mackay believes it could have a Chinese connection, maybe to do with the ending of the Chinese war in 1842. Now all we have to do is find out who Thoms betrayed and we will have our murderer."

"It's as easy as that?" Sturrock puffed blue smoke from his churchwarden pipe. "Was that all the surgeon had to say?"

"Not quite." Mendick scanned the second paragraph twice. "I can't quite believe this, Sturrock. Listen. The surgeon thinks he can identify the meat on the plate. He says it was human flesh."

For a moment the only sound was the hammer of rain on the small window. "Dear God in heaven." Sturrock lowered his pipe. "This case just gets worse." He shook his head. "Are you saying China Jim is a cannibal?"

"There is worse to come," Mendick tried to keep any emotion from his voice. "The surgeon is convinced the flesh was taken from the victim's leg and cooked in the shop."

"Oh, sweet Jesus in heaven," Sturrock's hand shook as he lifted his pipe. "We had better catch this monster quickly, Sergeant. So what exactly do we know about the unfortunate fellow who was murdered?"

Once again Mendick re-read his notes. Even augmented by the surgeon's report they did not reveal much. "We know he was David Thoms and he rented and ran the Oriental Emporium. To judge by the poor quality of his clothing and the calluses on his hands, the man came from the labouring class of the population. He was in his mid to late thirties, with strong muscles in his arms and upper body but lesser development in his legs, and had a number of minor, healed scars that suggested an active life. That is not a great deal to go on," Mendick said. "But we do have the tattoo."

Mendick put his papers down. "Now, let's put everything together. We have a murderer and cannibal in Dundee. We have a murdered man from the labouring class with a tattoo that says Rose. We have a ladder made by a seaman and a bag of thirty silver coins. That is what we know. We suspect there is a Chinese connection and there is the mysterious Mr Marmion who entered the flat above by a false key and who is definitely not Chinese."

He rose from his seat and slipped on his Chesterfield. "It's time to make ourselves known to the good people of Candle Lane." He grabbed his rattan walking cane and tapped the lead-weighted end into the palm of his hand. "Come, Sturrock, get into your civilian clothes and let's step out together, we have a murder to solve."

Mendick did not expect to learn anything from the shifting population that infested Candle Lane but he intended to try. He walked cautiously, checking each doorway as he approached, but although this dockland area was unpleasant and every fourth person appeared to be a prostitute or a thief, there was little possibility of two large men being assaulted unless they provoked the inhabitants. They paced Dock Street, the Seagate and the lanes and wynds in between, knocking at doors, entering lodging houses, asking about David Thoms and enquiring if anybody had seen suspicious activity in Candle Lane. They got the same negative answers from overdressed dolly mops, unemployed labourers and seamen without a berth.

"I don't know nothing. I never saw nothing."

"I wasn't looking out the window."

"Maybe these people don't believe we are police officers because we're not in uniform," Sturrock glanced over at Mendick in his battered hat and smart Chesterfield, with his cane rapping on the paved street. "You look like a gentleman out for a stroll, save for your hat."

"These people know full well who and what we are," Mendick told him. "And if there were a score of murders in broad daylight, they still would not have seen anything and would know nothing."

"Sometimes I wonder why we even bother . . ." Sturrock began until Mendick stopped him with a gesture.

"Trust me in this, Sturrock, I understand nautical people. Now, the entire parish has seen us asking questions, correct?"

Sturrock nodded.

"So nobody will think it amiss if we ask another man what he has seen." Mendick stopped outside the open door of a pub they had passed on two occasions. The sign, Greenland Inn, with a picture of a sailing ship against an icebound coast, hung above an open door. Although it was hardly past nine in the morning, the place was already buzzing, with men and women gathered around the tables and a swarm of children playing around their parents' feet. Alone in one corner, an elderly red-faced man whined an interminable dirge, stopping occasionally to clutch his stomach and mutter something to himself.

"We've been here already," Sturrock said.

"I know," Mendick agreed. "And that blind beggar watched everything we did," he pointed the tip of his cane at the man who slouched by the door.

Standing outside amidst a misery of rags that might once have been the proud scarlet of a soldier's uniform, the beggar proffered his cap in which rattled a worn farthing and a thin piece of metal. The label tied around his neck proclaimed: Please Help a Blind old Soldier.

Mendick dropped a single penny into the cap. "There's a shilling for you, my man."

The beggar touched a hand to his forehead. "Thank you kindly, sir. You're a gent, and there's not many going around nowadays."

"Talking of gents," Mendick leaned against the wall at the beggar's side, "my friend and I are searching for an old workmate of ours. His name is David Thoms and you might know him by the tattoo on his arm."

The beggar shook his head. "I am blind, sir. I can't see a tattoo."

"Of course you are; please accept my apologies old man." Mendick touched the man's arm. "I am not scholar enough to have read your sign. Tell me, which regiment were you in?"

"Twenty-Ninth Foot, sir." The beggar shuffled to a parody of attention and threw a salute that would have disgraced a first day Johnny Raw.

Mendick returned the salute and casually balanced his cane over his shoulder. "Ah the old Vein Openers, the two and a hook, the heroes of Mudki. You boys showed the Afghans, eh?"

"That we did, sir." The beggar's grin showed half a mouthful of yellow fangs. "We won that war all by ourselves."

"Heroes all," Mendick said. "I was in the Twenty-Sixth myself, the Camerons. Were we not brigaded together in the Punjab?"

"We were that, sir. I remember the Twenty-Sixth well."

"Well, for an old soldier of the Twenty-Ninth, I must give more than a single coin." Mendick reached into his pocket and hauled out a small handful of loose change, dropping two coins as he did so. Surreptitiously standing on one, he lifted the second and placed it in the beggar's cap. "Well my friend, there's a guinea somewhere around here, but I'm blessed if I can find it." Touching his cane to the brim of his hat, he sauntered away, followed by a confused Sturrock.

"Walk slowly," Mendick warned. "I want to watch that fellow."

"The blind man?" Sturrock said, "He can't help us, surely."

"Don't be so certain, Constable. That blind man sees more than most. Turn . . . now!"

He turned on his heel, just as the beggar snatched the coin from the ground. "Well spotted, Twenty-Ninth Foot!"

The beggar looked up. "It's a bloody farthing, not a guinea . . ."

"And you can see as well as I can," Mendick said. "Block him, Sturrock!"

The beggar jinked backward towards the pub but Sturrock was in his path, so he tried to weave sideways, slammed into Mendick's outstretched arm and crashed to the ground. He began to roar for help until Mendick placed the tip of his cane on his windpipe and pressed.

"There's none so blind as these who don't want to see. Now keep quiet, Twenty-Ninth Foot," he said, "or you won't be able to breathe either."

The beggar glared silent hatred. His eyes swivelled to the pub but with Sturrock's mighty frame blocking the doorway, staff in hand and grin on face, none of the denizens dared come to his help.

Mendick applied slight pressure to his cane so the beggar gasped for breath. "Now, Twenty Ninth Foot; you are guilty of a number of crimes and offences. I will not list them all but the least of them is begging under false pretences, that is theft. That would mean a nice long stretch in jail. So you and I are going to have a little talk. Let's find somewhere quiet, shall we?" Mendick looked at Sturrock. "We know the perfect place."

"Indeed we do," Sturrock agreed at once.

As they neared the shop in Candle Lane the beggar began to kick and struggle and Mendick clamped his arms around him to keep him still. The constable on guard at the door winked at Sturrock and then watched quietly.

The beggar pulled back. "Christ! Not in there! Don't take me in there!"

"What's the matter? You're a big brave soldier, are you not? Wounded in the service of your country, remember?" Mendick nodded to the constable to open the door and wrestled the beggar inside, where the smell of damp clothing and raw blood waited. "Come on, soldier boy and don't be afraid. We'll take good care of you!"

Mendick hauled the beggar inside and the constable

quietly closed the door at their back. Sturrock lit the gas but, if anything, the flickering light only emphasised the surrounding dark.

"You can't do this to a blind old soldier . . ." the beggar began. Mendick rapped him on the head with his cane.

"Firstly, you are not blind. You failed my farthing test. Second, you are no old soldier, you failed on every point: the Twenty-Ninth were not present at the Battle of Mudki, the Twenty-Ninth fought the Sikhs not the Afghans, the Twenty-Sixth are the Cameronians, not the Cameron Highlanders and the Twenty-Sixth and Twenty-Ninth were never brigaded together."

The beggar exchanged his whining for a bout of cursing. "You devious bastards!"

"That's us," Mendick told him. "I am Detective Sergeant Mendick of Scotland Yard and the Dundee Police. The gentleman with me is Constable Sturrock. We are going to ask you some questions and you are going to answer them quietly and truthfully, or . . ." he bounced his cane on the top of the beggar's head again. "Or this interview might become less pleasant."

"You bastard!"

"We already agreed on that," Mendick told him. "Is your habitual stance outside that pub?" He poised the cane above the beggar's head.

"Yes." The man's eyes swivelled, following the cane.

"That wasn't too hard, was it?" Mendick left the cane in position. "And your name is?"

There was a short hesitation. "Jones. James Jones."

Mendick brought the cane down hard and the beggar yelped and winced. "Now try your real name."

"John Hitchins, you bastard!"

"See? Tell the truth and there's no pain, is that not much easier?" Mendick lifted the cane again. "Right, John Hitchins, the civilian with two working eyes. I think you know everything that happens around here because nobody will hide from a man who cannot see. Correct?"

Hitchins opened his mouth, hesitated and nodded. "I know more than most," he agreed sourly.

"Then tell us all you know about what happened in here. Tell us all about the man who was murdered in this room."

Hitchins' eyes swivelled upwards to where the cane was poised above his head. "His name was Davie Thoms. He ran the oriental shop selling rubbish and acting as a pawnbroker. He was just a man trying to make a living." Hitchins shrugged. "That's all I know about him."

Mendick allowed the cane to fall. Hitchins yelled and tried to protect his head.

"Try again," Mendick advised. "A man like you watches everyone and listens to everything. Tell me about Thoms."

Hitchins swore but as Mendick raised his cane he started to talk again. "I know he was a seaman but that's all. He came shore-side a few years back and tried a job in the quarry at Kingoodie, but the gunpowder blew out his eardrums so he rented his shop. I swear that's all I know."

Mendick stored away the information. "Thank you, soldier boy. That may be of use. Was he on long haul voyages? Perhaps to China?"

"I don't know." Hitchins said, and yelled as the cane cracked down once more. "I don't know, I tell you!" He flinched as the cane poised once more. "You can

49

bullyrag me all year, Sergeant, but I still can't tell what I don't know."

"Have you seen any strangers around here?" Sturrock altered tack.

Hitchins laughed until Mendick smacked the cane down once more. "Aah! Careful Sergeant! Half the people here are strangers. There are draggletails and pickpockets, footpads and Greenlandmen and Baltic men in every pub from Craig Pier to the Ferry. Do you really think I know them all?"

Mendick lowered the cane. "You know more than you are saying, John, that we know. Why were you scared to come in here? And don't draw the long bow."

"Christ, man! There's no need for tales in this place. Did you see Deaf Davie? Did you see what they done to him? They castrated him, Sergeant, and stuck them in his mouth! Then they sewed his lips together! Jesus Christ alive, Sergeant! And you ask why I am scared to come in here?" Hitchins looked around as if expecting the mysterious 'they' to appear out of the dark shadows surrounding them.

Mendick nodded to Sturrock. "Who did it, John? Tell us who did it and we'll let you go. But if you don't tell us, we'll tie you up and leave you here."

In the dim gaslight, Hitchin's eyes glittered and swivelled right and left. His lips clamped shut.

Mendick smacked the cane down hard and the lead tip scraped Hitchin's scalp, drawing blood and causing the beggar to yell and grab at his head.

"Oh, my goodness! Look what has happened. Is it not fortunate you are blind and can't see the mess? Tell us who did it, John."

Hitchins raised his hand to his head then looked at

the blood on it. "You bastard, Mendick! You're as bad as they are."

"Oh, I am worse, Johnny boy, much worse." Mendick leaned closer. "You see, I have the law on my side. I am invulnerable. I know exactly where the law ends and my rules begin. Now, you have a choice. We can leave you here and spread the word you told us everything. We can arrest you and have you jailed or transported, or we can let you go, once you have told us exactly what we want to know. So who killed David Thoms, and why?"

Sturrock had been a silent spectator until that moment but now he stepped forward and winked. "Sergeant; we don't want to go too far here . . . remember what happened to the Irishman."

Mendick glowered at him. "The Irishman was a mistake. If he had done what I said he'd still be alive."

"But Sergeant . . ."

As intended, the conversation encouraged Hitchins into speech. "I never saw nothing."

"No, you never did," Mendick agreed, "because you are blind. But tell us what you heard, Johnny. Tell us what you heard."

"This!" Ducking suddenly, Hitchins made a lunge past Sturrock for the door, but Mendick had anticipated this and thrust his cane between the beggar's ankles. The man staggered and swore loudly. Sturrock threw him against the wall and held him firm.

"Shall I break his neck, Sergeant?"

Mendick frowned, then shook his head, "Not yet, Constable. We'll give him one last chance." He cracked the weighted end of his cane into the palm of his hand.

"There were four of them!" Hitchins yelled. "I saw four men go into the close beside the shop. It might not have been the murderers but it might have been."

Mendick pressed his mouth against Hitchins' ear. "You saw four men? Describe them to me."

With Sturrock's forearm thrust against his throat, Hitchins looked from one policeman to the other. He spoke in a hoarse whisper. "One was just normal, ordinary, but he carried a portmanteau. The others were smaller and wore cloaks and hats. One wore a wide-awake hat."

"Now we're getting somewhere," Mendick said. "Pray relax your hold on this most helpful gentleman, Constable Sturrock, but hold him secure."

Once he had begun to talk, Hitchins seemed reluctant to stop. "They got out of a coach. The normal man drove the coach there and back, it might have been a brougham but I'm not sure."

"Well done, thy good and faithful servant. Now their faces. What were they like?" Mendick intercepted Hitchins' glance towards the door and shook his head. "No, you won't get past us."

Hitchins looked at the floor. He answered in a whisper. "They never had faces. There was nothing there."

"What?" Sturrock slammed his forearm against Hitchins' throat again. "Don't give us any more fairy stories."

"Wait now. No faces? Did they have heads?" Mendick asked.

"Of course they had heads," Hitchins said, "but no faces, just a sort of blackness where their faces should be."

Mendick nodded, "Don't throttle him, Sturrock, he's doing his best. Are you saying they wore masks, John?"

Hitchins nodded as much as he could with Sturrock's

arm against his throat. "Yes! Yes, they might have been wearing masks."

Sturrock again relaxed his forearm. "Pray tell me again what their names were?" he asked with such casual skill that Mendick hid his smile.

"I never said," Hitchins was not so easily caught out.

"No, but you are about to," Sturrock retorted. "If you tell us, we will keep this as a little secret between ourselves. If you do not, then . . ." he shrugged, "the whole criminal class of Dundee will hear how helpful you were."

"Oh Christ, you wouldn't?" Hitchins looked from Sturrock to Mendick and back.

Sturrock nodded cheerfully. "Yes we would," he said. "And then we would use you as bait."

"Oh, Jesus, no!" Hitchins dropped his eyes. "It was the Ghost." He spoke in a soft whisper. "China Jim. Oh, dear God, I am a dead man."

"Not necessarily," Mendick told him. "Not if we get to him first."

Hitchins shrunk against the wall. "You don't understand, do you? You bluebottle bastards never understand nothing! Why do you think he's called the Ghost? Because nobody knows who he is and nobody ever sees him, that's why!"

CHAPTER FOUR

Mendick sat in his tiny office beneath the hissing gaslight, surveyed the litter of papers on his desk and sighed. He stuffed tobacco into the bowl of his pipe, struck a fusee to light it and pondered the new information. China Jim: the name sounded like a curse from the vilest alleyways of the city, a breath of foetid air into this room that smelled of beeswax and soap. What sort of name was that anyway? Perhaps it was a nickname given to a Chinaman who had some sort of association with Great Britain? Maybe a coolie from one of the ships that called at Chinese ports?

Mendick puffed blue smoke. "China Jim," he said. "Mr Mackay mentioned him and here he is. Dear God, maybe the Triads have indeed come over here."

Sturrock grunted. "I knew it was some foreign bugger that butchered Thoms like that. No Briton could act like that."

Mendick began to pace the room, tapping his cane against the furniture. "I think better when I walk," he said, before Sturrock asked. "Now. Mr Mackay does not want this China Jim's name mentioned. I don't agree. I want him to know we are after him. I want to flush him out of whatever pestiferous hole he infests." He stopped and cracked the cane on Sturrock's desk. "Right, Sturrock, we'll do it my way. Circulate the name China Jim to every police force in Great Britain; see if anybody has heard of it, and ask the beat constables if they have seen these three small men in cloaks and hats, or if anybody saw a brougham."

"It sounds like Chinese men in disguise," Sturrock said slowly.

"Do you have many Chinese in Dundee? Are they coolies off the ships perhaps?" Mendick could not think of ever seeing any in the streets. Chinese were a rare sight in London let alone a smaller town like this.

Sturrock shook his head. "I don't know of a single one, Sergeant." He had the transcripts of the court records in front of him as he continued to search for a seaman burglar.

Mendick sat back down and allowed the pipe smoke to haze around his head. "I don't like this, Sturrock. I don't like the idea of some foreign murderer butchering and eating people, and I don't like to think that criminals can conceal themselves behind aliases."

"Everything about this man is a mystery, Sergeant. We don't know who he is, we don't know which locality he infests or even what he does to earn his reputation and his money." Sturrock tapped the mouthpiece of his pipe on the desk. "All we know is the criminal classes are scared of him and now we see why."

"Is he a thief? Perhaps he controls the thieves, like Jonathan Wilde did in London last century?" Mendick looked up. "Has there been an increase in theft and housebreaking since China Jim appeared? Have there been more major robberies?"

Sturrock shook his head. "Trade is poor just now, Sergeant. There is always a slight increase in housebreaking and simple theft when trade is bad, and an increase in drunkenness and assaults when there's more employment and money around. There is nothing to suggest that China Jim is controlling our local criminals."

"This is a complete fudge," Mendick watched his smoke curl around the gas light. "We don't know what this Chinese fellow does. Maybe he doesn't even exist! Maybe he is just a wild notion of Hitchins."

"The murder was real enough, Sergeant," Sturrock reminded him. He pointed to the document that he had been studying. "What about this, Sergeant? I might have something. Here's a seaman who was sent to the Circuit Court for housebreaking."

"That's more the ticket!" Mendick said. "Was he convicted?"

"Lord Cockburn gave him 18 months with hard labour back in August 1847." Sturrock kept his finger on the entry.

"August '47. He'll be out now, hungry and resentful. That sounds promising, what is this enterprising fellow's name?" Mendick smiled, "He's not Chinese by any chance is he?"

"Josiah Oldbuck. Doesn't sound Chinese." Sturrock said.

"Not in the least. I had hoped the name would be Marmion. Do you have his address?" Mendick took his hat from its hook and lifted his cane. "We can step along there now."

Sturrock shook his head. "The only address we have is a lodging house in Couttie's Wynd – one of these penny-a-night hell holes for the transient. We don't have anywhere permanent for him."

Mendick replaced his hat. "All right. I want the town scoured for this fellow and for Robert Marmion. I'll tell Mr Mackay right now"

"It will have to be tomorrow, Sergeant," Sturrock said, "look at the clock. Wee Donnie went home hours ago."

Mendick swore and looked outside. Darkness swathed Dundee, penetrated only by the gas lamps that illuminated the main streets and the pinpricks of light at a hundred windows. He grunted. "We'd better get some sleep then, Sturrock, and start again tomorrow. At least we may have a name to pursue."

Thick with the smoke from a thousand fires, the night wrapped itself around Mendick as he walked to his lodgings. He heard the click of heels on paving stones and turned. The footsteps stopped immediately. Mendick waited a second and walked on, listening. He checked again before he entered the close that led to his house, saw the flick of a cloak, green in the ghostly glow of a gas lamp, then she slipped into shelter. He bolted his front door, locked his shutters, placed his single shot pistol under the pillow and his pepperpot revolver in his boot and went to bed.

Before he slept, Mendick allowed himself a small smile. He had expected a reaction from China Jim once Hitchins blabbed, and there it was. The woman in the green cloak was a sign he was pushing in the right direction.

Mendick eased the cramp in his hand and sighed at the ink stains on his fingers. Sometimes he felt more like a clerk than an active Officer of Police. He looked at the pile of letters and documents he had written, glanced up at the great circular wall clock whose sonorous ticking had kept time to the incessant scratching of his pen and shook his head. Eight o' clock. That was the day gone and what had he done?

He had scoured the country for references to Jonathan Oldbuck and Robert Marmion. He had had their names sent to the police offices in the surrounding towns and all the major cities of Great Britain. He had ordered the day constables to search and to ask for both men, and he had warned the coach operators and proprietors to keep a careful watch. He had contacted shipping companies in the hope they had him on the muster records of one of their vessels and he had asked the harbour police if the names were known to them. Nothing.

The door opened and a sergeant stepped in, the top of his head nearly brushing the door lintel. "Mr Mackay said you had orders for me, Mendick?"

Mendick heard the resentment in the man's voice. He looked up. "I want you to relieve the day watchmen at the railway station and the docks, Morrison. We are the same rank, so I cannot order you." He allowed himself a smile, but saw no responding warmth in Morrison's face. "However, Mr Mackay placed me in charge of this investigation and I intend to pursue our enquiries with the utmost vigour. I am sure you agree."

Morrison nodded stiffly. The use of the word 'our' may have thawed him a little, but Mendick was not prepared to unbend any further. His objective was to apprehend China Jim and leave Dundee.

"Wait, Morrison," Mendick lifted his hat and cane, "with your permission, may I join the night patrol?"

The request altered Morrison's attitude completely, as Mendick hoped it might.

"With pleasure, Mendick." Morrison did not smile, but he stepped aside to allow Mendick passage which was as genuine a gesture of respect as any. "I will detail Sturrock to accompany you."

Mendick nodded. He had got his wish and Morrison had retained his dignity so all parties were satisfied. He was gradually learning how to be a sergeant.

Couttie's Wynd was a narrow, slightly curved channel that made Candle Lane appear a residential paradise. It cut between four-storey high tenements, lined with cheeping houses, the lowest form of illicit drinking dens, and lodging houses. Mendick checked his watch, it was just past one. He blew on the face and rubbed it clean.

"That's the third time you have done that," Sturrock said.

"My late wife gave me this watch," Mendick told him. "She saved for months to buy it and it's about all I have left of her."

"I see." Sturrock nodded understanding. In common with most of the Dundee police, he valued family. "Here we are, Sergeant. We can try in here. It's a known den of predators and members of the light-fingered craft use it.

The sign said: *Mrs Kelly: Fine Lodgings*; the reality was a sunken door with peeling paint. Sturrock winked and cracked his staff against the door with no ceremony. The noise echoed around the wynd. Someone shouted for silence. There was a few moments delay and a middle-aged woman opened the door. She held up the stump of a candle to inspect her visitors.

"Oh. It's the thief-catchers." She made no move to let them pass until Sturrock pushed her aside.

"Have you any of our folks with you the night, Mistress?"

Mendick followed inside where the stench of damp and full chamber pots and unwashed humanity hit him like a fist.

"I dinnae think so, but ye can look. I keep a respectable house, mind."

Mrs Kelly glowered at Mendick through bloodshot eyes but handed Mendick the candle. Hot wax spilled onto his fingers. Sturrock led them into the first of two rooms and flicked the beam of his bull's eye lantern over the three couples laying in three beds that touched each other. Two of the couples wore their day clothes, the third had dispensed with that covering and were naked. The man had the letter D tattooed into his chest in three different places, and BC in one. Mendick knew the army had tattooed him as a deserter and a bad character, but Sturrock ignored him completely.

"Just labouring folk," Sturrock spoke without interest. "Who's in the closet, Mistress?" He shone his lantern into the corner of the room where a panelled door was wedged open. A young woman was propped up against the walls inside, her hair a tangled mess over her face, her dress soiled and filthy and her legs folded beneath her. Sturrock nodded.

"Jemima MacFarlane," he said. "She is a pickpocket, thief and lady of ill-repute. If anybody knows the criminal classes, she will." He nudged her legs with an ungentle boot. "Here! Jemima! Wake up! Sergeant Mendick has questions for you."

The woman opened her eyes, focussed on Sturrock and swore.

"That's right, Jemima." Sturrock bent over and helped her to a sitting position. "Just a few questions and we'll let you sleep again in your nice cupboard."

Mendick placed his candle on the window ledge where its light pooled onto Jemima's face. He knelt beside her.

"I am Detective Sergeant Mendick of Scotland Yard and the Dundee Police," he introduced himself. "I am looking for a man named Marmion. Do you know anybody of that name?"

Jemima tossed back her head. "No."

"You may have heard of a Josiah Oldbuck then?" Mendick moved the candle slightly so the light was full in Jemima's face.

"That's not a real name," Jemima closed her eyes and breathed out fumes that could have come straight from a whisky still.

There had been no hesitation in her answers, no wavering. Jemima's eyes had been no more or less focussed as she spoke. Mendick believed she was telling the truth. He raised the candle so the light was directly in line with her eyes. "You answered those questions uncommonly well, Jemima. I have just one more for you. Tell me when you last saw China Jim."

Jemima looked away. "Bugger off, bluebottle." Her tone had roughened, her voice slurred and the words came out quickly. "You come in here without a by-your-leave and ask your questions. Why can't you just bugger off and leave honest folk in peace?" She raised her voice into a scream, "Bugger off!"

Sturrock grabbed her hair and began to haul her upright, but Mendick touched his arm. "No, constable; she is scared. She will tell us nothing, or anything at all, to get rid of us."

It was the same in the crowded closes of the Overgate and among the Irish of the Scouringburn. Nobody admitted to knowing the names Marmion or Oldbuck, but when China Jim was mentioned, the response was either a shrug or a look of frozen horror that was quickly replaced by denial. Nobody volunteered any helpful information.

"You do realise China Jim will be more alert than ever once he realises we are actively searching for him?" Sturrock said as they breakfasted in Mrs Hunter's Eating House in Fish Street. Mendick faced the window, watching the busy passage of people as Sturrock finished off a plate of oysters and liver.

"That's the idea," Mendick said. "If he is nervous he may make a mistake and we'll catch him." He watched a carriage rattle past, the driver upright in his seat and the single horse obviously better cared for than some of the people in this town. There was poverty in Dundee, as there was in every British town, but there was money too. "How many broughams are there in Dundee?"

Sturrock stopped, with a forkful of liver half way to his mouth. "I don't know." He said.

"I want you to find out." Mendick said. "I am assuming that Marmion and Oldbuck are one and the same person."

"That's a very large assumption."

"Many criminals use an alias," Mendick said, "and we have a seaman with criminal tendencies here."

Sturrock shovelled the liver into his mouth. "If you say so, Sergeant," he said cheerfully.

Mendick sighed and smoothed a hand over his face as twenty-four hours without sleep caught up with him. "Let's see. We have a murder with a great many clues, but none of them make sense. A seaman who uses a ladder, a bag with 30 silver coins all dated 1842, a Chinese connection. Men who seem so ordinary nobody remembers what they look like, three mysterious small men, a man with two names and a murdered deaf man. Let's try and reduce that list."

Sturrock looked up, tore a hunk off a loaf of bread and wiped the gravy from his plate. "How do we do that, Sergeant?"

"We eliminate the impossible. You know Dundee better than I do. Now answer as accurately as you can. How many Chinese live in Dundee?"

Sturrock grinned. "Hold up your right hand, Sergeant . . . go on, hold it up."

Mendick did so.

"Now take away five fingers. How many do you have left?"

"Why, none of course . . ."

"Exactly. That is how many Chinamen live in Dundee." Sturrock said. "I heard what the beggar fellow said, but I don't believe a word of it. We can forget the Chinese triangle nonsense . . ."

"Triad," Mendick corrected.

"Aye, we can forget that too. Believe me, Sergeant, if there were any Chinese triangles living in Dundee, we would know about them."

Mendick looked him up and down. "And how many people live in this town?"

"Around 70,000 souls," Sturrock said.

"And you know them all?" Mendick asked. "Including the visiting lascar seamen and the Chinese cook who absconded from the ship from the East who slipped away one night and began a criminal organisation?"

Sturrock frowned, "I never heard of any such thing. This isn't London, Mendick. We know what happens here!"

Mendick considered. He remembered Dundee well.

Everybody knew everything and there were no strangers within the boundaries of the town.

"So if there are no Chinese, Sturrock, then there is no China Jim, or at least not a Chinaman called Jim."

He stood up, threw a shilling on the table to pay for the meal and stalked outside with Sturrock striding at his side. Early morning rain had washed the dust from the streets and spring sunshine reflected from a hundred windows, casting shadows from the masts of a score of ships onto the bustle of Dock Street.

"So maybe, rather than a Chinaman, we are looking for someone with a Chinese connection? Maybe we are looking for someone who trades with China?"

Sturrock frowned, shaking his head. "I don't think there is any Dundee trade with China."

"There may be no direct trade, Sturrock, but there may be indirect trade, perhaps via India or even America."

Mendick tipped back the brim of his hat and looked around. The docks were busy with men unloading timber from a newly arrived Baltic brig while a wagon heaped with unidentified bundles rumbled over the uneven cobbles. Carts and wagons crunched over the cobbles and the ubiquitous crowd of bare-footed children clustered around doorways, hoping for a chance to steal and run.

"I want a list of anyone with even the most remarkably small connection with China, and I want to know what they were doing in 1842."

Mendick stood aside as the topmost bundle on a passing wagon slipped and crashed onto the ground, sending fragments of pottery cascading in a wide arc. Two women shrieked and grabbed hold of each other.

"Find out what David Thoms was doing in 1842 and

keep looking for Marmion and Oldbuck. He might have been on a deepwater voyage." Mendick watched the carter sweep up the mess, with the gang of young boys and girls hovering around the tail of the cart waiting to swoop. "Maybe even to China."

"It all seems to hinge on China," Sturrock said.

"China and the sea," Mendick agreed. "Now. Mr Mackay posted you to me because of your local knowledge, so do you know that woman?" He nodded at the woman in the green cloak who kept pace with them step for step on the opposite side of the road.

Sturrock shook his head. "She's not known to me," he said.

"She's been following me for some days now. I think we should bring her to the office and ask her why."

Mendick turned as he heard footsteps behind him, to see a tall and evil-faced constable with a white scar running down the left side of his face. Mendick remembered him touching the pillars at the entrance of the police office.

"Is this the man Mendick?" The policeman addressed the question to Sturrock, who nodded.

"Aye, this is Sergeant Mendick of Scotland Yard and the Dundee Police."

"Aye, that's the fellow." The constable touched the brim of his hat in hurried salute. "Wee Donny says you've to come at once."

"I beg your pardon?" Mendick looked to Sturrock for a translation.

"Constable Deuchars is trying to say that Superintendent Donald Mackay requests your presence, Sergeant, as soon as is convenient."

"Aye." Deuchars glowered at Sturrock. "That's what

I said. Donny's in the Arctic. There's been another murder. There are bits of some bugger all over the place."

CHAPTER FIVE

Mendick thought there was always something sad about a workplace empty of people, and the Dundee Arctic Whale Fishing Company yard was no exception. He glanced around. Tall and slightly sinister, the shining copper boiling vats dominated everything in this long yard that stretched from the Seagate to Dock Street. It was littered with pieces of whaling equipment and thick with the lingering putridity of stale, boiled blubber. Despite the size of the yard the only building was the warehouse, situated a good fifteen yards from the Seagate entrance. Although only a seagull's call from the centre of Dundee, the yard seemed a bleak and lonely place.

"In here," a white-faced constable opened the great door of the warehouse.

There was no need to be directed to the corpse. It lay like a pile of raw meat and coiled intestines on the centre of the floor. Blood pooled all around and formed little rivers that ran along between the flagstones.

Mendick did not walk immediately to the body. Instead he paced the floor and looked around as a rising wind rattled the door against its frame and howled around the outside of the warehouse. He looked up, the fine weather had not lasted long and March was making up for its temporary smile with a roaring fury that battered for entry to the charnel house in the whaleyard. The interior of the warehouse was stark. Four oil lamps cast bouncing shadows on stone walls that rose to a timber-framed slate roof. Bloody footsteps around the body were small and many.

"More than one person involved then," Mendick said. "Three people, I think?"

"Hitchins saw four at the Candle Lane murder," Sturrock reminded him.

The Police Surgeon had arrived at the same time as Mendick. He pursed thin lips as he saw the bloodied pile of human body parts. "Good God! I've never seen the like!" He looked at Mendick. "You must be the Scotland Yard man. I am Dr Webster."

"That's the second atrocity inside a week, Doctor." Mendick shook his hand. "Is Dundee always as dangerous for its inhabitants?"

Webster looked away. "This is normally a quiet town, Mendick. Murders are quite a rarity here."

"So I see." Mendick moved closer, leaving Sturrock to stand against the wall, white-faced and shaking. This body had been spread-eagled on the ground and had been emasculated and eviscerated, with slices of flesh cut from the thighs and buttocks. Clothes were laid in a neat pile on the floor, slightly away from the congealed blood, and there was a small linen bag placed on the chest.

"Has anything been moved or touched in here?" Mendick prodded the body with the tip of his cane.

The white-faced constable swallowed hard. "Nothing, Sergeant."

"Very good," Mendick lifted the bag, opened the drawstring and looked inside. The silver sheen of shillings was not unexpected. He lifted the top coin.

"Eighteen forty two," he said. In case of coincidence, he checked a handful. All had the same date.

68

"We have a madman on the loose, Sturrock," he said.

"And a cannibal," Sturrock said quietly.

The oil lanterns gave sufficient light to see the plate of cooked meat that stood on the long wooden table which took up an entire wall of the warehouse. The ashes of the fire on the ground were cold, but when Mendick stirred them there was a faint red glow that quickly died.

"This unfortunate fellow was killed during the night, then." He looked at the surgeon. "Do you have a more precise time for his death, Doctor?"

Dr Webster probed a finger into the body and felt the muscles of the arms. "I would estimate around midnight, Mendick, to judge by the stiffening of the limbs."

"He was killed in a similar fashion to David Thoms in Candle Lane," Mendick raised his voice. "Do we know the identity of the victim?"

"He's – he was – Robert Milne." The white-faced constable did not look at the horror spread-eagled on the ground.

"How do you know that? Is he known to the police?" Mendick signalled for Sturrock to take notes.

"This is my beat, Sergeant. I used to speak to him most nights." The constable glanced at the body and away again.

"And your name is?" Mendick asked.

"Abbot, Sergeant."

"All right, Abbot, take your time now, lad. Don't think of the body, the man is dead and that is all there is to it. Just answer my questions as best you can. Do you know what Mr Milne's occupation was?"

Abbot took a deep breath. "He was a night watchman."

"Where?" Mendick stepped away so Abbot did not have to look at the mutilated body.

"Here," Abbot said. "He watched the whaleyard."

69

"That was providential for the murderer," Mendick looked up. "And you are the beat constable? Tell me what happened."

Abbot looked about ready to collapse but he pulled himself erect. "I checked the door every half hour and it was securely locked. I normally see Rab – Milne – when he comes out for a pipe, but not last night. When the day watchman arrived he found him like this, all cut to pieces."

"So either the murderer had a key, or picked the lock." Mendick said. He tipped back the brim of his hat and looked around. The ground was bare. "What is this place normally used for?"

Abbot swallowed hard. "It's used to store barrels of blubber when they're unloaded from the whaling ships and before it's boiled into oil."

Mendick nodded. That would account for the smell. "Is there only one entrance, where the barrels are loaded and unloaded?"

"Just the one," Abbot confirmed.

"I see," Mendick pointed to the furthest corner, where a green painted door carried a notice that stated:

Private: Keep Out. Property of DCC.

"What the devil does DCC mean?" He strode across and tried the door. "Who has the key for this, Abbot?"

"Rab – Milne – would have," Abbot could not look down at the body.

Sighing, Mendick went through Milne's clothes. His silver watch and chain were still intact and there was a handful of loose change and a single key. He had not been robbed and there was nothing else. "There is only one key here." He tried the key in the outside door, it fitted perfectly. "Has somebody told Mr Milne's wife?"

"He was unmarried," Abbot said.

"That is a mercy. It is always hard for those left behind." Mendick stepped to the interior door. The key fitted that door too, so he pushed it open and stepped inside. The room was empty save for a pile of stones, each one about half the size of a man's head, carefully shaped and polished and with a handle on the top.

"Curling stones," Sturrock had followed him in. "DCC must be the Dundee Curling Club, they will use this room for storage."

"Curling stones?" Mendick touched the nearest with his boot. "Why keep chunks of granite behind lock and key?"

"These stones are valuable property, Sergeant. Look," Sturrock lifted the nearest stone and tested it for weight. "This is blue granite from Ailsa Craig, the very best. The stones come from all over the place: Ailsa Craig, Perthshire, some are even made from Greenland stone . . ."

"I don't care where they come from," Mendick stopped him.

Sturrock shrugged. "Sorry, Sergeant. The DCC is a remarkably prestigious organisation."

Mendick grunted to show his opinion of prestigious organisations. "Thank you for that information, Sturrock. Since this key also fits the warehouse door, every member of this club is a suspect, however prestigious they may be. If they have access to this room, rest assured I will be talking to them." Mendick glanced around. "You will continue to search for China Jim and these other men. Have all the beat constables question their informants about anything Oriental. And Sturrock, contact every other major police office in the country and ask if there have been any similar murders. Check as far back as

1842." Mendick rapped his cane off the table. "I have some enquiries to make and a curling rink to visit. Step out, man."

Mendick coughed softly, so as not to disturb the concentration of the players. All around him the crowd was watching as Sir John Ogilvie, the club president, squatted upon the crampit and lined up his curling stone. The carriages of the players crowded the road that coiled up the Law to the curling ponds at Stirling Park, with most coachmen gathered in a patient huddle, smoking their pipes companionably. One nondescript man sat on the driving seat of a gig, reading avidly with his tall hat pushed back on his head. Mendick ran his gaze across each man, looking for the familiar signs of guilt but the faces were anonymous and he dismissed them as perpetrators of so-far undiscovered crimes.

Instead he concentrated on the players. These were the elite of Dundee: the linen barons, shipowners and merchants who knew little, and cared less, about the seething poor in the wynds and closes; these were the men who owned the chimneys he had once swept. Mendick watched them at play and wondered if one hid behind the alias of China Jim.

Scattered like butterflies among the monotony of dark-clothed men, a handful of women provided both distraction and colour. Presumably the wives of the merchants, they watched through bored eyes, clapped gloved hands together for warmth and spoke quietly, the condensation of their breath forming little grey clouds as they walked. Mendick narrowed his eyes when one of the women met his gaze; she was straight-backed with a wisp of auburn hair across her left eye. Alone of the women, she carried a curling stone, but with such casual grace it was obvious she was no mere spectator. She watched the progress of this particular match with keen interest. Only when she waved did Mendick allow himself to smile. He had not expected Johanna Lednock to be here.

He looked away. He had no time to admire women, however attractive. He had a job of work to do. One or more of these people could be his murderer, a monster hiding behind a facade of respectability. He could not afford the distraction of Johanna. As Ogilvie lined up his stone, Mendick looked down the steep hill and over the town of Dundee where the hazy light of late afternoon was already waning, street lights were being lit and smoke from a thousand chimneys congealed above the grey slates of tenement roofs. Beyond was the silvery streak of the Tay dotted with the pin-pricking lights of ships.

"Go on, Ogilvie," a man encouraged, and others gave sycophantic cries of agreement as the club president aimed, swept forward his arm and released his stone.

"That's a beauty for the final stone of the end!" someone yelled.

Mendick understood enough about curling to know that each game was termed an 'end' so this was an important moment. He watched as Ogilvie gave his wrist a subtle twist to impart draw to the stone which roared across the ice with the sweepers slithering in front, wielding their besoms frantically as they brushed away any loose particles of ice that might impede its progress.

One section of the crowd cheered as Ogilvie's stone crashed into that of another player, sending it spinning aside and out of the scoring area.

"Well done, Sir John!"

Ogilvie's stone continued, scraping across the ice to land within the centre of the three circles, side-by-side with a squat piece of blue granite.

"That's Johanna Lednock's Ailsa Craig beauty," someone pointed out, as the rest of the spectators shouted their triumph when it became apparent that the two stones were exactly level.

"It's a tie between Ogilvie and Johanna." The speaker looked up and caught Mendick's gaze. "And who the devil are you? You are not a member."

"The name is Sergeant Mendick of Scotland Yard." Mendick flourished his official staff. He examined the man. Middle aged, he tried to conceal his lack of height by standing erect, his weather-beaten face thrown into shadow by the flaring torches that lit the match, his dark waistcoat and trousers contrasted with the starched white of his shirt. His head was tilted back and his gaze held that of Mendick, unyielding. This was a man used to getting his own way.

"Pray tell me your name, sir."

The raised voice attracted the attention of others, and faces turned towards him. Some were merely inquisitive, others hostile, but all carried the unmistakable stamp of wealth, power and authority. Mendick allowed them to stare; he knew he would be speaking to them in the fullness of time.

The man remained silent and Mendick repeated his question, this time adding an edge to his voice. "Tell me your name, sir, if you please?"

"I am Gordon." The man spoke as if he expected Mendick to recognise his name.

Mendick did not. He nodded and raised his voice so

that everybody within five yards could hear him. "I am investigating the murder of Robert Milne, Mr Gordon. I will be questioning every man here."

The faces became expressionless until a younger man gave a hesitant smile. "You are investigating the murder of whom, Sergeant? I don't think I know the man."

"Robert Milne," Mendick explained. "He was the night watchman who was murdered beside the curling stone store of this club. And you are, sir?"

"I am Gilbride of the Waverley Shipping Company." Gilbride's suit was cut so close it emphasised the breath of his shoulders while disguising his lack of height. "Of course, he was the unhappy fellow down by the whaling yard. That was a desperate business, terrible."

Others added brief sympathetic noises before returning their attention to the curling.

"A bad business, certainly," Gordon agreed, "but obviously nothing to do with us, Sergeant. We are gentlemen. So I suggest you get about your business and let us get on with our game."

"Gentlemen or beggars," Mendick said, "we are all subject to the same laws."

Gordon gave a mocking bow, "You have your duty to perform, Sergeant. I leave you to get on with it elsewhere."

"Is that you, Sergeant Mendick?" This voice was jovial enough and the man who bustled forward had his hand outstretched in welcome. "Good God, man, why did you not make yourself known at once? You remember me? Adam Leslie – you saved me from pickpockets on the London!" He raised his voice. "This is a tale worth repeating, gentlemen. Two flicks of his cane and two blackguards sent reeling. 'Be off with you!' he said, and sent them scampering away as if the hounds of hell were howling at their heels!" The handshake was warm and firm, the myopic blue eyes friendly behind their thick glasses. However nervous Leslie had seemed in the boat, he was in his element here. "Now, sir, what's all this about a murder, eh?"

The warmth of his welcome almost brought a smile, but Mendick merely matched Leslie's grip. "You may have heard about the body that was found in the Arctic Whaling Company warehouse?"

Leslie's smile dropped away. "I did, Sergeant – terrible business, terrible. My wife was quite overcome: she fairly swooned away and poor Louise nearly had hysterics. Sarah had to apply smelling salts." He shook his head and turned away to remove and polish his glasses. "It was some poor fellow named Milne, I believe? My clerks speak of little else, Sergeant. It was a shocking business. The newspapers are full of speculation: wild animals on the loose, packs of stray dogs, a madman in Dundee. They are saying all sorts of things." He looked at Mendick with suddenly concerned eyes. "Is that why you are here, Sergeant?"

Mendick nodded, "I am afraid it is, Mr Leslie. The body was found in the warehouse where this club's curling stones are stored, so I fear I must make enquiries here." He pitched his voice to carry to the other club members but most had returned their interest to the curling or their own business affairs. Only Johanna continued to watch him, her eyes curious as she cradled the curling stone as if it were her son.

Leslie raised his hat, scratched his head with podgy fingers and asked. "Do you believe it was one of us, Sergeant?"

"I do not believe anything, Mr Leslie." Again Mendick spoke loudly so everyone present could hear. "I am merely investigating." He allowed the murmur of discontent to die down. "I will see you one at a time in the clubhouse."

The clubhouse was little more than a wooden hut a few paces from the side of the curling pond, illuminated by flaring torches and flanked by a group of men selling whisky and hot pies. Mendick stepped inside the open door and turned to watch as two new players placed their smooth chunks of granite on the ice and then stepped back. They laughed quietly as if unconscious or uncaring of the butchery only the previous night. Mendick was aware of breath clouding around cold faces, of men vigorously flapping their arms and ladies clapping kid-gloved hands together as they wished they were home in the warmth. When he shifted his head to the side he caught Johanna's gaze on him, and the startling clarity of her green eyes. She held the look for a few seconds before slowly lowering her eyelids.

Mendick could almost taste the wealth; it was in the scent of tailored clothes and the atmosphere of power, it was in the confident tones and movement of the players. There was something indefinable that marked these men apart from the mass of the population that crammed into the closes and tenements of the city spread out below. And yet, one of these successful, dynamic businessmen could well be the monster who had already murdered and feasted on two unfortunates. Most of these oh-so-respectable gentlemen were taller and broader than the average Dundonian, but evil could disguise itself behind a hundred cloaks. Mendick knew that Fate had made him an outsider, a man living on the precipitous oxymoron between respectability and chaos, protecting the one from the other, accepted by neither, distrusted by both. He could not allow himself to trust these men simply because of their position. He straightened, tapped his cane against the brim of his hat and looked around again.

"Whenever you are ready, Sergeant." Leslie was watching him, holding a nicky of whisky. He offered the glass to Mendick, who shook his head.

Lifting his cane, Mendick crashed it half a dozen times against the side of the hut. One of the ladies gave a small scream but the noise effectively broke the concentration of the players and they turned to face him.

"What the devil do you think you are doing, sir?"

"You blasted roughneck. This is a gentleman's club!"

Raising his voice, Mendick bellowed above their protests.

"Quiet! Now listen to me!"

Unused to being spoken to in such a peremptory manner, the club members stared at him. He brandished his staff. "By the authority of the Queen I am going to ask every person here a few questions."

"What the deuce for, sir?" Gordon glared at him. "I have already told you not to waste our time. Be about your business or I'll have your position!"

"Mr Gordon, I warn you not to interfere in the workings of the Dundee Police." Mendick pointed the tip of his staff at Gordon to alleviate any possibility of mistaken identity. The golden VR of authority reflected the torchlight. "We are none of us above the law, sir. You included."

"I am Gordon." The man spoke as if his name should be enough to subdue a mere police sergeant.

"And I am Mendick." Mendick saw Johanna smile

78

at that and cover her mouth with a gloved hand. "I am investigating two murders and you can be first to help me, Mr Gordon. Come this way, if you please."

"I am no murderer . . ." Gordon began, but Mendick opened the hut door and gestured. "This way, sir."

The interior of the hut was as stark as the outside. There was a small fireplace, a writing desk with an armed chair that Mendick appropriated as his own, two other hard-backed chairs and little else. Waiting until Gordon seated himself opposite, Mendick placed his staff on top of the desk and took his notebook from his inside pocket.

"This won't take long, Mr Gordon. At present, all I need to know is your whereabouts last night."

Gordon glared but responded. He removed his hat and placed it on the table. "I was at home," he said, "with my wife."

"And where is home, sir?" Mendick had already begun to write Unicorn Cottage when Gordon replied.

"Mandarin House." Once again, Gordon spoke as if he expected his address to be known.

"You have two addresses, sir?" Mendick raised his eyes to hold the level bar of Gordon's gaze. "I believe you also own Unicorn Cottage in Broughty Ferry."

Gordon snorted. "Unicorn Cottage belongs to my wife, Sergeant. It is hardly a place I would live. She uses it as a painting retreat during the day." He spat out the word 'painting' as if it were an oath.

"I see." Mendick noted that down. "Is there anyone who can confirm you were at home last night?" Mendick tried to keep the sharpness from his voice.

"Surely I am not a suspect?"

Mendick ignored the outburst and repeated the question.

This time Gordon replied. "My wife may confirm that, sir, and my servants, but I will see you at the devil before allowing you to subject them to this form of questioning." A deep groove appeared between Gordon's eyes as he glowered at Mendick.

"Indeed, sir. Now do you know of anybody by the name of Marmion or Oldbuck?"

Gordon grunted and shook his head. "I am sure I do not, sir."

"You may have met them some years ago," Mendick said.

Gordon snorted. "I have never encountered such names in my life, sir." Gordon lifted his hat and pushed back his chair.

"Mendick rolled his staff so the VR pointed at Gordon. "Pray remain where you are, sir. I will inform you when I have finished. Now, does the name China Jim mean anything to you?"

"China Jim?" Mendick saw a slight smile appear on Gordon's face before he replied. "No, I do not know that name."

Mendick watched his reaction. "And do you know of any Chinese people living in Dundee, or elsewhere?"

Gordon paused before replying. "No, sir, I do not."

"And do you have any business connections with China, sir?"

The pause was even longer. "I have been fortunate enough to have made sufficient money not to have to indulge in business at all, Sergeant."

"Your home is Mandarin House, sir. That is a Chinese name," Mendick pointed out.

"I like the term, Sergeant," Gordon said.

Mendick nodded. "I see, sir. Then that is all for just now, Mr Gordon. Thank you for your cooperation. I will be speaking with your wife shortly to have her confirm your statement."

"You shall do nothing of the sort, sir!" Gordon leaned forward in his seat.

Mendick held his gaze. "I shall, sir and if you attempt in any way to interfere with the workings of the law, I shall put such restraints on you that even you will not appreciate. Now, please ask the next gentleman to come in."

The club members entered one after the other, truculent, unhelpful and arrogant, and after two hours Mendick was utterly weary. He looked as the door opened again and Mr Gilbride limped in. He sat down carefully and stretched his leg out before him.

"A riding accident, Sergeant," he explained, as Mendick raised an inquiring eyebrow.

"When was that, sir, if I may enquire?"

"I had a tumble about six weeks ago, Sergeant. I was racing a point-to-point from the summit of the Law to Kilpurnie in the Sidlaw Hills and my horse decided to stop, while I continued." When Gilbride grinned he looked very young.

"So you are less active than normal," Mendick noted. "Are you still able to climb stairs or ladders?"

"I climb with care," Gilbride said, "but I will heal in time." He began to explain the extent of his injuries until Mendick stopped him.

"I am sure it was very painful, sir. Now could you tell me where you were on the evening of the 23rd March, pray?"

"I shall have to check, Sergeant," Gilbride frowned, "what day was that, now?"

"It was a Friday," Mendick reminded quietly.

"Of course, the 23rd March." Gilbride looked up quickly. "We had some trouble that day. One of my vessels was due to sail out on the evening tide but the boys refused to sail on a Friday; some superstition or other, and I had to go down and speak to them."

"You were at the docks then on the 23rd. Do you have anybody to verify that, sir?" Mendick made a note to check the tides and the shipping movements that day.

Gilbride eased his ankle a little. "I have, Sergeant. The master and entire crew of *Evelyn Berenger*: that was the vessel involved."

"Are they still in the harbour, Mr Gilbride?"

"They will be on their way to the Greenland Sea now, Sergeant." Gilbride seemed to find the question amusing. "But if you want to check, they will be back in August or September, perhaps October. It all depends how successful the fishing is."

"I see, thank you. And last night sir? Where were you last night?"

Gilbride retained his smile. "I was working Sergeant, I was paying suppliers and sending letters to old customers and new. Business is dull just now and one needs to use every artifice in order to keep afloat."

For a second a shadow darkened his eyes and Mendick thought of the recent Chartist troubles and the desperate poverty in the wynds and closes. If even a successful shipowner and businessman such as Gilbride was feeling the pinch, times must be hard indeed.

"Is there anybody who can verify that, sir?"

"I am afraid not, Sergeant. My staff finished at seven, while I was in the office until half past ten." He smiled again. "You may just have to take my word sir, as a gentleman."

Mendick did not smile, but he resolved to ask the beat constable if there had been a light at Gilbride's office window. "Could you give me the address of your office, sir?"

"Whale Lane, sir. I am the managing owner of the Waverley Whale Fishing Company . . ."

Mendick cut him off with gesture. "Yes, sir. Mr Milne's body was found in the whale yard of the Arctic Whale Fishing Company, is there a connection?"

"Good God, no!" Gilbride shook his head. "We are rivals, sir. We have no connection whatsoever."

"I see. Thank you, sir. I may have to speak to you again, but I have your address. I presume you do not intend to leave Dundee in the near future?" Mendick touched his fingers against his staff so it rolled slightly and the tip, with its gold crown and the VR letters, reminded Gilbride exactly with whom he was dealing.

When Gilbride nodded and left, Mendick completed his notes and barely looked up when the door opened once more and somebody sat gracefully opposite him.

"I suppose you wish to ask me questions as well?" There was music in Johanna's voice, and her eyes danced over Mendick.

"I do, if you have access to the storehouse key." Mendick had to suppress a smile.

"I have the same access as any other member," Johanna had no reservations about smiling at him.

"In that case, I have some questions for you, Mrs Gordon."

Johanna dropped her smile, sat upright in the seat, held Mendick's gaze and nodded. "Please continue, Sergeant Mendick."

Mendick wanted to say it was unusual for a woman

to be a member of a curling club as well as owning property, but duty came first. "May I enquire where you were last night, Mrs Gordon?"

"I was at home, Sergeant." Johanna said gravely.

Mendick nodded. "With your husband?"

When Johanna frowned, there was a little pucker between her eyes and a small groove formed at the side of her mouth. "My husband was at home also, Sergeant."

"You were together then." Mendick said. He waited for confirmation, but instead Johanna hesitated and shook her head. She looked up with her lips pressed tight together and her chin thrust slightly forward.

"We were not together, Sergeant. I live in Unicorn Cottage and he lives in Mandarin House."

"I see." Mendick thought it best not to pursue that line of enquiry at present. Mrs Gordon looked close to being out of temper with him. "Now this may sound a strange question, Mrs Gordon, but please bear with me. Does either of these names mean anything to you: Robert Marmion or Jonathan Oldbuck?"

Johanna frowned, "Marmion and Oldbuck? Now there is a strange question for a Criminal Officer! Of course I know these names, but what on earth have they to do with your investigation? What was it? Murder by literature?" Her laugh was not quite in keeping with the serious nature of the discussion but Mendick found it welcome nevertheless.

"I do not understand . . ." Mendick began.

"You don't read much, do you? Those names are from the books of Walter Scott. He wrote a poem called *Marmion*, and Jonathan Oldbuck is a character in *The Antiquary*." Johanna was smiling, shaking her head. "Is this some sort of game?"

"If it is," Mendick said, "it is being played on me. I had not worked out the Walter Scott connection." He looked at her with approval. He had admired her looks and was attracted by her personality, now he had to add respect for her learning and quick intelligence as well.

"Can you tell me more?" Johanna's eyes widened.

Mendick would have loved to tell her everything but duty forbade. "These names are alibis of possible suspects," he said.

"And as all these names are from Walter Scott's books," Johanna said, "they may have a connection?"

"That is possible," Mendick said. "But we have to investigate further." He watched her smile, "When curling and painting palls on you, perhaps you could join us in Scotland Yard."

When Johanna smiled, the left corner of her mouth lifted. "All my spare time is taken up by my son," she said.

Mendick noted that one thought of her son had altered Johanna. Her eyes had softened, with small creases at the corners. "Of course, but you would be a great asset to the force. Now, I am afraid I must ask more questions. Do you have any connection with China, or know any Chinamen?"

Johanna shook her head. "No, Sergeant. Save for my husband's previous business connections, I have no connection to China. I have never been to China and nor do I have any intention of going there. From what I have heard it sounds like a terrible place, full of disease and poverty."

Mendick wanted to agree with her and share his Chinese experiences but he forced himself to keep to the matter in hand. "You say Mr Gordon had business interests in China?"

Johanna's frown was unwelcome. "Did he not tell you? Well, if he said nothing about them, I am sure I had better not."

Mendick scribbled a note to speak further to Gordon but altered tack. "Do you know the Arctic Whaling boiling yard, Mrs Gordon?"

"Of course I do," once more her laugh was out of place but welcome, "by smell at least."

"Have you ever been there, Mrs Gordon?" Mendick tried not to smile.

"Why on earth would I ever want to go to a place like that?" She leaned closer, her eyes searching. Her smile entranced him and he had to force himself to concentrate.

"Why indeed? I do not think I need take up any more of your time, Mrs Gordon." Mendick fought the compulsion to ask more questions, to enquire how this woman with the musical voice and lightning mind could be so delightfully friendly to him but mix so easily with the elite of Dundee. Instead, he watched her leave the hut as elegantly and quietly as she had arrived. He sat for a long moment until there was a tap on the door and Adam Leslie peered in.

"I believe I am last, Sergeant." Leslie gave the expected answer. "My clerk was with me until around six, Sergeant, and then I was alone. Times are hard, you see, with this prolonged depression, and one needs make every shift . . ."

"I do understand that, sir." Mendick said. "Now, sir, do you know of any Chinamen in Dundee, or do you have any connection with China?"

"No, Sergeant. I have never seen a Chinaman in my life and I have never heard of one in Dundee. Nor do I have a Chinese connection; I've never been further east than London, nor further south either, now I come to think of it!" His laughter was shortlived. "I do apologise Sergeant. Laughing at such a time is unforgivable, with that poor unfortunate man not yet in his grave." Leslie took off his glasses and began to polish the lenses with a crisp linen handkerchief.

"Now, sir, could you tell me where you were on Friday the 23rd March?"

"Quite easily, Sergeant Mendick. I was on the boat from London, and then caught a cab straight home to my family." Leslie replaced his spectacles. "That was the day you saved me from those pickpockets, you recall." He smiled again, but tentatively. "I have never properly shown you my appreciation for that service, sir, and I would like to invite you home tonight. Have a bite to eat and meet the family."

Mendick was about to refuse when the prospect of a decent meal tempted him. He had not eaten properly since he came to Dundee and Leslie could hardly have a more solid alibi for Thom's murder. "That would be most acceptable, sir."

CHAPTER SIX

Mendick dismounted from the gig and surveyed the street as he waited for Leslie to join him. The Leslie residence was in Magdalen Place in the western suburbs of Dundee. It was one of a number of substantial villas arranged in a quietly curved street where trees rustled unseen in the dark. Mendick tapped his cane on the tall garden wall which sheltered this residential idyll. The name Juniper Lea was carved into the stonework beside the gate.

"This is really very good of you, sir . . ."

"Nonsense my dear fellow, you are more than welcome. Besides which, Mrs Leslie has constantly asked who it was who rescued me on the ship." There was sufficient moonlight for Mendick to make out the intertwined initials, AL and CC that formed the centrepiece of the wrought iron gates Leslie opened. "I do not oil this gate," Leslie explained away the terrible screech as he pushed the gates open, "so we can hear if a burglar enters the garden."

"Of course, sir," Mendick agreed. It was an old trick that sometimes worked.

Ranks of daffodils and crocuses ranged beside the gravel path leading to a bold doorway flanked by doric columns that denoted status to the outside world. The four stone steps were freshly scrubbed, the boot scraper clean, ready for the next dose of city muck, and the brass handles and nameplate gleamed. A maid-servant opened the door even before Leslie had fumbled out his key; she dropped a swift curtsey and failed to hide her smile.

"Welcome back, sir. Mrs Leslie is in the drawing room." She dropped her voice to a whisper. "I would walk warily sir, if I were you. The mistress was expecting you home this last hour and already the young ladies have heard the rough side of her tongue."

Leslie drew in his eyebrows, which unbalanced his spectacles so he had to grab them before they slid from his nose. "Thank you for the warning, Mary." He handed his coat and hat to the servant, and indicated that Mendick do likewise. "Mrs Leslie gets a little worried sometimes," he explained softly, "so pray forgive her if she seems a trifle short with me."

Mendick gave what he hoped was a reassuring smile. "I was married myself once," he said, and once more cursed himself for giving too much away.

"This way, sir, and shall I announce the gentleman?" Burdened with coats, hats and cane, the servant still managed another bobbed curtsey as she stood with her hand on the china handle of the door.

"I would rather like to do that myself, Mary," Leslie said. "Now, you had better be about your business before Mrs Leslie puts a flea in your ear." He smiled as Mary bustled away, her black and white dress neat around her ankles and a single strand of dark hair flopping free from her cap. "She's a good girl, Mary. Mrs Leslie rescued her from the poorhouse."

The drawing room was a haven of ordered peace, with a glowing fire contained within a tiled hearth, a longcase clock ticking quietly in one corner and a glass-fronted bookcase taking up most of the space on the back wall. A blonde girl played a rollicking but strangely melancholic air on an upright piano, a dark-haired girl sat, closely examining a piece of sewing beside an older woman who looked up, put down the sampler she had been working on and stood.

"You are back late, Adam." There was an edge to her voice, but her eyes were friendly. She glanced towards Mendick, "and you have brought company, I see." She clapped her hands and spoke sharply to the girl at the piano, "Sarah, desist! We have a guest."

The blonde girl stopped playing immediately, carefully folded away her sheet music, closed the lid of the piano and walked to sit beside her sister. She smoothed her skirt beneath her and sat with her hands folded demurely in her lap.

"I have brought very distinguished company, my dear." Leslie paused then, with his eyes bright behind the spectacles and obviously bursting with pride. He looked more relaxed than Mendick had seen him; a man at home, king of his own castle. "This is Sergeant James Mendick of Scotland Yard, the very man who saved my life when I was at sea."

"I have no wish to inconvenience you, Mrs Leslie," Mendick began, but Mrs Leslie shook her head. "Nonsense, Sergeant Mendick! Step inside and find some warmth, do!" Mrs Leslie gestured him inside. "Come on, man!"

Mrs Leslie held out a welcoming hand as the two younger women, obviously her daughters, looked up and smiled together. Mrs Leslie took control of the conversation. "Sergeant Mendick, we have heard all about you! Mr Leslie never tires of telling us about the brave Scotland Yard detective who chased away the pickpockets!" She frowned slightly and spoke over her shoulder, "Come along girls, say your good evenings to the Sergeant!"

"Good evening Sergeant Mendick!"

The voices came in a musical chorus from the two girls. They bobbed in a curtsey, and held Mendick's gaze. Although they behaved like identical twins they were as different in appearance as if they came from different worlds. The blonde piano player was a true beauty with a smile that lightened up her face; her sister was more solemn and in comparison, merely handsome, with dark hair drawn severely to each ear, high cheekbones and a hint of hectic colouring that could have resulted from shyness. Mendick judged them to be anywhere between the ages of eighteen and twenty-one.

"Our daughters," Mrs Leslie said as Leslie looked on, smiling. "Our oldest, Louise," she indicated the dark-haired girl with a slightly dismissive movement of her hand, "and Sarah." Her voice and attitude warmed as she gestured to the smiling girl.

"Good evening, ladies," Mendick tried to bow, but Mrs Leslie tutted her impatience at him.

"There is no need for that, Sergeant. Come, sit by the fire." She glanced at her husband. "It is a bit late for a formal meal, but I will ring for something."

"There is really no need," Mendick began, but Mrs Leslie had rung a small handbell and Mary appeared in seconds. Mendick noticed the maid curtseyed far lower to Mrs Leslie than she had to Leslie, and scurried away with all haste once she had her orders.

Leslie guided Mendick to the deepest armchair in the room, hard by the fire. When he looked up, both the girls were looking at him as if at a belted earl or a military hero. He smiled back as four big eyes fixed on him.

"The girls heard the story too," Leslie sat down in an armchair. "How you saved my life on the voyage home."

91

"Hardly that, Mr Leslie: they were pickpockets, not murderers."

"Maybe so, Sergeant, but you never know. A blackguard is a blackguard, and a pickpocket today could end up a murderer tomorrow!" Mrs Leslie settled down between Mendick and the girls. "Now girls, I am sure Sergeant Mendick would not mind if you had some questions for him."

"Not at all, Mrs Leslie," Mendick agreed.

"My father said you were a police sergeant, Mr Mendick," Louise's voice throbbed from her throat, "but you are not in uniform. Are you off-duty, perhaps?"

"I am a Criminal Officer, Miss Leslie and as such I am obliged to work out of uniform. It is my duty to detect crime."

"You are a police detective?" Sarah's eyes widened even more until they were nearly round in that perfect china-doll face. She glanced at her mother. When Mrs Leslie nodded Sarah continued, "I've never spoken to a detective before. May I enquire what your work entails, Sergeant?"

Mendick hid his smile. He could not count the number of times he had been asked that question, so he had his answer ready "We protect the respectable from the non-respectable, Miss Sarah." He stopped, realising how pompous he must sound. "In short, we try to catch criminals and ensure justice is done."

"I agree, Sergeant Mendick." Louise spoke very slowly. "I strongly believe that justice must be done."

Sarah nodded slowly and repeated the words. "Justice must be done. The Old Testament tells us 'an eye for an eye and a tooth for a tooth' and that is surely God's word."

"Louise is a very serious-minded young woman," Leslie said in the silence that followed. "She is a veritable bluestocking."

Mrs Leslie snorted. "Never you mind about her, Sergeant. I want to know if you are about to catch the monster who murdered that poor man Thoms." She shook her head, "And now there is this other terrible business in the whaling yard. Are you detecting that murder too, Sergeant?"

"That is my intention, Mrs Leslie," Mendick said.

"And are your investigations progressing satisfactorily, Sergeant?" Mrs Leslie looked up as Mary entered the room with a laden tray. "Put that on the round table, Mary, and bring it over here."

"I think I may have ruffled his feathers." Mendick said. He thought of the woman in the green cloak who followed him.

Leslie rose to help Mary carry a circular table to the front of the fire, but Mrs Leslie waved him back to his seat. He obeyed without a murmur and Mary struggled on alone.

"Sergeant Mendick is searching for a Chinaman," Leslie said. "I already informed him we are not aware of any Chinamen in Dundee."

The three Leslie women shook their heads. "Sergeant Mendick," Mrs Leslie said, "I can tell you with all my heart that I have never seen a Chinaman in my life, and I have travelled to Edinburgh and Aberdeen."

Mendick watched as Mary poured out tea from a porcelain teapot with a pattern of summer roses. "Perhaps you might be aware of a merchant with an Oriental connection?"

Leslie removed his spectacles and began to polish

them vigorously. "Indeed yes, Sergeant, many of the Dundee merchants trade with Bengal, if that is any help." He wriggled in his seat, rather like a dog wagging his tail to please his master.

"Do you have names, sir?" Mendick asked. He hoped to hear more about Gordon. He watched as Mary used a pair of silver tongs to place slices of cake onto plates with the same floral pattern.

Leslie nodded so vigorously that his spectacles nearly slid from his nose. "I certainly have names sir. I have a list of every merchant in Dundee and their areas of trade. I could have a copy made and dropped off at the police office tomorrow."

"Thank you, sir. I would be extremely grateful for that." Mendick bowed from his chair as Leslie beamed at him.

"I do hope you find this Chinaman, Sergeant Mendick. I fear for Mr Leslie sometimes, working all hours of the night." She lowered her voice. "We are all concerned in the administration of justice," Mrs Leslie said softly, with such an edge to her voice it merely confirmed who the head of this household was.

Mendick nodded assent. "If more people took that view, Mrs Leslie, my job would be easier and the streets would be a great deal safer."

Mrs Leslie sipped noiselessly at her tea. "I believe it is everybody's duty to help remove blackguards and the unworthy from the streets, Sergeant. I have brought up our daughters to think likewise and they are both actively involved in making Dundee a safer place."

Mendick looked over to the two girls. Louise had her earnest, serious gaze fixed on him but Sarah seemed more intent on studying her profile in the glass front of the bookcase. He tried to imagine them walking the beat as constables, but the idea of female police officers was so ludicrous that he could not help but smile.

Mrs Leslie explained, "Louise helps teach the intermediate class at the Castle Street School, Sergeant, and Sarah does charity work at the King Street Infirmary."

"It is our Christian duty." Louise told him, unsmiling.

"Your parents must be very proud of you both," Mendick said.

"We are a very affectionate family," Mrs Leslie claimed, although Mendick noticed there were no supporting nods from her children. She completed her lecture on the importance of justice and retribution before dismissing the maid with a flick of her hand and passing round the plates.

As they ate the superb cake and the girls bowed their heads to sewing, Mendick admired the family portraits that covered two walls. There was a splendid oil of the sisters as toddling infants, another of them as young girls with solemn faces and a third when they entered their teen years, all arms and legs and satin clothes. Their brother, however, seemed destined for the sea from childhood, to judge by the paintings. He wore a white sailor suit as a baby, a blue one as an infant and blue and white as a gawky youth.

Mendick frowned. Although he could trace the development of the children from infancy to near adulthood, the only picture of Mr and Mrs Leslie showed them in middle age. Mendick smiled at the pride behind these pictures and stifled the surge of sadness he felt for loss of his wife Emma and stillborn daughter. The black frame around the solitary portrait of the young man told its own story.

Leslie noted his interest. "Do you like them, Sergeant? A professional artist painted the earlier ones but now Mrs Gordon has honoured us with her skills."

Mendick nodded. "She does it well." He had no knowledge of art, but he liked the way Johanna had caught the character of each member of the family, from the hesitant Leslie to the dominant Mrs Leslie, the captivating Sarah and Louise with her straightforward gaze. Yet even as Mendick looked, he could see the difference between the professional and the amateur; in Johanna's images every face had a slight flaw so that when the candle flickered their characters altered. He looked away. He was glad Emma had never been painted in that style.

"Mrs Gordon is a lovely lady, so unlike Mr Gordon." Louise put her sewing down. "There now Mama, I think I am finished."

"Do you indeed?" Mrs Leslie took the material, examined it closely and pointed out an infinitesimal flaw for Louise to correct.

Mendick watched Louise return, uncomplaining, to her work. "You don't approve of Mr Gordon, then?"

"He is anything but a pleasant fellow," Louise was surprisingly candid. "And I do not like how he made his money."

This was what Mendick wanted to hear. He raised his eyebrows. "Oh? And why is that, pray? I heard he was a respectable merchant. Was that not the case? What was he, a slave trader?" Mendick tried to sound humorous but there was no laughter on Louise's stern lips.

"He was every bit as bad, he dealt in opium." Louise said the word as if it was obscene. "Mr Gordon was an opium trader."

"Opium trading is a respectable business, Miss Louise." Mendick tried to hide his surge of interest.

It was Sarah who looked up, her blue eyes bright with tears. "No, sir, I fear you are mistaken. You perhaps have never seen the harm it can do, Sergeant Mendick. You have never seen the wasted figures and the dead eyes of men who indulge? Well, I have. I have come across a few in my infirmary work. The overuse of opiates is a terrible thing, Sergeant, and Mr Gordon supplied it by the ton!"

Despite the seriousness of her words and his interest in their content, Mendick smiled. He enjoyed the passion of these young ladies. "I understand your reasoning, Miss Louise and I completely agree with you. I too, have seen the damage opium can do."

"Oh?" Louise faced him squarely. "And where was that, pray?" Her words were so direct a challenge he was surprised.

"Chusan, mainly, but other parts of China too." Mendick found Louise's intense stare fascinating. "Where did you say Mr Gordon traded in opium?"

"I did not say," Louise was sharp, "as well you know, Sergeant." She stared at him for a full ten seconds longer than most of his suspects would, then dropped her gaze. "He was in China, Sergeant. That's where he made his money."

Mendick nodded. He was not surprised that Gordon had been an opium smuggler in the China Seas. He had seen opium clippers in harbour in Hong Kong. Long, low, raking craft with smooth lines, built for speed. He had admired them for their seamanship but, when he had been a soldier of the queen, he had not thought twice about the morals of their occupation.

97

"Thank you, Miss Louise. You have been most helpful."

He looked at the clock, "I really ought to be on my way now, thank you for your hospitality . . ."

"Oh, Sergeant Mendick, you have only just arrived." Ignoring Mendick's protests, Mrs Leslie insisted on showing off her house. He spent an uncomfortable hour on a guided tour, from the comfortable withdrawing room to the door of the private chapel at the rear of the house, although Mrs Leslie did not take him inside, as it "was not seemly unless it is the Lord's Day." Only then was he allowed away, with Mrs Leslie rousing James, the handyman and coachman, from his quarters in the basement with orders to take Mendick home.

"Here we are then, sir." James seemed not in the least put out by having to take Mendick across half the town at one o'clock on a wet morning. He pulled up the gig outside the High Street tenement where Mendick lodged, tipped back his hat and opened the door. "You be careful how you go now, sir." He looked into the darkened close, "Would you like me to accompany you, in case a blackguard may be prowling?"

Mendick shook his head. "Thank you, James, I am but one flight up. I am sure I can make it." He gestured to the pedestrians who slouched past, cowering from the wet. "This street is busy at any hour of the day, so there is plenty of help at hand."

"Aye, aye, sir, as you say," James touched a hand to the brim of his hat. He watched Mendick enter the close, flicked the reins and rumbled away.

When Mendick looked out of his window he saw the woman in the green cloak; she was standing in a shop doorway directly opposite his flat, staring upward.

CHAPTER SEVEN

Mandarin House stood within a large well-tended garden just outside the planned village of Newtyle, where the smiling fields of Strathmore stretched from the flanks of the Sidlaw hills across to the distant Angus Glens. Mendick turned the hired gig through the pillars of the front gate and pulled up in front of the door. He waited for a second as the dust settled around him and the horse stamped within its harness, then mounted the two steps to the front door. The square pilasters reached to an austere pediment that guarded the arched door itself, while birdsong sweetened the sky.

Mendick grunted; he thought of the weeping villages he had seen in China, where men lay in the slow death of opium addiction, and agriculture and work was neglected in favour of the drug. That horror had been caused by the owner of this property and men of his type. Louise had been right to term him evil, but she had only seen the shadow of his crime, never the full appalling reality or the contrast between the palaces of those who profited from opium and the misery of those who suffered the effects. Mendick pulled the black knob of the bell and listened to the rapid patter of a servant's feet.

An aroma of oriental spices wafted towards him as the door opened.

"Yes?" The servant was small and obviously unimpressed by Mendick. "Tradesmen use the back entrance."

"Do they indeed?" Mendick pushed the man aside with his cane and stepped inside without being invited. "Pray inform your master that Sergeant Mendick of the Dundee Police is here to see him."

"Sergeant Mendick of the Dundee Police?" The servant looked Mendick up and down as if he was something unpleasant he had stepped on in the fields.

"And be quick about it," Mendick put the edge of authority in his voice. He looked around, tapping his cane against his leg.

The outer hallway was decorated like a miniature Chinese palace, with a pair of man-sized urns immediately within the door and quilted wallpaper with dragon designs covering the walls. A large Chinese throne squatted in one corner.

"Mendick?" Gordon carried a Purdey shotgun broken over his shoulder as he pattered down the stairs. "What the devil are you doing inside my house?"

"I am about to ask you why you did not tell me you were an opium trader in China," Mendick tapped his cane against the nearest urn, "and have brought half the country back with you."

"My business has nothing to do with you, Mendick," Gordon inserted a cartridge into the breach of his shotgun and snapped the weapon shut.

Mendick rapped the barrel of the gun with his cane. "I sincerely hope you are not carrying that weapon to threaten me, sir?"

"I have no need to threaten in my own house, Mendick." Gordon said. "A house to which you were not invited and which I demand you leave."

"We are searching for a man who calls himself China Jim," Mendick ignored Gordon's outburst, "and you seem best qualified for that title." He indicated the Chinese memorabilia that decorated the house.

"How dare you, Mendick," Gordon moved his shotgun but did not point it towards Mendick. "I am a gentleman!"

"Indeed, sir, but even that does not necessarily mean you are honest." Mendick kept his voice even. He fought the surge of anger he always felt when faced with the high-handedness of self-proclaimed gentlemen. He knew gentlemen liked to believe their position made them invulnerable, but he had dealt with embezzlers and card sharks from all walks of society and saw nothing special about presumed gentility. "I would seek permission to search your house, sir." He watched Gordon's face flush with fury.

"Get out!" Gordon's hands twitched on his shotgun.

Mendick kept his cane poised to deflect the barrel.

"It would be easier for us both if you were to agree, sir, else I have to obtain a magistrate's warrant and return with a group of uniformed constables." He tapped his cane on the wall, just below a shelf on which stood an intricate jade chalice from the Ming dynasty. "Could you imagine their great clumsy boots clattering around your beautiful house?"

"Good God, Mendick! Do you think you can threaten me with your bully boy tactics? Do you know who I am?"

"At present, Mr Gordon, you may be a murder suspect." Mendick told him. "Do you wish me to leave and return with a platoon of police? Or shall I stay and search your house on my own, quietly and without fuss?" He helped Gordon ponder his choices by tapping his cane around the priceless artefacts in the hall.

"Damn you, Mendick," Gordon said at last, "search if you must, but be assured I will put in a strong word with your superior."

"Thank you, sir," Mendick gave an ironic bow. "My superior's name is Donald Mackay. I am sure he will be pleased to hear from you."

Mandarin House was not a huge mansion but every room was more splendid than the last, all decorated with Chinese art and crammed with Chinese artefacts. Mendick walked around slowly, not sure what he was looking for and more concerned with unsettling Gordon than finding anything incriminating.

"Well?" Gordon followed him step for step, "See anything, Mendick?"

"Not a thing, sir," Mendick said.

He glanced in the bedroom – a man's room without a doubt. The large, plain bed sat squarely in the centre of the room, on bare, polished floorboards. The walls were of panelled wood, with three hunting prints for decoration, a leather armchair in one corner and not a single piece of Chinese artwork in the room.

There was nothing of Johanna. No dressing table, no mirror, no female fripperies and not a single scrap of feminine clothing. There was no reciprocal bedroom for Johanna, or for John. It was as if Gordon's wife and child did not exist. He lived a bachelor's life in this grand house, and they lived their life in Unicorn Cottage.

The gun room hosted an impressive display of firearms, with shotguns sitting beside the latest rifles and smoothbore sporting pieces by Joseph Manton of London. The wine cellar was stacked with barrels of port, sherry and French wines, with brandy and gin in reserve.

"No whisky?" Mendick rapped the nearest barrel with his cane.

Gordon snorted. "Not unless I purchase it from the Scouringburn Distillery, which is rotgut, or from some glorified shebeen keeper. I really wish you people would do something about that."

Mendick grunted, "I will be sure and mention it to Mr Mackay, Mr Gordon but at present we are a trifle too busy to concern ourselves with the supply of your whisky."

"It's a damned inconvenience, Mendick." Gordon poured himself a brandy and swallowed it in one gulp.

Mendick nodded. "I am sure Mr Mackay will act immediately. We can't have you inconvenienced by a mere murder. Just one point, Mr Gordon," Mendick stopped at the head of the stairs, beside a life-sized statue of a Buddha. "You told me you spent the night of the murder at home with your wife, yet there is no trace of her here. She does not live with you. Could you explain that to me?" He held Gordon's eye.

"My domestic arrangements are my own concern," Gordon said.

"You were alone in the house then, on that night." Mendick said. "Now, if you will just show me your stables, I will leave you for the present."

There were six horses in the stable block. Four were thoroughbred, fine, blood horses for riding and hunting. The remaining two were carriage horses used for drawing the black brougham that sat just within the arched doorway of the principal stable.

"The men who murdered Mr Thoms travelled in a brougham," Mendick said. He replaced his hat.

"Thank you for your cooperation, Mr Gordon. You

may depend on me to further pursue this investigation, and I may well return later."

CHAPTER EIGHT

"So there we have it," Mendick sat on top of his desk and addressed Sturrock and Deuchars. "We are slowly gathering a great deal of information, but none of it seems to make sense."

Deuchars fingered his scar. "We keep hearing about this China Jim fellow, Sergeant, but nobody knows anything about him. We don't even know what he does or what he looks like. How the devil are we to find a man nobody knows anything about?"

"Well," Mendick said, "let's see what we have got and maybe one of us will spot a connection."

Deuchars sighed and slumped into a chair. "On you go then, Sergeant."

Mendick lit his pipe. "We have a tenuous link between two of the people who may be involved. They both have names from Walter Scott's novels, so they may be pseudonyms for the same man. We also know that Gordon owns a brougham and had an extensive connection with China."

"Scott's novels?" Deuchars snorted. "Of course, you know that Gilbride names all his ships after Scott's characters? Hence the Waverley Whale Fishing Company, after the Waverley Novels."

Mendick thought of the young businessman with the bad leg and the lack of witnesses the night of the murder. "In that case we should interview Gilbride again. We also know Gordon hid information from us but that just makes him an uncooperative fellow rather than a murderer."

Deuchars grunted. "Now there's a gentleman I would love to see locked away for a very long time." He shrugged. "It seems that both Gordon and Gilbride are suspects: neither have witnesses to support them on the day of either murder."

"The only man who has is Leslie," Mendick said. "He was with me."

"Mendick," Superintendent Mackay pushed quietly into the room, "I am sorry to break up your conference but China Jim has done it again, and this time he's killed a soldier." His eyes were bleak. "Here are the details," he handed over a single sheet of foolscap and raised his voice. "Now get out there, gentlemen, and for Heaven's sake sort things out! The last thing we need is trouble with the army."

"Another one?" Mendick sighed and reached for his hat. "Dear God. Is this monster determined to kill everyone in this town?" He nodded to Sturrock and Deuchars. "Right, lads, let's step out together now."

Dundee Law rose five hundred feet above the town, a landmark for seamen and a guardian for the spreading tenements beneath. In summer it was bright and clear, with views across the Firth of Tay to Fife and around to the Sidlaw hills, but on this spring morning of howling wind it was cold and stark and unforgiving. Mendick stopped for a second to gather his thoughts. He gazed over Dundee, seeing a panorama of blue-grey tenement roofs and tall factory chimneys. The whim of the wind gusted smoke eastward towards Broughty or south towards the silver-grey sheen of the Tay, where the ships waited with furled sails for the weather to improve.

"Let's hope this one's not as bad as the last." Deuchars grunted his doubt. "Wee Donny said it was China Jim's work, so don't expect anything pretty."

They walked the final few steps and stopped. The latest victim had been killed in the open and his remains spread across the southern slopes of the hill. A dozen policemen guarded the spot, holding their tall hats firmly against the assault of the gale and with their faces closed against shock and disgust. Mendick tried to envisage what had happened up here, and when. A killing in this wild and windy place was unusual, it was unlikely to be a drunken brawl or an argument between a man and his wife.

Within the circle of uneasy policeman, what was left of the victim lay in the usual hideous mess of blood and flesh. A few yards outside the circle, a hostile group of soldiers and bystanders were hunched under the battering storm.

"Aye, there's plenty bluebottles now," a scarlet-coated soldier glowered at Mendick through poisonous eyes. "What were they doing when the lad was being murdered? Sitting in the warmth drinking drams, that's what."

When Sturrock turned to face the soldier Mendick took his elbow and hustled him onward. "You can't argue with a frightened and angry man," he said, "particularly when he's wearing a scarlet jacket."

"What was the victim's name?" Sturrock asked.

"David Torrie," Mendick said, "He was a private soldier."

"You'd better catch him, coppers," a saturnine corporal shouted. "Or we bloody will!"

"Oh my eye!" Sturrock looked away, "this one is even worse!"

Mendick nodded. As before, the man had been stripped stark naked but this time he retained all his limbs. His intestines had been neatly removed and the now-expected linen bag placed in the bloody cavity. There was a piece of what looked like bone placed on his forehead.

"What sort of man would do that?" Sturrock shook his head. "We're dealing with a monster here, not a man."

"I do not know what sort of man," Mendick said quietly. "But there are some terrible people out there." He knelt beside the victim and lifted the bone. He pointed to the silhouette of a woman's face that was carved on one side. "I wonder if her name was Rose," he said.

"Do you think this was the work of a jealous lover?" Sturrock examined the face. "Not much to look at is she? She looks foreign anyway. Look at the shape of her eyes."

"Chinese, perhaps," Mendick said, "a Chinese Rose?" He ran his thumb over the object. "I don't think that's bone though. What do you make of it, Deuchars?"

Deuchars took one glance. "It's scrimshaw work, Sergeant, baleen from a whale's mouth. Lots of the old Arctic hands do it, but I've never seen it on a soldier before."

Mendick stared at the face in the carving. "So this may be Rose. This woman may be the cause of three murders. One thing's certain. China Jim did not leave this here for nothing. It's a message."

"Aye, Sergeant. Either for us or for somebody else." Sturrock said. "Maybe he is warning the criminal class that he is top dog and they had better behave themselves." He looked downhill at the growing crowd. The noise was increasing. "Do we have any more details of Torrie?"

"Not many." Mendick re-read the piece of paper Mackay had handed him. "He was a new recruit, he'd only been in uniform for three weeks."

"Only three weeks?" Deuchars frowned. "He's a bit old for a Johnnie Raw isn't he? He must be five and thirty if he's a day. The army are really dragging the bottom of the barrel now." He turned the body over. "Sergeant! Look at this."

Mendick looked closer. Both Torrie's thighs and buttocks were mutilated with great chunks of flesh hacked off and the remainder punctured and torn in the same manner as he had seen with Thoms and Milne. "It looks like he's been chewed. Those are teeth marks or I'm as Chinese as Jim." He shivered. "What in God's name are we dealing with here?"

"A monster," Sturrock took a deep breath. "I always hoped to be involved in a murder case, Sergeant, but I never expected anything like this."

"It's no monster, constable," Mendick tipped out the bag. As expected, there were thirty silver shillings all dated 1842. "Just a very evil man."

"We had better catch him then," Sturrock said quietly. He tapped his fingers on the haft of his staff, suddenly looking very much older than his twenty-one years.

"We need to ascertain why China Jim selected these particular victims. The bags of silver would tell us a lot if only I could work it out, and I suspect this woman Rose is at the crux of the matter. Maybe she was China's girl and she betrayed him." Mendick examined the scrimshaw again, the woman's face was enigmatic; she seemed to mock him.

109

"With three different men?" Deuchars shook his head. "She's not the sort of woman I want to have anything to do with, then."

"Nor I," Mendick agreed. He tucked the scrimshaw inside his pocket. "I want to know why Torrie joined the army, and I want to know if he was out alone and where he was going. I also want to know where he was in 1842."

The bottle landed beside them with a soft thud, followed by a stone. While they had been inspecting Torrie's body, more soldiers had arrived and now there were about fifty with the crowd still increasing; some in regimental scarlet, others in shirtsleeves, but all uniformly angry. Their voices came in fitful snatches, partly carried away by the now dying wind.

"Hey, bluebottles! Why haven't you caught the beast yet?"

"You buggers are useless! If you can't catch him, we'll get him ourselves."

They pushed forward, angry young men who had learned about the murder of one of their own, all searching for someone to blame. Another stone bounced from the scrubby spring grass and the noise rose as the soldiers encouraged each other. The police line withdrew as the soldiers advanced. Mendick frowned. "Sturrock. Run to West Bell Street and warn the Superintendent there's trouble brewing. We might need reinforcements." He frowned. "Top speed, man! I've seen redcoats on the batter before. It's not a pretty sight."

A small shirt-sleeved soldier swaggered forward, thrust his thumbs into his braces and faced Mendick.

"Are you in charge here?" When Mendick nodded he said, "We want to know who murdered Torrie and why you haven't done something about it, eh?"

The crowd was now sixty or seventy strong, mostly soldiers. While some were probably out officially from Dudhope Castle barracks a mere quarter mile away to the south, Mendick suspected others were absent without leave, men who were already in trouble and careless of causing more. Voices rose to support the small man.

"Aye, why haven't you done something about it? Who killed Davie Torrie eh?"

"Why isn't this Chinese beggar hanging from a rope, eh?"

"We want China Jim!"

The faces were angry, confused, some flushed with drink, some fearful and staring towards the mutilated corpse. As the noise increased, Mendick took another step forward.

"Calm down now, men," he shouted. "Show some consideration for poor Mr Torrie here!"

"Consideration! If you bastards had any consideration for us you'd have caught the monster by now!"

"Aye! Maybe it's you who should show consideration!"

Holding his staff high, Mendick took a third step forward to show he was not afraid. He was now a full five yards in front of the police line and wondered if he could withdraw to safety before the soldiers caught him. The prospect of being kicked to pieces by iron-shod army boots was unappealing.

"I assure you that we are doing everything we can to trace this killer."

"Was it China Jim?" A large and muscular redcoat joined his shirt-sleeved companion. "If it was China Jim, why have you not got him under lock and key?"

"We are following lines of enquiry," Mendick

attempted to sound confident. "And that is all I can say just now."

"It was that bloody China Jim again," a small man with a neat moustache said. He had the olive complexion of long service in the East and eyes hard enough to drill through granite. A blue-tinged scar on his left arm revealed he had been in a gunpowder explosion at some time. "We'll get the bugger!"

"No!" Again Mendick brandished the official staff. "You cannot take the law into your own hands. If you want to help then return quietly to the barracks and let us get on with our job. Every soldier who knew David Torrie will be questioned by a police officer and can then pass on any useful information."

"Oh aye? By that time the monster will have murdered half of Dundee!"

"Then don't delay us now!" Mendick held the scarred soldier's gaze until he turned away and began to walk down the slope of the Law. The others followed, in ones and twos and then in groups, some mumbling, others glancing back over their shoulders.

"That was well done," Deuchars murmured.

"Aye, but I doubt it's finished yet." Mendick slid his staff back into its pocket. "Take two men and follow the soldiers, but be discreet. Don't provoke them."

"Oh, I won't be provoking them," Deuchars said, "I like to keep my head attached to my shoulders."

It was nearly an hour before Mackay arrived with reinforcements and Dr Webster, and then the work of removing Torrie's remains began. Mendick kept hold of the scrimshaw silhouette. He knew it was significant in some manner, but could not figure out why or how. He held the scrimshaw as he read the list of women named Rose he had asked the beat constables to compile.

"Rose Arnold?"

The woman looked up from the clattering machinery. She brushed the hair back from her face and nodded. Her eyes were sunk into a face lined with tiredness. "Yes. If it's about the rent, I will find the money. Just give me time."

Mendick showed the crown on his staff. "It's not about the rent, Mrs Arnold. I am Sergeant Mendick of the Dundee Police and I am asking about a man named David Torrie." He mentally compared her face with the silhouette on the scrimshaw. She looked a good ten years older and there was nothing oriental about her features.

"I don't know any David Torrie." Her eyes flickered with indignation. "Here! What sort of person do you think I am? I'm a respectable married woman! Just because I got a little behind with the rent doesn't mean I know every Tom and Dick in Dundee . . ."

Mendick stopped her with an upraised hand. "I was not suggesting that for a second, Mrs Arnold." He sighed as Sturrock reached in his pocket and produced a few shillings.

"How far behind with the rent are you, Mrs Arnold?" Sturrock asked.

She narrowed her eyes in suspicion. "Not far enough that I take charity from a thief-catcher, anyway. I keep my own house."

Mendick gave a small smile. "Come on, Sturrock. If you tried to give money to every woman in arrears in Dundee you'd need a never-ending purse."

They left the factory and stood in the narrow confines of Brown Street with the cliff-like walls crowding them on either side, and carts growling past.

"That was the last Rose." Sturrock consulted his

list. "There were eighteen names and she was number eighteen. That's another possible hope gone."

Mendick nodded. "You better get about your business, Sturrock. I will get back to the office and write this up. He glanced again at the face on the scrimshaw and was still clutching it when he passed the square pillars of the entrance to the police office.

Deuchars was bustling past, straightening his hat with one hand and trying to push his staff into its inside pocket with the other. "Don't get yourself settled, Sergeant. Wee Donnie wants everybody in the High Street. The lobsters are rioting. There's blood and guts and broken heads all over the blasted place."

CHAPTER NINE

"Get the Chinese! Kill China Jim!"

The chant echoed and re-echoed around the centre of Dundee, accompanied by the smashing of windows and the crash of stones and bottles. Acrid smoke from a burning cart coiled across the street, obscuring the topmost storey of the tenements and stinging Mendick's nostrils. He heard the buzz from spectators who had gathered to watch or who hoped for easy loot. Mackay had formed the police in a line across the High Street, and they moved slowly towards the mob gathered around the Old Steeple and the ruined remains of the City Churches that dominated the Nethergate.

Mendick frowned as he hurried along, watching the slender line of blue swallowtail coats and tall black rabbit-skin hats advancing with staffs drawn, and the much larger crowd of soldiers, youths and hangers-on, some in scarlet, others in shirtsleeves or ragged civilian clothes surging around the High Street. A group of youths kicked at a shop window while others threw stones at the police or passers-by.

"Get the Chinese! Kill China Jim!"

As Mendick moved closer, the soldiers coalesced into a tighter group and turned against the police, a barrage of assorted missiles arcing through the space between them. Carters whipped up their horses and tried to flee, congesting Union and Lindsay Streets and the narrow closes that plunged north and south. The hackney carriages that stood waiting for custom at the Town House began to flee, with the leading cab having to swerve to avoid a loaded jute cart. Women screamed in terror, some running with children in tow, others dropping recently purchased parcels from the still-open shops. A gaggle of bare-footed girls gathered at the tail of the soldiers, adding their own raucous voices to the noise.

"It's a full-scale battle," Sturrock shouted. He pulled free his staff and looked eager.

"Not at all," Mendick ducked as a bottle hissed past, turning end over end until it exploded in a shower of shards against the shutters of a shop window. "It's only the lobsters letting off some steam. They're angry and confused and they've lost one of their own. They want revenge and they've nobody else to attack."

Mendick had left his cane at the office and carried the regulation baton. "This might get a bit unpleasant, gentlemen, so keep together." He stamped his feet on the ground. "Mind you, I used to quite enjoy a good turn-up when I was in the army. Most of these lads will be looking forward to this."

The soldiers withdrew before the advancing police officers and gathered again in an untidy bunch beyond the Steeple. They shouted insults and chanted about China Jim but already their aggression had dissipated and some of the girls lost interest and began to drift away.

Mackay halted the police line outside the Town House, whose classical pillars were partly obscured by drifting smoke. The police stood shoulder to shoulder and on an order from Mackay began to tap their staffs on the ground in a rhythmic, menacing drumbeat that echoed from the surrounding buildings.

Mendick looked along his line. The men stood firm, their tall hats adding to their height, the long coats adding to the impression of lean strength, the array of staffs looking formidable. The Dundee Police were a powerful force when seen in this mood. Up beyond the blue-white smoke, the evening sky was dull grey, with low clouds pregnant with rain and a few seagulls circling lazily, their screams melancholic in the troubled street.

"Right, lads." Mackay sounded as calm as if he was reading the duty roster on a Sunday morning. "We want to contain the redcoats here and prevent them from destroying the town. I've contacted the barracks commander and he'll be sending a company of men in support, but until they get here, it's up to us."

The number of soldiers had increased again as stragglers joined them, and the noise rose until it was hard for Mendick to think. He frowned as he saw a carriage at the back of the crowd. Who would want to stop in such a perilous place? He tried to see who was inside but the shifting movement of the soldiers blocked his view. Another bottle arced above, to shatter against one of the pillars of the Town House in a hundred shards of glass.

"It's building up again," Deuchars said quietly. He did not appear displeased.

Mendick looked to the east where an island of buildings narrowed the High Street and the name altered to the Murraygate. A handful of redcoats drifted from that direction, shouting and waving their fists. Fifty yards west, the high-quality Reform Street, where Adam Leslie had his crockery shop, led off at a right angle, while behind him Crichton and Castle Street arrowed down to the docks with some narrow wynds giving alternative dark passage.

"We'll have to keep them from Reform Street and the Murraygate," Mackay said. "Mendick, hold this line here. Keep them from advancing further." He refused to duck as another bottle spiralled past and shattered on the cobbles underfoot.

"Now here's trouble!" Deuchars pointed as a small body of lascars, Indian seamen from a newly arrived ship, wandered up from the dock and stared at the riot as if it was a public entertainment. "These lads had better get out of the way before the soldiers lynch them."

"They're Indian, not Chinese," Sturrock said.

"Do you think the redcoats care? They wouldn't know the difference between a maharaja and a mandarin."

Within seconds one of the soldiers, more sober or more alert than his companions, pointed to the lascars.

"There's the bloody Chinese! That's China Jim and his friends! Get the bastards, boys!" The roar increased and a group of soldiers advanced towards the bemused seamen.

Mackay pointed to the breakaway group, "Sergeant!" but Mendick was already stepping forward, staff in hand.

"Sturrock! Deuchars! You're with me!" He moved to get between the seamen and redcoats. British soldiers were notorious for their drunken brawls and he knew that in their present temper they were quite capable of murder. "You men! Stop there!"

The soldiers ignored him, as he had known they would. One whooped loudly, encouraging his fellows to battle. Suddenly aware of the threat, the lascars turned to run, watching over their shoulders as the redcoats broke into a ragged charge.

"There they go lads! After them!" Two young redcoats, one giggling in drunken excitement, raced ahead to cut off the lascars from the narrow wynd which offered the best escape route. "Don't let them escape, boys! Kill the Chinamen!"

The main body of redcoats yelled, whistled, roared in their triumph. Mendick saw one smallish soldier leap high in the air to land with both heavily-booted feet on the back of the rearmost lascar and knock him to the ground. The lascar's scream was high-pitched as the soldier swore and twisted his boots deep into the man's back.

"Get off him!" Mendick smashed his staff across the back of the soldier's head, sending him reeling forward. "He's not China Jim!"

"He's a bloody Chink!"

Mendick sought to quieten the soldiers, "He's a bloody seaman, you stupid bugger!"

Two soldiers had joined their colleague. They glared at Mendick. "Who the hell cares? He's bloody Chinese."

"He's Indian!"

"Same difference." The voice was flat and vicious, reared in the gutter of some English Midland slum. "We're going to string these bastards up, and if you don't get out of the way, we'll have you too." Unfeeling eyes glared at Mendick.

"Will you, now?" Mendick placed his staff diagonally across his chest as he stared the soldiers down. He watched Deuchars turn the screw to close his handcuffs over the wrists of the fallen redcoat.

Other soldiers snarled drunkenly at him, both sides a few paces apart in that street of tenements and shops, with the flare of the burning wagon puncturing the

119

growing dark. One by one the soldiers unfastened their leather cross belts and began to swing them menacingly. Mendick had seen those army belts and in the days of his wild youth he had used one as a weapon himself. Broad and heavy and with massive brass buckles at the end, they could easily break an arm or a skull. Now he heard their sinister whirr as they were swung, gathering momentum as the soldiers crowded round.

"Don't wait, lads" Mendick shouted, "if we hit their hands and arms they'll drop the belts. Step in together!"

There was no quarter given as the three policemen attacked the mob. The first belt buzzed past Mendick's face with a sound like a skein of geese passing close overhead, but he cracked down his staff on the holder's knuckles, feeling immense satisfaction from the shock of contact and the man's instant yell of pain.

Something hard and heavy thumped against Mendick's back. He shortened his grip on the staff and thrust it hard into the throat of the nearest soldier, leaving him gasping and writhing on the ground. Mendick looked up to see Sturrock using his staff like a sword, parrying the buckle end of a soldier's belt, withdrawing and slashing right and left at the man's upper arms. The belt dropped and Sturrock felled the bearer with a sharp blow to the head.

"Watch that one!" Mendick gestured to a tousle-haired soldier who was dragging clear his bayonet, but Deuchars was there first, smashing sideways with his long staff so the man shouted and dropped the weapon. Mendick recognised the vocal soldier from the Law but had no time to arrest him.

"Keep going, Sergeant!" Deuchars was grinning, enjoying the challenge of a fight. Something had knocked flat the reinforced leather of his hat and there was a trickle of blood on his face, but he sidestepped a swinging belt and thrust out accurately with his staff, catching the soldier in the belly. "And that's done for you!"

The chanting rose high, "Get the bluebottles! Kill the peeler bastards!"

"At least they have lost interest in China Jim," Deuchars grinned despite his bloodied face.

There were more soldiers now and more supporters, a rabble of beery, swearing faces shouting oaths as they lunged at him, but Mendick knew there was no turning back. There was no sign of the lascars, and the High Street took on the appearance of a battleground as redcoats fought blue and the inevitable casualties crumpled in pools of blood.

"There's too many of them," Sergeant Morrison shouted as two soldiers converged on him, kicking viciously with their heavy boots. A belt buckle smashed against his face and he yelled and staggered back. The soldiers laughed and closed in, boots hammering. Another redcoat, diminutive in stature but large in animosity, leaped high in the air and swung his belt so the great brass buckle crumpled a constable's hat. The policeman stumbled and another soldier thrust at him with the jagged edge of a broken beer bottle.

"Hot work, Sergeant." Deuchars shoved the bottle holder aside, reeling as a stone thumped against his chest. He took a step backward, and Mendick thrust his staff between the ankles of a running soldier, bringing the man clattering down. Another constable was writhing on the cobbles, with the broad cross belts hissing and heavy buckles crashing down on his screaming form.

"Get the bluebottles! Kill China Jim!" Now a different chant started, one that arose from a small group of soldiers but soon spread amongst the rest.

"Burn the place! Burn the place!"

The cry was accompanied by a new approach from the soldiers. Intense groups smashed shop windows and threw burning rags inside so flames ripped skyward from half a dozen different locations.

"What the devil is that about?" Deuchars asked, "I've never known redcoats do that before."

"Nor have I," Mendick said. "We can discuss it later; here they come again!"

"Kill the bluebottles! Kill China Jim!" A volley of bottles smashed and rolled on the cobbled ground, announcing another surging charge of soldiers who erupted from the direction of the Overgate.

Mendick and Deuchars stood apart from the others and the police line looked thin and weak as it rallied once more to face the onslaught. Five constables were crumpled on the ground and others swayed in the ranks, white faces streaked with blood. Most officers nursed some sort of injury. Superintendent Mackay was in the centre, brandishing his official sword and giving loud orders but even he looked shaken, while the flames from burning shops illuminated the night. Smoke, dark and acrid, coiled between the buildings.

"Talk about the squares at Quatre Bras, eh?" Deuchars altered his grip on the staff. His face was scarlet-streaked with blood, but there were three soldiers on the ground immediately in front of him, one secured by handcuffs and the others in groaning immobility.

"And here come the French cavalry." Mendick nodded at the next onrush of soldiers.

He saw the carriage again, the dark-coloured brougham. He craned his neck to see past the soldiers, but a drift of wind blew smoke from the burning cart between them. When it cleared the carriage had vanished.

"Get the bastards!" The soldiers rallied again and the noise multiplied. It was like nothing Mendick had heard since China. A constant background roar, punctuated by coarse voices screaming obscenities, the drumbeat of army boots on cobbles and the crash of breaking glass.

"Watch your front, boys. Here they come again."

As Mendick stepped forward the redcoats seemed more numerous and even more determined. He blocked one hissing belt, slammed his staff against an unwary bicep, staggered as something thumped into his side, sidestepped a clumsy kick and slipped on the blood-greasy cobbles. He felt himself falling, saw Deuchars leaping to help, and then a knot of soldiers closed over him, boots and fists swinging.

Mendick yelled as an iron-shod boot scraped down his shin and lunged savagely upward with his staff, catching somebody a shrewd blow in the groin. The man shrieked, and crumpled on top of him. Mendick shoved the body away, tried to rise, flinched as a boot crunched into his ribs and curled into a foetal ball as a crowd of soldiers concentrated on kicking him to pieces.

"Sergeant!" That was Deuchars, his voice sounding distant. He heard sharp commands, the rhythmic crunch of disciplined feet, and a hard hand helped him to his feet. An army captain was nodding calmly to him, a cheroot bouncing from the corner of a moustached mouth.

"You'll be Sergeant Mendick, then?"

"I am." Mendick took a deep breath to calm the

rapid hammering of his heart. "But not for long if you hadn't turned up."

"Captain Chambers, Twenty-First Foot on attachment." Chambers spoke as if he was introducing himself in a drawing room rather than in the heart of a riot.

Mendick looked around. There were at least three shops ablaze, and a couple of carts, with orange flames leaping skyward to illuminate what now seemed like a battlefield. "How many men do you have?"

"Three piquets of thirty men each." The captain said. "We'll have your town tidied up before you can snap your fingers." He drew heavily on his cheroot.

Mendick saw a group of soldiers drag another face down along the ground and throw him onto the flat bed of a wagon. "Your boys are a bit rough, are they not?"

"Different regiments tend to have a little rivalry." The Captain sounded casual, as if regimental difference allowed for any level of violence. He watched unemotionally as two of his men kicked one of the rioters senseless. "That lot let us down in the Peninsula, so we don't like them much."

"So it would seem."

Mendick watched Deuchars push two of the rioters onto the back of an omnibus the police had commandeered to transport the prisoners to the police office. "Well, before you kill them all, I'd like to interview a few."

The captain shrugged. "As you wish. Any in particular or shall I pick them at random?"

Mendick walked to the flat wagon and raised his voice. "Anybody here know Private David Torrie, the man whose murder caused all this mayhem?" He looked round the battered faces of the redcoats just as the firelight gleamed on a brougham pulling up from Castle Street. Ignoring the bedlam, the driver negotiated the knots of fighting soldiers, cracked his whip and growled past Mendick. For a second he looked up, eyes bright behind a black mask; then pushed his tall hat further back on his head and whipped on the horses.

Mendick raised his voice. "Stop! Stop that carriage!"

"What's that, Sergeant?" Sturrock looked at him as if he was suddenly insane.

"That was China Jim! Stop him!" He nodded to Chambers, "Excuse me, Captain," and began to run, but the coach picked up speed as it rattled along the now quiet High Street and he knew he would fail.

"You!" He pointed to the constable in control of the omnibus, "Follow that coach!"

"But Sergeant . . . I have prisoners . . ." the officer stared at him in astonishment.

"I don't care," Mendick began, then realised the futility of trying to follow with a bus full of truculent soldiers. He could see the brougham clattering along the cobbles, its narrow body already fading into the night. He followed on foot and hoped for some miracle that would delay its progress. The carriage turned right into South Tay Street, and the driver whipped up.

"Damn and blast and buggery!" Gasping with fatigue and frustration, Mendick stopped. He knew he would never catch the brougham and by the time he organised a proper search, it could be anywhere in Dundee or within a ten mile radius. It was another victory for China Jim. He stared at the disappearing coach and swore softly.

"Here come the fire engines now," Deuchars tied a handkerchief around a bleeding wound in his forehead.

"They've got a job of work ahead of them."

Dundee's entire force of three engines and fifteen firemen arrived a few moments apart and started to pump water into the burning shops. Those of the crowd who had not fled gathered round to watch this new entertainment.

"I still don't understand why the soldiers started fires," Deuchars said, just as the western sky was lit up. The flame shot fifty feet above the roofs of the tenements, as if a new sun was rising in the west, remained constant for a good five minutes then began to settle down.

"Dear God in heaven," Deuchars said quietly. "What the devil was that?"

"I don't know," Mendick said. He watched as the captains commanding the fire engines debated with their superintendent which fire was more important, and eventually one of the engine crews began to gather their equipment together for this new conflagration.

"By the time it gets there, there will be nothing to save," Sturrock continued to stare at the western sky where the fire silhouetted the stark tenements.

"Leave the fire to the fire engineers," Mendick said, "we have our own job to do. Come on lads, we have murders to solve."

Since all the cells in West Bell Street were full of battered and truculent soldiers, it was not difficult to find people to interview. One by one, Mendick hauled them out to the interview room and he and Deuchars interrogated the men while Sturrock took notes. All gave very similar answers.

"Yes, I know Davie Torrie. He's that Johnnie Raw that was murdered."

"No, he had no enemies within the regiment, he hadn't been there long enough to make any. Did you not hear me, you peeler bastard? He was a bloody Johnny Raw!"

"How should I know why that Chinese bastard picked him out? I told you he was a Johnnie Raw, a no-nothing, a recruity, less than dog shit on my shoe. I never spoke to the bugger."

"Did he have any connections with anything illegal? I don't know and I don't care."

There was only one constantly recurring answer that interested Mendick:

"Why did Torrie join the army? I think he was scared."

"Torrie was running from something or somebody."

"He was hiding behind the uniform, plain as the snout on your ugly face."

When Deuchars asked if they thought rioting and burning shops would help, some glowered and said nothing but a few gave a sly grin and looked away which Mendick found intriguing. When the small soldier with the poisonous eyes openly laughed, Mendick's patience gave out.

"What the devil are you laughing at?" He leaned across the table and grabbed the man by the throat.

"I'm laughing at you," the soldier gasped. "Trying to bullyrag me. You're only a bloody bluebottle."

"And what are you? You're only a broken-down redcoat." Mendick allowed the man to drop back into the chair.

"Maybe I'm broken-down, but I'm a redcoat with a golden boy," he gave another grin. "Look at this!" Diving deep into his pocket, he produced a sovereign.

"That's why I rioted. I never knew Torrie, I never knew he existed until yesterday, he was just another shit-scared Johnnie Raw."

Mendick lifted the coin. It was genuine, and more than a month's pay for the average soldier. True, a redcoat officially earned a shilling a day plus a penny beer money, but with stoppages for damages and barrack room expenses he was lucky to see a third of that. A sovereign was a small fortune to him.

"So where did you get this from?"

"Some woman gave it to me." Closing a grimy fist over the coin, the soldier breathed stale alcohol into Mendick's face.

Mendick exchanged a glance with Deuchars, who raised his eyebrows. "What did she look like, this woman?"

"That's for me to know and you to wonder at," the soldier sneered.

"It doesn't matter anyway," Deuchars said. "That's stolen money so we'll have it." He reached out for the sovereign but the soldier snatched it back.

"Hey! That's mine." He closed his fist tight. "The woman gave one to each of us, and a half dozen bottles of beer to start us off."

"Why?" Mendick leaned across the table and pressed his forehead against that of the soldier. "Why did she do that? Do you mean to say that this entire riot was arranged? Who was she?"

"How the hell should I know who she was?" The small soldier gave another short laugh. "She just came to us this morning when we were gawking at Torrie's body."

"Tell me exactly what happened." Mendick retreated a little, but glared at the soldier's unrelenting eyes.

"We were up the Law, watching the fun and laughing at the bluebottles buzzing around, useless as ever, when this woman wandered up, all smiles and cheeriness. She bumps herself against me, friendly like. 'Hello' I sez, and 'hello yourself,' sez she, 'would you like to earn yourself a sov?' I smiled at her and gave her the look, 'I thought it was more normal for me to pay you,' I sez, but she just laughed and told me to gather as many boys as I could and come to the High Street at five and I could earn a golden boy for a job I'd enjoy. So I told a few of the fellows and we came down, and she came in her coach and handed out sovs as if they were sweeties. She sez we were to start shouting about China Jim and start as many fires as we could."

"Describe her." Mendick said. "Was she tall, short, well-dressed, a gentlewoman, a weaver, a fishwife . . .?"

"Oh, she was no gentlewoman," the soldier said. "She was maybe a prostitute or a fishwife, and her in her green cloak and feathers."

Mendick grunted. "All right, that will be all."

"When you get out of the cells," Deuchars said, "I hope the army flogs the skin off you."

The soldier shrugged. "It wouldn't be the first time, nor the last, and worth last night's fun any time. And I got a golden boy for it." His grin was triumphant. "It isn't every day we get paid to ram the boot into some bastard peeler!"

CHAPTER TEN

"So, are we any better off?" Deuchars faced Mendick across the desk while Sturrock listened, puffing at his churchwarden pipe.

Mendick shrugged. "Not much. All we know is that Torrie was a recruit and the woman in the green cloak wanted to start fires. We don't know why yet, but we can assume she works for China Jim."

"Maybe China Jim was just causing trouble for trouble's sake?" Sturrock blew thick blue smoke across the room. "I can't think of any other reason."

"I think we can assume China Jim had a reason, we just don't know what, yet." Mendick said.

"Oh, he had a reason all right." Superintendent Mackay arrived with his usual silent grace. "When three quarters of the police force and all the fire engines were busy around the High Street, the Scouringburn Distillery was burned down."

"We saw the flames, sir," Mendick remembered.

"We suspect it was deliberate fire-raising," Mackay said. "I want you to go with James Fyffe, the superintendent of the Fire Brigade, and see what you can find out."

"Yes, sir," Mendick reached for his coat.

"And when you return, Sergeant," Mackay's voice was like cut glass, "come and see me in my office."

"Nobody hurt, Sergeant Mendick," Mr Fyffe lifted his tall hat and scratched the top of his bald head. Smuts of soot settled on his bushy eyebrows. He surveyed the damage to the distillery, "But it's made a fine mess of the building. The place went up like a bomb, we were lucky the burning spirits did not spread to the houses nearby."

Mendick looked at the Scouringburn. Blue smoke sat trapped by low housing, tenements and high-walled mill buildings. The streets were narrow, dark and noisy with tall chimneys adding to the smog. Newly idle distillery workers gathered in disconsolate groups, muttering about unpaid bills and hungry children. Mendick glanced at the nearest chimney and shivered.

He looked upward to where the flue ascended forever, the sides black and slippery with soot and the exit a tiny circle of light diminished by distance.

"Move you bugger! Or it will be the worse for you."

That voice still haunted his nightmares. He forced himself back to the present. Even in the street outside Mendick could hear the unending clatter of the mill's machinery, the noise seeming to repeat one phrase '*more profit, more profit, more profit.*' This was an area of densely packed buildings with small factories and workshops wedged between tenements and low houses, there were scores of children gathered everywhere and a number of pubs that sold kill-me-deadly whisky and watered beer. If the fire had spread in this neighbourhood, there could have been many hurt or killed. Water flowed slowly down the cobbled street, carrying all the debris of a gutted building amidst the smuts of soot. Mr Fyffe moved to speak to the manager of the distillery, a man made round-shouldered by the sudden uncertainty of his future.

"Do you know what caused it?" Mendick asked the

nearest fireman. The man shrugged and continued to coil up his canvas hose and load it into the wagon. The matched brown horses flicked their ears as smuts of soot irritated them.

"Our job is to put out fires, Sergeant, not to find out how they started."

The fireman slammed shut the hinged compartment that held the hoses, checked the water pump was secure and clambered onto the engine. "That's it out now, so I'll leave you to it." Raising his hand in farewell, he cracked his whip and the horses jerked the machine away. The crowd switched its attention to Mendick who ignored them as he peered through the charred doorway to the still-smoking remains of the building.

He stepped inside the mill, coughing as warm ashes and smoke engulfed him. The interior was more cramped than he had expected; two storeys high with little space between the copper stills and the mash tubs that stood on a slabbed stone floor. The ground was a mess of sodden ash, with pieces of charred paper seemingly everywhere. Light filtered in from the open door.

"You'd better be careful, Sergeant," Fyffe said, "This is no place to walk around."

Mendick nodded. "Aye, you're not wrong there, Mr Fyffe. Are fires like this common?" He stood in the centre of the floor, surveying the devastation.

"That was one too many," the distillery manager said. "There will be no whisky distilled here again." He shook his head. "That's the second fire this month. The engines put out the first one before it caused too much damage, but not this time."

Mendick stirred the ash with his cane. "Is there some weakness in the building perhaps, that makes this distillery more vulnerable to fire?"

"We have had a spate of fires in Dundee lately," Mr Fyffe said. "There have been three pubs burned out in the last month. I think it more likely to be carelessness than anything else, though." Fyffe spoke with a broad Dundee accent, a man who had educated himself. "There are many reasons for a fire starting where there is raw spirits." He sighed. "It could be something as innocent as a man dropping a match when he's having a sly smoke, or a spilled lantern of oil, or something similar. I doubt we will ever know. We can only thank the Lord that He did not see fit to take any lives."

Mendick only grunted. "I have my suspicions, sir, that this fire may not have been quite as accidental as you think."

Mr Fyffe waved a hand at the remains of the distillery. "Well, Mr Mendick,we shall never know what started this mess, but who this side of Bedlam would want to start a fire in a distillery?"

Mendick recalled the mutilated remains of the three murdered men. He tapped his cane against the nearest copper still. "I am not at all certain that the man I have in mind is on the right side of Bedlam, sir. Indeed, I am certain he would be better off locked inside there forever, if a gentle judge spared him the noose." He touched the brim of his hat. "I shall leave you now, sir. Thank you for your help."

Mackay's office was the largest and plushest in the building, but was still permeated by the austere atmosphere of the police office. Mackay sat back in his leather armchair and pressed together the lean fingers of his hands. "So far you have not been as successful as the reputation of Scotland Yard would have us believe,

Mendick. There have been three murders since you arrived, one serious riot and at least one possible case of major fire-raising."

"Yes, sir," Mendick wondered if Mackay blamed him personally for the outbreak of mayhem in his town.

Mackay leaned forward in his chair. "Catch China Jim, Mendick, and catch him while there are still some people left alive in Dundee." His Caithness accent became more pronounced as he held Mendick's gaze. "Do I make myself understood?"

"You do sir," Mendick agreed.

"I want to see you back in here in fifteen minutes, Mendick, with a full record of what you have achieved."

"Yes, sir, a full record." Mendick's salute was not entirely ironic as he left the office.

"Wee Donnie seems a trifle upset," Deuchars had obviously been listening at the door. He did not appear concerned as he stuffed tobacco into the bowl of his pipe with a huge thumb. "I think we had better catch this blackguard, Sergeant."

"So we continue as before," Mendick felt a wave of weariness wash over him. Thus far his investigations had got him nowhere, he had only reacted to China Jim's crimes and had not succeeded in preventing a single one. He walked across to his own office, stood in the doorway and put an edge to his voice. "I want the boys reminded about that carriage. I want every brougham stopped and searched, and the driver and occupants questioned and noted."

Sturrock looked up from his notebook and frowned. "There could be a score of broughams in Dundee; you might alarm a completely innocent man . . ."

"What is more important, Sturrock," Mendick

lowered his voice, "alarming an innocent man and perhaps catching a murderer, or being concerned about such things and having that innocent man murdered?" He lifted his hat and cane from the coatstand. "Sometimes it is necessary for a police officer to be less than pleasant to get the job done."

Sturrock nodded. "Yes, Sergeant."

"And now, I am looking for a coach." Mendick jammed the hat on his head.

Deuchars looked up, "Yes, Sergeant, but what about the Superintendent? He expects a full report from you."

"The Superintendent can go and bless himself." Mendick marched out of the room.

Freshly painted in green and gold, the sign hung proud on the outside of the Nethergate office and workshop:

Walter McLauchlan, it proclaimed, *Dundee's Premier Coachworks: Makers of Carriages, Two and Four Wheeled Dog Carts and Gigs.*

Mendick tapped his cane against the wide door and stepped inside. He entered a cobbled courtyard with a litter of timber and wheels, busily sawing and hammering workmen, a watchful collie dog and the inevitable cat that sat on a pile of wood shavings, overseeing everything. In the corner, two men were busy painting a completed coach.

"I wish to see Walter McLauchlan."

"That would be me." McLauchlan was of middle height, with neat whiskers that matched his grey eyes. His handshake was firm.

Mendick showed his official staff and came straight

to the point. "My name is Sergeant James Mendick and I am seeking information about a brougham."

McLauchlan narrowed his eyes. "Do you want me to build you one? They don't come cheap." He gave a slight smile.

"Not on my wages." Mendick noticed the collie come closer but it appeared friendly enough to be ignored.

"Nor on what this yard brings in," McLauchlan said sadly. "Come into the office, Sergeant." He led the way through the yard, stopping twice to give advice to young apprentices. "You'll be asking about that China Jim fellow, I suppose?"

McLauchlan's office was nothing more than a wooden shed with a plank desk and two chairs, but there was a small stove on which sat a battered kettle, and his tea was strong and sweet and welcoming. "Right, Sergeant, tell me what I can do for you."

Mendick removed his hat and lowered himself into a chair. "We think that China Jim uses a brougham to travel about Dundee."

"Aye, I can believe that." McLauchlan nodded slowly. "I'd pick a one-horse fly myself but I can see the advantage of a brougham. It has a tight turning circle, you see."

"That would be useful in Dundee's narrow streets," Mendick agreed. "Do you have a list of your customers?"

"We don't need a list for broughams," McLauchlan said. "We've sold two, one to Mr Gordon of Mandarin House and one to Mr Gilbride of the Waverley Company."

"Gordon and Gilbride?" Mendick smiled. Both were suspects so this piece of information did not help him in the slightest. "Are you the only coach manufacturer in Dundee?"

McLauchlan waved his mug. "I am, but there are plenty in Edinburgh and Glasgow. Anyway, maybe your China Jim fellow bought a coach privately and did not have it made for him."

"That is always possible," Mendick said. "What colour were your coaches?" Mendick asked. "The one we are looking for is dark blue or black."

McLauchlan opened the door and gestured with his cup to the coach the men were painting. "There's one there, dark blue. All of ours are dark blue because it's the most popular colour this season."

Mendick nodded. He recognised the brougham with its elevated driver's seat. "Thank you." Replacing his hat, Mendick flicked the brim with his finger. "You have been of some assistance. And the tea was most welcome."

Now he was back to Gordon and Gilbride. Gordon, the one-time opium trader who had lied to him about the night of the second murder and Gilbride, with the sore leg that made it impossible for him to slide down ropes, and the strong Walter Scott connection. The trail just led in small, pointless circles.

"They're like smoke," Deuchars grumbled. "China Jim, the seaman with a hundred names and that woman in the green cloak all just vanish when they please."

"They're not like smoke," Sturrock said. "Maybe that old beggar was right. They are like ghosts. They're spirits, that's what they are."

"They're solid bone and flesh," Mendick hardened his voice. "They are here, hiding amongst us and I want them. Check every stable for that coach, and that

137

includes private as well as public. Note every brougham. Note everything." Yet despite himself he remembered the uncanny way China Jim had manipulated the police and vanished. His identity was unknown even to the criminal classes. They only knew how to fear him, as he had feared his master as a child.

His world was restricted to the circumference of a flue, the exhausted slumber of end-of-work and the cringing acceptance of his master's belt.

"Faster you wee bastard! There are two more to go after this one."

The memory brought goose pimples to his spine and for a terrible moment the ranting face of his old Master merged with his mental image of China Jim. Mendick shook away the thought and concentrated on reality, but the fear remained to gnaw at his consciousness.

Blue broughams joined China Jim in Mendick's mind as he spent the next few days walking Dundee's streets, following coaches and checking stables. He listed every brougham he found, lost some in frustrated chases and compared his list with that of Sturrock. It was a Wednesday evening when he called his small team and they sat around his battered desk, sipping at vast mugs of tea as they reviewed their progress.

"There should be a registration system for carriages," Deuchars grumbled as they copied out their piecemeal notes, "so we can just look it up when we need it. They do it for ships, so why not coaches?"

"It would make things easier for us," Sturrock agreed, "but the people would never stand for it. Maybe the continentals would do something of the sort, but we value our freedom higher than that."

"So what do we have so far?" Deuchars asked. "Six broughams. I had no idea there were so many in Dundee.

You know about Gordon's and Gilbride's, of course?"

"Both men I would not trust the width of the street," Mendick said. "And the others?"

"That leaves four: the merchants Josiah Scrymgeour and Walter Rennie, one that's lacking wheels and one owned by Farquhar Jamieson, the ship master." Deuchars finished.

"A ship master? How can a ship's master afford a private carriage? This bears some investigation. Has he ever been to China?"

"I have no idea," Sturrock said. "I know Jamieson though, he's master of Bride of Lammermoor and he's been at sea since December. He's somewhere between here and Quebec."

"Damn and blast!" Mendick banged his palm on the desk top. "Every possible lead goes nowhere!" He walked to the window, stood with his back to it, pushed tobacco into the bowl of his pipe and applied a Lucifer. He enjoyed this first pipe of the evening best, when the day's work was behind him and the ease of the night was ahead. "We have spread the word we're searching for China Jim. We have a permanent watch on Mandarin House and Gilbride's office in Whale Lane. We have men noting every dark brougham they see and who the owners are. But what have we discovered?"

Sturrock sat back in his chair, his legs stretched before him and his churchwarden pipe emitting blue smoke. "We're making progress, Sergeant. These things take time."

Mendick glanced outside for a moment, noting the forest of chimneys that punctured the dimming sky. God, but he hated this place.

"We have two main suspects," Mendick said, "the first being James Gordon the Chinese opium trader. He's top of our list, but what could have been the motive for murdering these three men, and in such a barbarous manner?"

"Perhaps they were rivals?" Sturrock hazarded.

"Gordon is a wealthy property owner, Milne was a night watchmen, Thoms a pawnshop proprietor and Torrie a recruit and an ex-seaman." Mendick shook his head. "They were not business rivals. They could hardly have been love rivals either. Gordon has a beautiful wife and would not associate with the type of woman that Thoms or Torrie would know." He shrugged. "Second is George Gilbride of the Waverley Whale Fishing Company."

Sturrock removed the pipe from his mouth. "Gilbride is one of the most respectable gentlemen in Dundee."

"There are three things that give rise to suspicion about him," Mendick said. "One: he has a bad limp and claims it was a riding accident. Men with bad legs cannot climb down a rope, they would need a ladder–"

"Might as well arrest half the cripples in Dundee then." Sturrock broke in, but Mendick stopped him with a lift of his hand.

"Two: he is a whaling ship owner and Milne was found in a whale boiling yard."

"He worked there–" Sturrock said.

"Three: our invisible seaman of the many aliases always chooses a character from Scott's novels as a false name, and Scott is Gilbride's favourite author."

"So, after three murders we have two people who may possibly have been involved," Sturrock said. "I have always thought Gordon an arrogant sort of fellow ever since he arrived in Dundee, but a murderer?" He shook his head. "No. I can't see it. Why? He's already as rich as Croesus. Why should he want to butcher people? It doesn't make any sense."

"You are correct," Mendick agreed. "This case is all about reason: what was the reason for murdering these men, and what was the connection between them? There must be one. The method was the same, and we have the coins with the date 1842."

"So we are looking for a connection between a seaman turned soldier, an ex-seaman who owned a shop and a night watchman?" Sturrock shrugged. "I cannot think of any, except for the fact two had been at sea, but so have half the men in Dundee."

Mendick frowned. "Including me," he said. "You said 'ever since he arrived in Dundee,' when would that be?"

Sturrock exhaled smoke. "Let's see. It was at least four, maybe five years ago. Yes, about five years, say 1844."

"Two years after the date on the coins, then." Mendick began to pace the room. "Have we any news of Marmion or Oldbuck, Sturrock? A description, perhaps?"

Sturrock shook his head. "No, Sergeant. The man who arrested him has left the force and nobody else knows him at all. He was just an itinerant sailor."

Mendick grunted. "Itinerant sailors do not suddenly turn into housebreakers. They may be drunken rioters or steal a bottle of whisky from a toll house, but going to all the trouble of manufacturing a complex rope ladder?" He turned to look out of the window, "There is more to our sailor man than meets the eye; a thief, yes, but . . ."

"Yes, Sergeant," Sturrock pressed more tobacco into his pipe "but do you know what he was caught stealing?"

"Not until you tell me," Mendick said.

"I only found out this afternoon," Sturrock opened his notebook. "He was caught leaving the office premises of the Waverley Company with documents – wage sheets, crew lists, articles – no money or valuables."

Mendick shook his head. "Who in the devil's name would risk their freedom to steal rubbish like that? This whole case makes no sense at all. Nothing adds up." He reached for his hat. "I think I will have a little walk to see our beggar friend. He knows more than he says. I want you to trace the history of the murdered men. See where they were in 1842."

Darkness was falling when Mendick lifted his Chesterfield and pulled it on. As usual the pepperpot was clumsy in his inside pocket but he felt safer carrying it. He passed the stone columns that marked the door of the police office, placed his battered hat on his head and strode towards the docks. Already the atmosphere of the town was changing as the honest bustle of the day dimmed into the hidden scurry of the night. Around him the flicker of gas lanterns illuminated the main thoroughfares, with the unseen masses huddled in concealing darkness. Somewhere in those shrouded wynds and lanes there lurked a monster and his policeman's instinct told him that there were depths he had not yet plunged. As he paced towards Dock Street he looked around, mentally reviewing his pitifully thin list of suspects.

Well, China Jim, I'm after you now, and if you're in Dundee then I will find you, no matter in which noxious close or salubrious suburb you hide.

He jammed his hat further down his head, gripped his cane, lengthened his stride and strode along, his footsteps ringing on the paving stones of the High Street. He watched a brougham as it whirred in front

142

of him and noted the driver who stared at him over a lean shoulder. The face was not familiar, it could have belonged to anybody; an anonymous man in a bustling city, but it was a brougham and he must check.

"Hey!" Mendick raised his cane, "Dundee Police! Stop!"

The brougham neither slowed down nor increased its speed. It continued along the street with the gas lights reflecting from the glossy paintwork of the body and the blurred yellow spokes of the wheels. Mendick shouted again and watched in frustration. He gave an ironic smile and muttered "There is never a policeman when you need one."

He strode downhill through the dark streets. After spending hours on administrative work and attempting to piece together evidence that seemed to have no relevance to anything, he needed some exercise and it was always useful to see the town at night; he might catch a drift of conversation even before he reached Hitchins.

He passed a trio of spinners returning blank-faced and exhausted from the mill, and glowered at a striding sweep with two climbing boys trailing at his side. As always, he examined the Master sweep, wondering how he treated the youngsters, but moved on, heart-sick, as he fought the memories. The lights of small shops flickered as shopkeepers tried desperately to drum up custom from people who had barely enough to keep from starving. There was a group of young would-be pickpockets hanging around, hopeful for a victim. With luck they would find nobody tonight for he was not in the mood to chase children, or to see their tousled heads barely above the bar in the court.

The sudden prickle at the base of Mendick's skull alerted him. It was more than instinct; a combination of knowledge and experience that warned him something was wrong. He stopped at the corner of Reform Street and the High Street, thrust his cane under his arm and struck a Lucifer. As he pretended to light his pipe he looked around as nonchalantly as possible, disregarding the group of promenading females and the battered butcher's dog cart. He heard a commotion – the raised voice of an indignant man, the shrill denial of a woman, the patter of scurrying steps on the paving, but with so many people milling around he could not see who was involved.

"Stop, thief! Police!" The words were familiar, he had heard them a thousand times in his life, and if the Dundee accent was different to that of London, the meaning was just as clear. "Stop that woman!"

There she was – a lone female with a wide skirt and a voluminous dark green cloak – trying to find anonymity amongst a gaggle of strollers. The woman looked at him and recognition was instant and mutual. He did not know her name but she was the woman who had been dogging him for the past few days.

"Here, you!"

Mendick stepped forward and the woman lifted her skirt to mid-calf and ran. He followed, crossed the High Street with its buzzing traffic, dodged a cursing carter and looked around. The woman hesitated for a second beside the pillars of the Town House, glanced at him and disappeared down a narrow close that ran southward towards Dock Street.

If he had still been a beat officer he would have sprung his rattle to summon assistance, but a criminal

144

officer carried no such device. He knew he should not get involved, he should wait for help, but by the time he did so the woman would have vanished into the labyrinth of closes and medieval alleyways that criss-crossed Dundee behind the main streets. He had to follow, it was his duty.

"Stop that woman!" He rattled his cane against the wall and thrust into the darkness, breathing the familiar stench of poverty and decay.

The victim had followed, an undistinguished man half-seen in the gloom. "Catch her, she's a thief!" Mendick ignored him. He did not need any support.

Voices murmured all around and shadowed forms shifted in the dark. The quick, rough Dundee accents mingled with the longer vowels of Ireland to create an echoing cacophony between stone walls that wept foul water. Mendick stopped and listened for the click of footsteps. If the woman was clever she would ease into one of the side doors and remain still, invisible in the dark, but no, she was still running, the sound of her boots fast and sharp in the whispering dim.

Mendick followed, ignoring the comments from either side, the furtive attempts to trip him as he passed, the bottle dropped from above that crashed to the ground a second after he passed; such things were as normal in the London rookeries as in the unsavoury closes of Dundee. "Police! Stop right there!"

As expected, his words only spurred the woman on. The click of her heels increased in volume and he was able to follow her with more ease into the stygian dark. The close merged into a junction with another, in a combination of poverty and run-down houses, but rather than jink back to lose herself in the crowds the woman ran straight down the steep slope and out into Fish Street.

Mendick stopped to get his bearings. Although broader than the close, Fish Street was still a dark thoroughfare running almost parallel to the High Street, but nearer to the docks. The buildings stretched four storeys towards the sodden sky; crumbling tenements and town houses that had once belonged to the elite of Dundee but which were now abandoned to the lowest classes. In ones and twos and family groups, the wealthy families had fled the factory smoke of central Dundee and migrated to the cleaner air of West Ferry or the Perth Road.

Down here, ragged people grouped in front of doorways, preferring the relatively fresh air of the squalid street to the foetid stench and overcrowding of the much-divided interiors of the houses. Eyes watched him pass, some shorn of hope, others bereft of interest, a few predatory, and one or two people shouted obscene insults but Mendick did not stop. The woman hesitated at the door of the Ship Tavern, wailed, lifted her skirt even higher and clattered past and down the street.

"Here! Get back to your own bit!" A couple of gaunt youths, toes protruding from broken boots and knees from frayed trousers tried to block his path. He pushed them aside.

"Go and find a job," he advised roughly, knowing full well that such luxuries were scarce when trade was depressed and mills idle.

The woman had stopped halfway down the street, a vague dark figure leaning against an abandoned cart. She glanced back, caught sight of him, swore and dived through the door of the nearest building.

"Police!" Mendick ran down the sloping street. He

mounted the two steps leading to the slightly inset front door, pushed it and grunted in surprise when it opened without a sound. There was the usual underlying stench of damp and decay, mingled with a more acidic, sharper smell that he did not immediately recognise. He heard the staccato click of hurrying feet and then thick silence. He stepped inside.

The darkness was pitiless. Outside there had been the tang of sooty smoke and the scent of the sea, the grind of wheels on cobblestones, harsh voices and the raucous scream of seagulls. Here, silence closed like a clamp and the dark blocked all his senses. The woman had vanished as completely as if she had never been. Mendick raised his voice, "Police!"

Emptiness swallowed the word. Cautious, feeling his way, he stepped forward, wishing he had the lantern that all beat constables carried. He knew he should call a halt now and return with reinforcements, but he also knew he could not retract as long as there was a chance of success. He had set himself the task of catching this woman in the green cloak, and that is what he would try to do.

As his eyes became accustomed to the light he saw a flight of stone steps spiralling downward. He checked his inside pocket, felt the reassuring bulk of the pepperpot revolver, held his cane ready and descended, step by step until he came to another wooden door. Again it opened when he pushed and he walked in to the room beyond.

A sudden flare of lights blinded him. "What the . . .?" He put his left hand over his eyes as he held the cane in front of him ready to repel any attack.

"Are you Sergeant Mendick of Scotland Yard?"

The voice was disembodied, coming from everywhere

147

and nowhere. Mendick heard footsteps behind him, turned in time to see the vague shape of a man and then the door through which he had entered slammed shut. He heard the grate and draw of a bolt and looked around, blinking in the harsh light that held him like a rat in a trap. The simile was quite apt, he realised, for he was in a stone cellar with a vaulted stone ceiling. Intense darkness crowded beyond the pool of light, filled with the terrors of his infant self.

"Who are you?" Mendick peered upwards into the dark as his voice echoed around the chamber.

"Are you Sergeant James Mendick, of Scotland Yard?" The question was repeated.

"I am Mendick, who are you?" Mendick looked around the chamber but the lamps above his head blinded him, he could not even see a shadow. "Show yourself!"

"Here I am, James." A different voice mocked him and a woman slid into the periphery of the light. She stood still, hugging her green cloak close. "Oh, James! Don't you want me any more? And I thought you liked me, too. After all, you followed me here."

She laughed again – without humour – her voice harsh as she stood at the edge of his vision, her pinched, slum-reared face lined with poverty, soured with hardship, scarred with her loathing of the world. "Aren't you going to arrest me? Look! I'll show you everything." Tossing back her cloak, she reached to the front of her skirt, unfastened a hidden hook and allowed the material to fold back. The entire skirt opened and a rent in her threadbare petticoat allowed a glimpse of the white flesh of her thigh.

Mendick grunted. "You are a common thief."

From the pocket down, the skirt was lined with fine canvas, so creating a large space that now held a variety of small articles, from a pair of shoes to a selection of cheap ribbons. The combination of cloak and wide skirt acted as a perfect disguise for this cache of treasure.

"I may be a common thief, Sergeant Mendick, but I am running free as a bird, while you . . ." She pushed forward her right leg so her skirt fell back, and hauled up her petticoat. "You will be dead in twenty minutes, James, and so disfigured that even your own mother won't recognise you."

"You vile harpie!" Mendick stepped forward but the woman slid away into the dark. There was the ominous thud of a door closing and then silence. Mendick thought of the mutilated remains of Thoms, Milne and Torrie, all found within half a mile from where he stood. He gripped his cane and felt for the butt of his revolver. He had no intention of dying down here, in some dark Dundee cellar.

"Come on then, you blackguards!" He shouted.

There was a curious grating, the sound more sinister in the dark, and a deep baying that raised the small hairs on the back of his neck. "Sweet Jesus!" A dog! Mendick felt his pulse quicken: these people were going to set a dog on him and he was trapped with nowhere to run. There were more sounds, the ominous pad of multiple sets of paws and Mendick knew there was more than one dog in this cellar with him.

He had a choice: remain in the light where he could see whatever attacked him, and be seen, or retreat against a wall. If he remained where he was a dog could get behind him, best withdraw to the wall.

"Who's first?" If he was going to die, he would die

game and neither China Jim nor anybody else would hear him cry uncle.

"Come on you slavering bastards! Come on!"

He transferred the cane to his left hand and rapped it on the floor, simultaneously hauling his pepperpot from his inside pocket. It was bulky and clumsy, but in a situation such as this he was glad of the five barrels. He had learned in the army that an enemy would often wait until the act of reloading before attacking and he had no desire to be caught out.

Mendick waited for the sound of the animals. He heard the padding of their feet, one to the right, another to the left, and a third directly ahead. He swore. Three of them; if they all came at him he would have little chance. This was not how he wanted to die, mauled by dogs in a Dundee cellar. He kept his attention on the dogs. They were circling the chamber, occasionally passing through the pool of light, heavy and ugly and panting.

"Are you China Jim? Am I speaking to China Jim?"

"You are speaking to the last man you will hear before you die. You made a mistake in coming into my territory, Sergeant Mendick."

"If you kill a policeman they will hunt you forever." Mendick shouted. He could hear the dogs patrolling outside the circle of light. Their paws were heavy on the stone floor and their breathing was harsh.

The first of the dogs burst into the pool of light and headed straight towards him with its head down and mouth agape. It was a bullmastiff, a massive man-killer that could rip him to bloodied shreds. Raising the pistol he shot it clear through the skull. The report was loud in the cellar and gunsmoke erupted in a choking cloud. The dog continued its run; he stepped aside and it slammed against the wall, bleeding and kicking but still alive.

Mendick watched in sick horror as the remaining two dogs leaped on it, jaws working and for a minute there was a stramash of clashing jaws and terrible squeals. Mendick backed away, lifted his cane and peered around the chamber; if these dogs had got in, there must be a way out.

"That's one dog less, China! I hope you have a supply in reserve!"

The squeals faded to a long drawn whimper then died altogether. There were a few moments of growling and sounds of tearing flesh and then that ominous padding again.

"Mendick's got a gun! He's gone and shot one of the dogs!" That was the woman's voice, harsh and ugly, as she was herself.

"Douse the light!" That was a man's voice. "Don't let him see them!"

"No!" The woman replied. "He's fired his shot. They will be on him before he reloads and I want to watch."

Mendick thought of the three mutilated bodies and wondered if this woman had watched them die as well. He shook his mind clear and waited for the sound of the animals. He heard the padding of their feet, one to the right, the other to his left. If they attacked simultaneously he would have to fend off one with his cane while he shot the other.

"Die slowly, Sergeant." The female sounded less confident now. The grating noise sounded again and Mendick was left with the dogs.

They prowled around, sniffing, aroused to savagery by the scent of blood. Mendick kept his back to the wall and moved sideways around the perimeter of the chamber. He stepped quietly, trying to make no noise, thankful the raw stench of dead dog would mask his own scent. The floor was stone slabs: cold, smooth and occasionally uneven. He stumbled and froze. Only the harsh breathing of the dogs broke the silence, and the rapid, sinister patter of their paws.

The first came from his left, a bounding, snarling mountain of muscle and aggression and teeth that leaped through the darkness. More by instinct than intent, Mendick lifted his cane to meet it, just as the second dog came from the front. He fired again and the muzzle flash presented him with a tiny vignette of his position; he saw the dog in mid-leap, mouth wide and double rows of teeth gleaming, spittle drooling from its mouth, twin eyes pale and staring, then came the intense blackness of the after-flash. He heard the high-pitched yowl as the bullet connected, and the scuffled thump as the impact slammed it against the wall. But before Mendick could turn the final dog was on him.

He lifted his cane, aimed for the gaping mouth and thrust as hard as he could. The dog moved, the cane bounced off bone and scraped along the fur of its muzzle. Mendick continued the push and the tip entered the dog's eye. The animal howled, Mendick pushed harder, thrusting the narrow, lead-weighted end as far as he could and the dog broke away, yowling. Mendick pushed the muzzle of the pistol close to the dog's neck and squeezed the trigger; the barrels rotated, the hammer rose and fell – nothing. The pistol had misfired. He tried again – nothing. The dog opened its mouth wider and emitted a snarl just as Mendick tried his final barrel. This time the pistol fired. The report was deafening and the dog staggered backward, howling and still alive.

It faced him, the cane a hideous unicorn horn through its eye, and he jumped forward, grabbed the cane and pushed, working the lead-weighted end through the back of the eye socket and into the brain until the dog lay at his feet and he was gasping in reaction and the aftermath of fear.

"He's killed the dogs!"

The woman sounded furious. She added a bevy of foul language.

"Shut him in and let him rot!"

The light was doused.

Mendick swore. The darkness was oppressive, crushing him in its intensity. He backed against the wall, found the handful of cartridges in his pocket and fumbled to reload. The pepperpot was not the easiest of pistols to load, even in daylight, but in the dark and with hands still shaking, Mendick took a good three minutes. By the time he was finished his eyes had adjusted to the dark and he could see his surroundings.

The chamber was rectangular with two heavy doors. It only took a moment for Mendick to realise both were locked, and a couple of trial pushes to ascertain there were bolts at the top and bottom; he could not get out that way. He felt around the wall, searching. If the dogs had got in, then there must be another way out.

He stumbled into something and cursed softly. It was a barrel, waist high and heavy. This gloomy chamber had probably been a wine cellar so presumably this was full of wine. He moved on slowly, cautious in case the woman released more dogs.

The stones were rough under his fingertips. He probed, searching for the gap he knew must be there, somewhere. He almost shouted in triumph when his hand slid into nothingness. The hole was set two feet above the ground and was just large enough for a dog but there was no alternative. Replacing his revolver in its holster, Mendick wriggled into the opening. He had no idea how long the shaft might be or if there were any bends, but, he reasoned, if a large mastiff could negotiate it, then so could he.

The shaft was of smooth stone and had possibly been created for rolling kegs or barrels to the basement. Mendick inched upward, using his elbows and knees for leverage as he fought the steep incline. Twice he cursed as he heard the stonework scrape against the watch in his fob pocket: he valued that above all his few possessions.

The air stank of foetid dog. He gagged and ignored the stone that tore his clothes and scraped the skin from his elbows and knees. After a few moments the incline increased and he was slithering up a steep slope. He looked ahead but saw only darkness. For a moment he was a child again, climbing a flue for his master, but he shook away the memory and moved on, feeling for invisible handholds in the dark.

The passage ended abruptly. Solid darkness engulfed him and he could not tell where the stone ended and the foul air began. Mendick probed with his free hand, feeling wood rather than stone blocking his path. This must be the door. He pushed without effect, ran his hands around the edge, unable to find either hinge or handle. For a second he felt frustration and fear building inside him. He was trapped, unable to escape and unwilling to return to that dungeon with its dead dogs, there to wait until China Jim saw fit to release him.

He forced himself to think rationally. The dogs had come this way, so the door must open; if it had been intended for rolling down barrels there would be a simple catch. No! It was not a catch. He remembered the grating sound that had perplexed him. Rather than a hinged door, it was a square piece of wood set within two vertical slides.

Mendick braced himself against the sides of the chute, pressed against the door and exerted upward pressure. The door moved, very slightly. He kept pushing, wincing at the noise he made. He was so close to the door it screamed rather than grated, a noise that set his teeth on edge. He stopped, put one hand on the butt of his revolver and waited. Nobody came. He continued, pushing the door up, inch by noisy, painful inch. The darkness beyond the door was intense, the silence forbidding. Finally he was able to haul out his pepperpot and wriggle through to fresher air.

He landed on a wooden floor and lay still for a second, listening. There was no sound, he was alone in a dim room. He stood up, stumbled slightly and moved towards a thin vertical bar of light that shimmered from somewhere to his left. As he had hoped, the light came from the slight gap between two ill-fitting shutters. He fumbled for the catch and hauled them open. The bustle of the night-time street was welcome – the high chatter of women, a drunken laugh, the rumble of wheels on cobbles as a cart lurched past. Mendick checked his watch. It had been less than an hour since he followed the woman in the green cloak into this house, although it seemed far longer.

He looked out through the tiny windowpanes and saw rain cascading onto Fish Street, only one storey below. He had escaped the dogs and the cellar; he had light and he was free. China Jim had thrown his dice and lost, now it was his turn. China Jim had made a big mistake in revealing his address.

Mendick grinned. He would get a few hours sleep, borrow some uniformed policemen and turn this house upside down. Somewhere in this building would be a clue to China Jim's identity, and now the attempted murder of a policeman was added to his list of crimes.

The blackjack crashed off his skull so suddenly he had no chance to look round.

CHAPTER ELEVEN

He was flat on the floor, unable to move, looking at a collection of legs and feet. Six legs; there were three people then. He tried to rise, reached for his revolver and saw a foot casually kick it away from him.

"So what do we do with him now?" The man spoke as if there was gravel in his throat.

"Take him out to sea and dump him." The voice was so muffled that Mendick knew he would never be able to identify it again.

"It would be easier just to shoot him," the gravel-voiced man said.

"No," the muffled voice came again. "Any fool can shoot a man. I wanted him ripped to shreds by the dogs but that can no longer be, so I want him to vanish without trace. Make sure there is nothing on him that can be identified."

"His face will identify him." That was the female with the harsh gutter voice.

"Not after the fishes have been at him," gravel-voice said. "They go for the eyes first and then the soft flesh." His laugh echoed around the room. "Within two days he will be half gone. Within a week he will be a skeleton."

Mendick moved his hand, his revolver was too far away. Instead he formed a fist and punched hard behind the nearest knee. The gravel-voiced man staggered backward and Mendick rolled over, braced himself and stood up, just as the woman landed a mighty kick in his

157

ribs. Mendick grunted with surprise at the force. He tried to push up, but somebody jumped on his back, thrusting him to the floor and the woman began to kick again, remorseless, gasping at each blow. The light glinted on the steel caps on her boots.

"Bastard, bluebottle bastard!" Her vocabulary was limited, Mendick thought, but she was handy with her boots. He tried to catch her ankle to trip her and she dodged, crashing her boot into his ribs then his face. Mendick saw the green cloak swirling then curled into a ball as the kicks hammered on.

"Beth is doing fine there. We could just kill him here and now," the gravel-voiced man said casually, "and just dump the body."

"Take him on board and pitch him over the side." The other man gave the order.

"As you wish," gravel-voice grunted.

Mendick felt a powerful grip on his collar hauling him upright. He allowed himself to be lifted, winced and swore as Beth slapped him hard across the face, and looked into her bitter eyes.

"You're going to die, bluebottle," she said, rolling the words around in her mouth. "Your wife will be waiting for you to come home, day after day after day . . ."

For a second, Mendick remembered Emma lying dying in childbirth. Her eyes liquid with love, her voice gentle but racked with pain in their bedroom that smelled of life and blood and her imminent death. The memory was agony.

He kicked out, catching Beth on her knee and sending her yelling to the ground. He lashed backwards with his elbow, missed the floating rib of gravel-voice by a whisper but made him relax his grip a fraction. The third man was tall and bulky with a dark mask concealing his face. He stepped back as Mendick lunged for the mask, but the woman had recovered quickly, slipped on brass knuckle-dusters and landed a powerful punch that slammed Mendick's teeth against his lips and sent him staggering sideways. He shook the blood from his mouth, just as gravel-voice wrapped an arm around his throat.

"Burke the bluebottle bastard!" Beth screamed, "Go on Captain! Burke the bastard!" She came closer and spat in Mendick's face. "Hold him like that, Captain."

Mendick felt the pressure on his throat increase and the captain's hand clamp over his mouth and nose. He was being burked; suffocated. He struggled but the Captain was immensely strong. He kicked and the woman stepped back, smiling. She swivelled, aimed and punched him in the stomach. The impact of the knuckle-dusters seemed to tear his muscles apart.

"Burke him now, Captain," she said, watching.

"Wait." The masked man approached Mendick. He was the largest of the three, slow-moving and clumsy, his voice hissing as if he were a foreigner struggling with the language. "You disappointed me, Sergeant. You really were so easy to trap." He shook his head. "And you told me your weakness yourself."

"The hunt is not finished yet, China!" Mendick kicked backward, but the captain had his legs splayed well apart and Mendick's heels missed their target.

"It is." The masked man said. He nodded, and the woman checked her knuckle-dusters and swung, first low into Mendick's belly and as he doubled up, hard at the point of his jaw.

He was not unconscious. He felt the bone-cracking

159

pain and the dissipation of his strength as he slumped. He heard voices as if from a distance. He felt himself dragged down the stairs, saw the dim shape of a coach and felt hard contact with the floor as he was thrown in on top of rustling straw. Beth and the man called Captain came in beside him, with Beth landing the occasional kick as they rattled through the streets.

Mendick drifted in and out of consciousness as he was hauled out of the carriage again. He saw masked faces, heard the snort of a horse and smelled the familiar twist of the sea mingled with tar and wet canvas.

"Cover him up securely," gravel-voice spoke again, "and get him down below."

Mendick looked up, saw the gently swaying masts of a score of ships and then a canvas was thrown over him and he was hustled away again. He struggled for a moment but the canvas pressed against him, stifling him in darkness and he passed out again.

Mendick could feel the surge and sway of the ship. He understood ships. He recognised the tang of salt, the friendly scent of tar, the rough feel of planking beneath his face and body, the never-ending creak of deck and bulwarks, the whine of the wind through the rigging and the flap of canvas from a sail somebody had badly stowed. He was on board a ship, or some sort of vessel anyway. Why? He could not remember. Had he signed articles? He tried to recall the previous few days. Had he been in a dockside pub and had some boarding master drugged his drink or blackjacked him so he was thrown aboard some hell ship bound for Sydney or the West Coast of South America?

He shook his head, the pain did not help. Random

images crowded into his mind; the dark tunnel of a flue; the packed forecastle of a coaster, reeking of sweat and damp, with Larsson the Swede coughing his consumptive lungs out; the sweat patches under the arms of the scarlet uniforms as his colleagues of the 26th Foot marched into action; Emma smiling into his eyes as she waited for him before the altar; that rocking swaying carriage beneath him on the nightmare attempt to rescue Queen Victoria.

Who was he? He was Sergeant James Mendick of Scotland Yard and now of the Dundee Police, trying to find China Jim and solve the murders of David Thoms, David Torrie and Robert Milne. Mendick tried to rise but something was stifling him, pressing him to the deck. He shoved upwards, struggled with folds of stiff canvas and gradually wrestled the cover to one side. He rolled over and swore again at the various pains throughout his body. His head was pounding, his jaw, stomach and ribs ached and he had a loose tooth or two where Beth had punched him with the knuckle-dusters.

He pushed himself upright. It was dark so he knew he was below decks, probably in the hold or the 'tween decks of some vessel. There was no engine sound so she was a sailing vessel, and judging by her lively movement in the water, she was not very large and under way. He put out his hands and touched something wooden and curved, with metal bands around it; definitely a barrel of some sort. A few more moments fumbling confirmed he was in a hold jammed with barrels and kegs. They were stacked eight high, leaving him only a small space in which to move. A quick tap on each told him they contained liquid. What, he could not tell. It was much more important that he find a way out.

Fighting the pain in his head and the nagging ache of his stomach and ribs, Mendick tried to climb up the nearest barrel, but his fingers slipped on the convex bevel; he could get no purchase on the smooth sides and slipped back down to the deck. He tried again, broke two fingernails as he clutched desperately at the iron hoops, but dragged himself up, inch by agonising inch until he was wedged between two barrels. He used the most immediately adjacent for support and thrust with his feet, walking himself up the curved staves towards where the hatch had to be. The strain on his arms and legs was terrific, but he managed to scale the first six barrels and reached upward towards the hatch that was secured so close above his head. He reached up again, balanced with his feet and knees and tried to ease back the hatch cover.

The ship was bouncing, rising and falling in short, steep seas and Mendick guessed they were not far from shore, perhaps still in the Tay. He tried to push upward again but his feet slipped from the curve of the casks. He swore, clutched at the iron bands, missed and clattered in a cursing heap to the deck below. He lay for a moment as a sharp, familiar scent surrounded him. He grunted: whisky. It was whisky leaking from one of the upper casks.

China Jim had taken his revolver and his cane was broken, but he still had his packet of lock picks. He extracted a long sharp spike and thrust it into the nearest cask, twisted until he penetrated the wood and slowly withdrew. He licked the blade. "Whisky again," he said. He moved along the casks, testing at random and in each case tasted whisky on the blade of his spike.

"So," he said to himself, "China Jim is transporting

an entire boatload of whisky. Let's see what we can do to reduce his profit."

Returning to each barrel he inserted the spike and gradually made each hole larger, soon the tiny trickles of whisky increased to a slow stream. After half an hour he had penetrated only five barrels, but there was a growing puddle on the deck, swilling from side to side as the ship gyrated with the sea. Mendick gave a grim nod. "You might kill me yet, Jim, but that's a few pounds less for your pocketbook my lad!"

The vessel heeled right over and Mendick had to clutch at the barrels to avoid falling. He heard the patter of bare feet on the deck and dim light eased in as the batons securing the cover scraped open. Two faces peered down: one, a thin-faced seaman, the other was Beth.

"He's conscious again," the seaman sounded nonchalant, as if holding a man captive in his hold was an everyday thing.

"Good," Beth said. "That way he'll know when he's drowning. I want to watch him suffer. Fetch him up."

Mendick stepped back, ready to fight. A rope uncoiled slowly from above and thudded onto the deck at his feet. Two men appeared with a net and dropped it on his head, as he struggled in its mesh a succession of seamen slid down the rope. They dragged the net tight, pinioned his arms and hoisted him to the deck with such ease it was obvious they had performed this task before. As he fought within the net, Mendick saw that he was on the deck of a small sloop; black-painted and with weather-darkened sails bent on a tall mast of Baltic pine.

"There you are," Beth gave him a casual kick as he lay entangled within the rope mesh. "Strip him of anything that might be recognised and throw him overboard."

Mendick snatched for her ankle in a gesture of pointless defiance. "You bitch!" He writhed and struggled until the nearest seaman grabbed a marline spike from the bulwark and cracked him over the head. He slumped into semi-consciousness. Three men grabbed hold of him, their hands hard around his arms and legs. Mendick retaliated weakly as they unravelled the net, dragged him free and and stripped him naked. Beth watched, smiling.

"Cold, Sergeant?" She leaned closer, "Never mind, when you get to hell, Lucifer will keep you nice and warm." She nudged one of the seamen with her boot. "You! Check his pockets for money or anything valuable."

The thin-faced seaman lifted Mendick's waistcoat. "I'll have his watch. It's only silver but it will pawn for a few shillings."

A second man rubbed finger and thumb over Mendick's shirt. "I'll have this, it's good quality linen."

Beth stood on Mendick's hand and smiled down on him. "You're not so arrogant now are you, Sergeant?" She twisted her foot, driving her heel into his palm. "Right, boys, bind him securely and toss him overboard."

The thin-faced seaman looked over the side. "We're not clear of the Tay yet. That head wind held us back, and the currents here are uncertain . . ."

Beth kicked Mendick again. "I want rid of this rubbish before I leave the boat. Throw him over and let the sea have him."

"Another twenty minutes and we will be out of the Tay and heading south; the current off Fife Ness could take him anywhere."

"Get rid of him," Beth ordered.

The man shrugged. "As you will." He signalled to the other seamen "Right, lads! Over the side with him." He clasped Mendick's watch tightly in his hand and winked. "Thanks for this, Sergeant."

With his hands and feet tied, Mendick could only writhe as two men lifted him and carried him to the low gunwale.

"You look after that watch, you blackguard," he warned as they balanced him on the rail. "I'll be coming back for it."

When the thin man laughed his lower lip writhed around the remnants of an old scar. For an instant Mendick wondered where he had picked that up: a dockside brawl perhaps, or in some sterner encounter with Mindanao pirates or African slavers.

"Davy Jones has other ideas," the seaman said and they tossed him overboard with as little concern as if he had been a bucket of dirty water. The last thing Mendick saw was Beth's face, smiling.

CHAPTER TWELVE

The short fall between the deck of the sloop and the sea seemed to last an eternity as Mendick waited for the impact, and then the sound of the splash deafened him and he was sinking down forever. Water roared in his ears, louder and louder until the terrible noise dominated his brain and his thoughts. He let the sound take over, embraced it with all his being and became part of it. Noise and pain and he were one being, sinking in the chill waters of the Tay as the world ended. He swallowed water until the pain was like fire enclosed in his chest and then he surfaced in an agonising explosion of water and air.

"Jesus God in heaven!"

He was still alive but for how long? More than that, he was moving. A current gripped him, pushing him further out to sea, away from the Tay and to his death. He was sinking, helpless against the force of the Tay when he felt something firm beneath him, the sea surging back in a sucking hiss that left him gasping but only half-submerged. He looked around. He was on the edge of one of the shifting sandbanks that made the entrance to the Tay so treacherous, but he was not alone. A small colony of seals howled and wailed on top.

Mendick rolled out of the sea onto the yielding sand and lay still as the waves splashed over him. His throat and lungs burned from the salt water he had swallowed, his head thumped as if it would explode, but he was safe, at least for a while. He knew the tide would change soon and this sandbank would vanish but he had a few minutes, perhaps a few hours grace. Mendick didn't care – he was alive.

He wriggled further up the sand and looked straight into the face of a seal. He had seen seals by the thousand as a seaman and had never paid them much heed. Now, close to, he saw them as they were: wild animals, and with their young to protect, they were dangerous.

Close to, a seal was not pretty. However much children and their nannies might exclaim and point to them as they lie on the shore, they were ugly creatures, particularly with their mouths open and their vicious teeth exposed. Mendick tried to move away but, tied hand and foot as he was, his movement was restricted and there was nowhere to go. He looked over his shoulder, hopeful that some miracle had improved his situation, but nothing had changed. He was still lying on a sandbank at the entrance of the Firth of Tay, shivering violently and so cold he could barely move at all. He had had a temporary reprieve but when the tide rose he would certainly drown. His life had come full circle from birth in some festering close in Dundee to death in Dundee's own river.

High up, an easterly wind drove clouds across the moon. Mendick could no longer see the seals or the sandbank. Only the faint phosphorescence of the surf illuminated his predicament as the tide hushed in from the North Sea to meet the powerful current of the Tay. Mendick struggled to sit and then to stand but his legs, numbed by the freezing temperatures, would not respond to his brain's commands. Maybe, he thought, maybe if he could get to his feet somebody would see him? Somebody might be standing on the Fife side of the Firth or on the long beaches of Broughty and notice his pale, white figure against the black of the sea? It was a forlorn hope, the only one he had. The reality was that anybody looking to sea would be searching for ships and no ship would dare attempt the entrance to the Tay at night, with its notorious sandbars and treacherous currents. He was alone, save for the seals.

There were a whole family of these seals sharing his sandbank: huge grey things with snub noses and wicked teeth, capable of tearing his arm off without any difficulty. One began to flop across the sodden sand with so little grace it was hard to believe it was the same creature that slid so effortlessly through the seas. Mendick wriggled backwards, trying to put as much distance as possible between himself and this creature. He knew men hunted them for their oil and pelts. Now he was the prey as the seal closed in, its nostrils distended and mouth open.

Mendick opened his mouth to shout, hoping to drive the creature away, and instead vomited an acrid gush of salt water onto the dull sand. He lay there, gasping and shuddering, but at least the noise had given the seal pause. It stopped for a second before it moved again, now joined by one of his companions. They approached, eight-foot-long monsters with sharp shining teeth, totally at home in this environment in which he was so obviously the intruder.

Over to the north, the lights of Broughty glinted through the dark. The village was only a mile or two away. A long swim for a strong man but impossible for a man with his limbs securely fastened. Mendick looked and longed but knew any attempt would merely hasten death. The lights teased him and he imagined the comfortable houses of the wealthy and the crowded, tar-scented cottages of the fisher-folk with the women redding the long lines and the men preparing to go back to sea.

The surf was rising. Spindrift sprayed his freezing legs. He crawled crabwise, yards further from the sea, but equally, closer to the waiting seals. Which was best? To die in screaming agony under those sharp teeth or to choke as the sea burned his throat and lungs? It was sickening to die knowing he had failed. China Jim would continue to terrorise Dundee; the murders would continue and the police would chase their tails and find nothing. Mendick grunted in terrible frustration; it was worse now he understood how China made his money. If he had only been granted another few weeks he could have had China Jim hanged.

The patch of sand diminished as the tide rose. Each surge of the sea meant a few seconds less to live, yet still Mendick planned his campaign. He knew now that China Jim was a large-scale whisky smuggler and certainly not Chinese, but he could not yet work out the connection between the criminal activities and the murders. There must be one; those unfortunate men must have crossed China Jim in 1842. That was the only possible conclusion. He had to discover what they had been doing in 1842.

But he could not. He would drown here, naked and alone, a few miles from the place of his birth. Would anyone ever find his corpse? Or would the sea spirit his dead body away and drive it deep under water for the fish to slowly devour? The tide rose fast, forcing him further up the sandbank, still closer to the seals. They were calling now, cracking open the night with their eerie, high-pitched voices sounding like the souls of the damned. Mendick shuddered. This was not how he wanted to die, alone and uncared for, surrounded by wild beasts and in this place of evil memories. He moved closer to the gaping jaws of the seals.

The rising easterly wind brought rain, increasing from a smirr that had smeared the friendly flickering lamps of Broughty to a skin-lashing torrent that erased the lights completely and left Mendick alone with the dark and the leaping waves, the crash of the surf and the hoarse wails of the seals. Unable to stand, he lay, feeling the water rise around him, and then the seals were gone. One second they were there, a terrifying presence all around him, and next they had vanished into the sea as if one mind controlled all their bodies. In their place came the most sickening smell Mendick had ever experienced. He looked up, just as the sea covered the last few square inches of the sandbank and surged the length of his naked body. A shift of wind tore a gap in the clouds, he could see the lights of Dundee glimmer faintly to the north. Christ, but he hated that place and now he must die on its sea gate, unloved in death as he had been in life.

Unloved, that was, except by Emma. He spat the salt from his throat. "I'm coming, Emma," he shouted. "Hold out your hand for me!"

But what was that terrible stench?

CHAPTER THIRTEEN

The stench increased, causing Mendick to gag even as the sea slid up the length of his body. He rolled over and pushed himself upright, straining for air. The swell increased, surging up his body, breaking against his chest, splashing water against his face and into his nostrils. He closed his eyes: this was not how he had visualised his death, a slow drowning on a sandbank at the mouth of the Firth of Tay. But Emma would be waiting, always with that soft smile. He could almost see her, pointing, shouting something he could not understand.

"Man ahoy!" The voice was male, the accent born in the streets of Dundee. The voice faded slightly but the words carried above the hush and spatter of the sea.

"There's some lunatic standing on the sandbank, lads. Pull closer and we'll have a look."

Mendick's knees buckled as he tried to turn and he slipped beneath the surface and emerged, choking and spluttering, "Ahoy! Who's there?"

The boat was so close to him the port oars almost cracked his head, but the oarsmen shipped in time and glided alongside. Bearded faces stared at him as if he were a ghost. A man with an iron-grey beard and huge hands hauled him on board and left him lying face down on the thwarts. "You lie there a minute, son, and get your senses back."

Mendick glanced along the line of legs to the stern to

where a cloaked and hooded figure held the steering oar.

"He's naked," the man with the beard spoke again.

Mendick retched and vomited seawater into the boat, heaving and gasping as he emptied his lungs and stomach of the burning salt.

"Tied up, too," somebody said. "There's been foul work here, I wager."

There was the snick of metal in leather and a knife sliced through Mendick's bonds. He wriggled his hands and feet, gasping at the prickled torture of returning circulation. He tried to thank his rescuers but he could not speak. Salt sea water had combined with the biting cold to rob him of the power of speech. He tried to stand, to see who steered this providential boat, but the bearded man thrust him hard down onto the middle thwart. "You just sit there, lad. Keep still or you'll have us over."

The muffled figure in the stern gave an order in the light voice of a youth and the oarsmen thrust in again. The boat pulled for the northern shore of the Tay with all four oars dipping and rising simultaneously in the practised stroke of an experienced crew. Despite his exhaustion, Mendick admired their skill and watched the phosphorescence gleam from the oar blades and reflect from the bubbling wake. He began to shiver until someone threw a soft cloak over him. It smelled of salt mingled with a strange, floral aroma he recognised, from where he could not say.

Iron-beard tapped his shoulder. "Rest easy, lad. You're safe now." He nudged Mendick's arm and passed him a flask. "Go on, drink. It'll help." The voice was rough but not unfriendly and the eyes that scrutinised him were worldly-wise, bright blue behind a web of wrinkles and deep with knowledge and compassion.

"Thank you." Mendick sipped from the flask. He coughed on fiery rum and sipped again. Liquid fire seeped into his throat and exploded inside his stomach. He breathed out slowly and closed his eyes. It seemed an age since he had followed that green-cloaked pickpocket across the High Street although he guessed it was just over 24 hours ago. He swayed slightly but righted himself as the oarsmen eased past the towering bulk of Broughty Castle and towards the lone gleam of a single lantern. The second the keel of the boat kissed and furrowed the soft sand of Broughty Beach, the oarsmen shipped oars in unison. Hard hands helped him gently from the boat and onto the beach.

There were six men in the boat. Iron-beard and another guided Mendick, two carried bundles carefully wrapped in oiled canvas, one carried a cask and the slim, hooded figure walked the length of the boat from the stern to the bow before stepping dry-shod and erect onto the beach.

Lights flickered from the windows of the clustered fisher cottages as the men headed directly for the solitary yellow glow of a lantern in the upper window of a larger house.

"That's Unicorn Cottage," Mendick's voice was harsh in his own ears. "That's Mrs Gordon's house."

The men ignored him, their feet silent in the soft sand as they hurried to a door in the garden wall. The young man in the hood unlocked it and without hesitation they marched to the back door and eased inside, where the young man lit the gas light.

They were in a stone-flagged kitchen dominated by a range black-leaded to a gloss, with racks and spits and spoons dangling from hooks. The room smelled of soap

173

and polish. The men carefully placed their burdens on a scrubbed deal table, while iron-beard pulled out a chair for Mendick.

"Sit you there, lad." He guided Mendick down. "You'll be fine after a wee rest."

The young man stepped inside the pool of lamp light and pulled back his hood. When he shook his head his auburn hair cascaded around his shoulders. "Thank you," Johanna said softly. "You'd better get back to the old Rose now."

"What shall we do with the castaway?" Iron-beard hesitated, one hand rested on the hilt of his knife. His eyes were no longer so friendly.

"Leave him to me," Johanna said.

"He's naked under your coat," his bearded escort reminded her.

"And I am naked under my clothes too," Johanna smiled and shook her head. "Thank you, Iain. I know this man. I am in no danger from him." She waited until the last man left. "That was Iain Grant, he is a harpooner on the whaling ships, and a good man. But you, Sergeant Mendick, you seem to have got yourself into a pretty pickle."

Mendick rose from the chair, swore softly as Johanna's cloak flapped open and did not fail to notice the humour in Johanna's eyes. "So have you, Mrs Gordon; you have a naked man in your house and if I am not mistaken, those are smuggled goods sitting on your table."

"Indeed they are, Sergeant." A dimple appeared on Johanna's left cheek as she smiled. "Do you intend to arrest me for a little fun, Sergeant?" Her eyes laughed at him. "Don't tell me you have never done anything just for the excitement of the thing?"

Mendick frowned, "Normally when I challenge somebody about their activities, they respond with evasion or defiance. Not by questioning me."

"A question you did not answer, Sergeant, so I will ask again. Have you ever done anything that was not right?" She swivelled one of the kitchen chairs and drew it beside him, so close he could feel the heat from her body. "I am waiting, Sergeant."

"I think I should be asking the questions . . ." Mendick began, but Johanna was having none of it.

"I don't think you should, Sergeant. I really don't." As she stood up her hip brushed against his shoulder. It was an accidental, fleeting touch but it sent a thrill through him and he gasped so audibly he knew she should have heard.

Johanna stood over him with her mouth slightly twisted and her dimple deep beside her mouth. "I think you just follow the path of duty and never spare time for fun or for yourself," she said.

Mendick shook his head. "We are discussing your illegal activities, Mrs Gordon, and what I should do about them, not my pursuits."

As Johanna shook her head a few tendrils of auburn hair snaked across her left eye, an imperfection that made her appearance all the more entrancing. "Not so, Sergeant Mendick. It is more important to wonder what I am going to do with you?" Her smile broadened. "How can I explain to my husband that I have a naked man in my house?"

"If you send a message to the police office that I am here, they will send a constable with some clothes." Mendick tried to rise but swayed and sat down heavily.

Johanna's smile combined sweetness with iron

in a manner Mendick had not seen since the death of his wife. "You wish me to inform the police? That is undoubtedly the most effective way of informing all of Dundee, including Mr Gordon, that I have a naked man here." The flash of anger in her green eyes altered quickly to concern as Mendick slid down the chair. "Well, it seems the solution to that little problem will have to be postponed, Sergeant. You need rest." She leaned closer and touched the purple bruises on his jaw and the top of his head. "And some patching up, I see."

The slavering jaws of the dog were gaping around his throat, the fangs polished ivory, sharp as a curved row of razors. Then they changed, flattened; evolved into the dark hardness of that chute and then again eased into the liquid surface of the Tay, soft surging around his head as he sunk slowly down, down to the depths. His feet struck something solid and he swore. Death was so easy when Emma was waiting for him, her eyes wide in promise and her arms wide in welcome, the jolt meant he had to continue the struggle. He rolled with the sea roaring in his ears and the white hot agony of expanding lungs in his chest. Onward, rolling, pushing, he thrust towards the agony of life, away from the delights of peaceful death: the light was there, glaring in its brightness, harsh in its offering, and he surfaced in an explosion of pain.

Mendick woke to the sound of seagulls and the scent of beeswax, paint and perfume. He sat up with a jerk, unable to recognise his surroundings.

"Relax, Sergeant." Johanna sat at the bottom of the bed; her perfume wafted towards him. Light and floral, it was pleasant rather than heady, relaxing rather than stimulating. "Or perhaps it is I who should be afraid? I have a bold man in my bed."

Mendick breathed in deeply, enjoying the scent. "You are safe with me." He thought he saw a flicker of disappointment in Johanna's eyes, but knew he must be mistaken. "But am I safe from your husband?" Mendick considered his position − naked, unarmed and lying in the bed of a woman who might be China Jim's wife. Even more dangerous, no-one knew his whereabouts or even whether he were alive or dead.

Johanna shrugged. "If I am safe, Sergeant, then so are you. Gordon never calls here unless he wants me for something, and that is a rare event." When she looked away Mendick saw the hurt in her eyes.

"That is undeniably his loss," he said softly.

"Did you sleep well, Sergeant?" The briskness was back as she rose from the bed and walked to the window. He realised he was watching the swing of her hips and looked away quickly. Johanna was another man's woman and the wife of a possible suspect. He could not, should not look, but her skirt was neat around her hips and reached to just below her ankles. It matched the loose grey mantle that thumbed its nose at a fashion which demanded a tight waist and balloon sleeves. Johanna then, was a woman who wore what she liked in defiance of what was expected.

Her sudden turn took him by surprise and her eyes were bright and clear as they met his. "You were unconscious for long enough," Johanna said, "so you must have slept well. Now," she clapped her hands together as if making a decision, "you must be hungry. I know I am." She lowered her head so her hair flopped forward. "Do you swim, Sergeant?"

"Do I what?" Once again this woman had caught Mendick by surprise.

"Swim, Sergeant. Can you swim?" She smiled at him, "You do understand the word?"

"Why, yes, but I do not understand why . . ."

Johanna patted his arm. "Good. Then you shall join us in our morning swim." She stepped towards the door. "John and I always take to the water in the morning. Eat first though, you need to build up your strength."

He knew he should report to the police office. He knew he should be hard on the trail of China Jim now he had new information and new knowledge, but as soon as Johanna gave him that slightly lopsided smile, and spoke with that laughing voice, his resolve melted clean away. Duty disappeared and something else took its place. He did not know or perhaps he did not want to admit what it was. He only knew he had not felt this way since Emma died.

"I have no swimming clothes," Mendick temporised.

Johanna smiled. "I can provide them." She looked down for a moment and smiled again, "unless you are too good to go swimming with me of course."

Mendick thought of all the questions he should be asking. About Gordon and his movements, about his business, about the night of Milne's murder and Torrie's murder. Instead he bit into a hunk of fresh bread and cheese, sipped tea from a chipped, china cup, enjoyed the childish chatter of young John and worried vaguely about swimming clothes and what he might wear when he eventually rose from this bed. Somehow, when he was in Johanna's company he did not care. She would work something out, he was sure.

Johanna took hold of John's hand and slipped through the door in a shiver of skirts. She reappeared ten minutes later, still holding her son but dressed in an

178

outfit so shocking that Mendick spent a long moment simply staring before he recollected himself and paid a mumbling compliment. Her dress was of thin linen, with a bodice top and baggy trousers that reached only to mid calf, leaving the lower leg, ankles and feet quite exposed.

"You like it?" Johanna gave an unselfconscious twirl. "I designed it myself. It is far more comfortable than these heavy serge things that weigh you down and drag you to the depths." She tossed a small bundle onto the bed. "This is yours, I will leave you to get changed," the light in her eyes was pure mischief, "unless you want me to help?"

"I think I can manage." Mendick waited until Johanna left the room before he rose and quickly pulled on his own linen costume. It was light and simple but left him feeling very exposed. Designed to the same pattern as Johanna's, it was tight around his chest and baggy at his waist and hips. He felt supremely self-conscious when he padded out of the bedroom but within seconds Johanna put him entirely at ease.

"It's all right," Johanna had waited for him just outside the room. "There are no servants here, just you, me and John." She slid her gaze over him. "If you do not mind me saying so, Sergeant, you cut a fine figure!"

"And you are utterly enchanting," Mendick said, and looked away. The words had escaped before he had the chance to stop them. However it seemed that Johanna had not heard for she merely smiled and gestured for him to follow down a short flight of stairs into a room whose walls seemed to be entirely glass.

"My studio," she said.

Paintings filled the room. There were seascapes and

landscapes, paintings of ships and of breaking seas, but mostly there were portraits. Mendick stopped to admire Johanna's skill, looking at a group of men who posed on the deck of a ship. There were six of them, from a handsome youth with an embarrassed smile to a familiar iron-bearded man with knowing eyes. The bearded man also featured in another portrait as he sat on the deck of a ship, splicing a line onto a harpoon.

"That is one of my favourites," Johanna said quietly. "That's Iain Grant. You met him yesterday morning."

Mendick nodded. He knelt down to study the canvas. "You have caught something of his character there. I can see more than just the face. There is a light in the eyes and an expression of something." He struggled for the word, "Durability I think, yes, durability."

"Do you think so?" Johanna touched his shoulder, a light touch although her fingers left an impression like fire on his skin beneath the thin linen. "Thank you, James. Nobody has ever said anything like that before." There was a catch in her voice that intrigued him and for a second he sensed a vulnerability that he craved to ease, and a loneliness he would not have understood if he had not already learned of her loveless marriage.

"It's beautiful," Mendick said. He meant, "You are beautiful," but he could not say that. Not to another man's wife.

"I try to catch the character of all my subjects," Johanna said, "people, ships, places. When I paint, the light is important. Some ships have their own atmosphere, and people . . . I love portraits, and capturing the hidden sides of people." She stepped back and looked away, "It is good to be appreciated, Sergeant Mendick. I only wish that Mr Gordon . . . shared my interest."

"You have a rare talent," Mendick said. He was unsure if he meant her painting skills or something else. He waited for a response but Johanna seemed unable to accept a compliment.

"Come, Sergeant, before the morning's sun has gone." She took John's hand and hurried out of the door.

Sunlight sparked from a myriad waves, glittering like a layer of diamonds scattered on a carpet of undulating blue. Mendick watched as Johanna waded deep, ducked under and began to swim with strokes more powerful than he had ever seen from a woman. John followed, as fearless as the divers Mendick had once seen off Ceylon, as he gambolled in a display of splashing water.

"Come on, Sergeant!" Johanna shouted back to him, waving her arm. "Race you!"

She was like a puppy, Mendick thought; all fun and frolics, teasing and tormenting for his attention. She turned and dived under water, jack-knifing. For an instant he had a splendid view of her rounded bottom with every curve and contour closely caressed by wet linen and then she was gone, swimming beneath the surface. He smiled and shook his head. She was a creature of the water, a nymph, an auburn mermaid. He should be asking her about Gordon, but that would be to acknowledge the fact she was married and he did not want to do that, not yet. Dear God, he never wanted to admit that, not even to himself.

The hands took him by surprise, grabbing at his legs and he floundered and ducked under. Johanna was there, smiling at him and for a second they grappled like lovers then surfaced in a fountain of water that rose, suspended in the air for a long instant as the morning sun played a hundred rainbows with the water droplets and then cascaded downward to join the surface of the sea. For some reason Mendick knew he would never forget that tiny fragment of time. It encapsulated his feelings about Johanna – a magic escape from reality, a relationship doomed by circumstance yet blessed by fate and the God of Love.

Love. He had admitted the fact to himself. He was in love with Johanna Lednock and there was not a thing he could do about it.

"I just could not resist that," she said. "You looked so staid and respectable, and good of course. I thought you were obviously thinking of your duty when you should have been enjoying yourself for once."

"I am enjoying myself," Mendick told her, and he was not lying.

From their vantage point he could see the sunlight reflected on the great glass windows of Unicorn House with the village of Broughty Ferry spread on either side. Mendick looked to the west, where the factory chimneys of Dundee serrated the horizon, some extinguished in this time of depression but others oozing smoke into their already leaden sky.

He saw the steeple tower of St Mary's, prominent despite the fire of 1841 that had destroyed much of the fabric of the church, while the great green mound of the Law provided a backdrop like a mother caring for her brood. Dundee: the town of his nightmares and here he was spending a day in a dream more perfect than he had experienced since Emma died. An oxymoron of experiences jostled his senses, but at that second he would rather have been here and with Johanna than anywhere else or with anyone else in the world. Including Emma, God forgive him, including Emma.

They bobbed together on the surface of the sea, and Mendick was content to just be. He glanced over at Johanna and she was watching him, her eyes narrow, thoughtful and green; or were they grey? He could not decide. He did not really care, he just enjoyed the sensation of her gaze.

"You look better now, James." Johanna said quietly. "You looked terrible when we picked you up. I think it's time you told me what happened."

Mendick nodded. When had she started to call him James? He shrugged. Did it matter, as long as she did?

Unicorn Cottage greeted them with warmth and a ready-laid fire that Johanna lit even before she dried and changed herself. Mendick watched as she walked around with the wet linen clinging to her, moving with her, enhancing each contour and curve and when she looked up and caught his gaze he did not look away.

"I know," she said so softly he almost missed her words. "I feel just the same way." She pulled a towel from a corner cupboard and passed it to him. "Best get dried, James." She smiled again, the mischief so evident her eyes sparked. "I won't watch." When she left the room Mendick's eyes were busy on her.

She returned with a small bundle of clothes, withdrew politely until he dressed and took him upstairs to the room in which he had first interviewed her, with the tall windows looking out to the Tay and the pictures adorning the walls. John was running around like a boy demented, with the same cheerful maid serving tea and the same fire casting its heat. Johanna, who had been so confident in the water, made straight for the heat and shivered in front of it.

In borrowed clothes and without his notebook and

pen, Mendick hardly felt able to conduct a proper interview.

"You mentioned that your husband habitually lived in Mandarin House. Does that mean he was there on the night of the murders and you were here?"

Johanna accepted a cup from the maid and sipped gracefully. "He is there every night, Sergeant, unless he is out hunting or shooting. And I am here every night unless he requires me for some reason."

Mendick raised his eyebrows but made no comment and Johanna laughed and shook her head.

"No, Sergeant. Not for the reason you are thinking!" She pointed to where John lay on the floor making strange noises and looking up at the ceiling. "He is the only reason David and I ever indulged in that sort of activity. He wanted an heir. I gave him one."

"And a very handsome young heir, too."

Johanna smiled. "I like to think so." She was quiet for a minute. "John is my life," she said at last. "John and my painting, and water. Here I have the sea. At home I had the rivers."

"So you must get a little bored," Mendick said, "which explains the smuggling of duty free rum and tobacco."

The sadness was fleeting but definite. "It could be a lot worse," Johanna said. "I have a lovely house, a lovely son and everything I need except affection and adult companionship." She shrugged. "But I am very lucky compared to most . . . I think that is enough information about me, now."

"Not quite," Mendick said. He would have liked to listen to Johanna speak all day and every day, but he had to focus on his duty. At that moment he detested his duty, keeping him from her. "Mr Gordon made his money in the Chinese Opium Trade, is that correct?"

"I believe so," Johanna said.

"So tell me, how does he spend his time now?" Mendick lifted his cup, watching changing emotions chase across Johanna's eyes.

"Are you asking this as Sergeant Mendick or as James?" The smile was back, still slightly lopsided, but her eyes were cool. The laughter had disappeared.

"Both," Mendick said.

"In that case, Sergeant Mendick, I do not know." She faced him directly and her voice dropped. "He is my husband, James, and the father of my son."

"If I was your husband . . ." Mendick stopped himself. He had learned while in the army never to venture unsupported into dangerous territory.

"James . . ." Johanna held out both hands. "I think there is something we need to do."

"Johanna? Or Mrs Gordon?" He smiled. They were both living dual lives. He was the duty-bound policeman, she the dutiful wife, but beneath the mask of duty lay the turmoil of emotional reality. Life was a matter of layers with the truth concealed behind the public face.

"My name is Johanna Lednock," Johanna's voice was soft. "Come to my bed, James." Her hand was held out in invitation and her eyes wrapped their love around his heart.

They lay side by side under the tangled sheet with the afternoon sun ghosting through the window and their fingers entwined. Mendick looked at her as she slept. With her eyes closed and her mouth relaxed she looked

185

very young indeed and for a moment Mendick thought of Emma, but he shook away the memory. That was unfair to both women. Emma had been his wife; loyal, devoted, loving. This was Johanna; another man's wife but now joined to him by a bond he could neither define nor deny.

Her eyes opened, focussed and smiled. "Hello James."

He smiled back. "Hello, yourself, Johanna."

Her hand squeezed his. "That was unlike anything I have experienced before."

"I hope that is not an insult," Mendick smiled.

He lay back. Love-making with Emma had been gentle and soft, he had needed to take his time and woo her. Johanna had been ready before he was, had matched him in every way, anticipated his desires and climaxed as fully as he had. She had been a ready and willing partner, laughing with open glee and enjoying their mutual pleasure. He had thought he had known about women but Johanna's reaction had been so unlike Emma's he had been at first astonished, and then met her energy with his own.

"Gordon is not . . ." Johanna hesitated, "I do not like to be disloyal, James, but Gordon is not . . . the most enthusiastic of husbands in the bedroom." She stirred and looked away. "We have been married seven years, James, and he has bedded me less than that number of times."

There was nothing Mendick could say to that. For a moment he wondered if Johanna was merely using him because of her naturally frustrated desires, but one glance at her eyes assured him she was not. What they felt, whatever they felt, was genuine.

186

"You have me now," he said, and she smiled and moved closer.

"I have you now," she confirmed. As she moved, the sheet slipped clear of her breasts. Rather than cover them back up as Emma would have done, she left the sheet where it was and lay natural and unashamed at his side. "You know a lot about me, James, but I know so little about you."

Mendick could not escape the magic of her eyes. "I think that after the last couple of hours you know a great deal about me, Johanna."

Her hand slid down and patted him. "Not the physical, James. We all share some needs there. I mean you. Who are you, where are you from, what made you a police sergeant?" She turned to face him with her head propped up on her hand. "Tell me about yourself, James."

He had been a climbing boy for as long as he could remember; he had been a climbing boy since his father had died of fever and his mother had signed him onto a seven year apprenticeship. He knew nothing else except that life was a nightmare of misery, pain and work.

Mendick shrugged. "There is nothing much to tell," he said. "I was apprenticed to a chimney sweep as a boy, ran away to sea and then joined the army."

He knew she was looking at him, watching every expression on his face as she tried to work out what made him tick, but he did not care. For a second the images returned; the horror of his early life, the hardship at sea and the mud and humidity of India and China. "The regiment came home in 1843 and I joined the police."

"Tell me more," she demanded. "Tell me all."

Mendick did so. For the first time in years he revealed

his inner self. He spoke of his fear as a climbing boy, his adventures at sea and the sordid horrors of the Chinese campaign. When he finished, there was interest and even compassion in Johanna's eyes. "I will never look at a chimney sweep in the same way again, James."

Mendick looked around the room, so fresh in its bright colours, so civilised with its paintings and books. He could not imagine Johanna understanding the persistent misery of his early life and for a moment he resented her casual acceptance of her wealth and position. He chased that thought away as being unfair to a woman who had shown him nothing but kindness. She touched him, softly.

"Are you all right, James?"

No, he thought; it was not kindness. It was something far greater than kindness. He did not dare to admit the depth of her feelings for him, but as he watched that small dimple, and the slightly lopsided smile, he knew she felt as he did, or nearly so. As her fingers sought his, some of the bad memories faded; they would never disappear completely, but Mendick knew he could push them to the back of his mind, at least when he was with Johanna.

"So you were a seaman as well, James?" Johanna sat up, allowing the covers to slide further down her body. She smiled as Mendick's eyes followed and did nothing to cover herself up.

"Seaman and soldier both and now I am a policeman." Mendick felt suddenly embarrassed and looked away. The room was obviously a woman's domain. The wallpaper was light and simply patterned, and vases of spring flowers adorned most surfaces, while the oval mirror on the dressing table reflected the whalebone mirror, comb and hair brush and the collection of pots and potions that reminded Mendick so much of Emma. "Are these all your paintings?"

"All mine," Johanna said.

He heard the pride in her voice, and the undertone of doubt.

"They are beautiful." Mendick slid out of bed, unconcerned about his state of undress, and examined the pictures once more. He stopped before the largest, a canvas a full three feet square. Two ships sailed side by side down the Tay with Dundee as a backdrop. In the foreground four men pulled at the oars of a small boat while a slim, hooded figure sat in the stern. He did not need to be told who that slim figure was.

"That could be in an art gallery," Mendick said. "Are these real ships or from your imagination?"

Johanna did not smile. "They are real ships of course: that is *Evelyn Berenger* and *Rose Flammock* of Gilbride's Waverley Whaling Company."

Mendick turned around and ignored Johanna's wicked smile. "What did you say their names were?"

"*Evelyn Berenger* and *Rose Flammock*," Johanna pointed to the names painted on the stern of each ship. "They are characters in Scott's *The Betrothed*. Gilbride names all his ships after Scott's characters . . ."

"Dear God! Of course!" Mendick suddenly remembered Johanna had ordered the smugglers to get back to the old Rose but he had not thought anything of it at the time. "Rose. It's a ship's name and I have been wasting my time dilly-dallying with you." He stopped and turned as he realised what he had said. "I did not mean that as it sounded. I did not mean that I had wasted my time with you in any way at all."

Johanna was lying on her back, her head propped up on her pillows, watching him. "I did not think you did, James," she paused and sighed. "No, you are not my James now. Sergeant Mendick is back, all duty and gruffness."

My James. Mendick closed his eyes. My James. The phrase spoke of ownership and belonging; it spoke of someone who cared for him, and a home and hearth to call his own. While duty compelled him to thrust on, search for China Jim and solve these horrendous murders, there was a huge part of him that wanted to forget he had seen that picture, to forget about *Rose Flammock* and climb back into bed with Johanna. But he knew he could not; life was not so easy. He had made his commitment and he must stand by it. He looked down at her. She suddenly looked so alone.

"I must go back to the police office," he said.

"I know you must." Johanna slid out of the bed and stepped towards him. She held him close, her head against his chest and the scent of her hair sweet and clean. "I know."

When she stepped back, the mischief was back in her eyes. "But you had better put some clothes on first. Maybe James can parade himself around as stark as nature intended, but I do not think Sergeant Mendick should arrive at the police office in quite so unclad a condition." The laugh gurgled in her throat, but now Mendick knew there were hidden depths behind Johanna Lednock; and deep desires.

CHAPTER FOURTEEN

A trio of blackbirds were singing when Mendick dismounted from the cab, paid the driver with money borrowed from Johanna and walked self-consciously into the police office. He ignored the stares of the office sergeant and mounted the steps to the office he shared with Sturrock and Deuchars.

"What in the devil's name are you doing here? You're dead!" Sturrock sat on Mendick's chair with his feet on Mendick's desk, busily engaged in stuffing Mendick's tobacco into the bowl of his own pipe.

A quick sideways gesture of Mendick's thumb ejected Sturrock from his seat. He grabbed Sturrock's pipe and emptied the tobacco onto the desk before planting himself firmly in the chair. "No, Sturrock, I am very much alive and wanting to kick back." He thumped his feet on top of the desk.

"That's what we heard, Sergeant," Deuchars slurped from a large mug of tea. He did not look perturbed to see Mendick back from the dead. "Wee Donnie has probably stopped your wages."

"Wee Donnie has not." As silent as always, Superintendent Mackay arrived. He pointed to Mendick's feet. "Being dead does not give you the right to destroy the property of the Dundee Police, Mendick. Put your feet on the floor where they belong." He waited until Mendick complied, gestured Sturrock move from his chair and dragged it across to Mendick's desk.

"We've thought you dead for the past 48 hours."

"I assure you sir; I have never been dead in my life." Mendick began, Mackay held up a slender hand.

"Well you are now." His smile was as friendly as a cat spotting a nest of mice. "A young lad found your hat lying in Dock Street all covered in blood and gore, and your Chesterfield turned up ripped and bloody on the harbour protection wall."

"How did you recognise my hat, sir?"

"It's unique, Sergeant; no-one else wears a hat that battered," Deuchars said.

Mendick glanced down at his borrowed clothes and was glad nobody asked him from where they came. "Was there any news of my watch? My wife gave me that watch and the bastards stole it from me."

"There is no need for foul language, Mendick," Mackay said. "The entire Dundee underworld is alive with the news that China Jim has murdered a Scotland Yard detective, they are crowing to the world how clever they are."

"Are they, by Christ?" Mendick thought of the time he had spent with Johanna when he should have been pursuing China Jim. He had forsaken his duty for personal pleasure and his professional worth was therefore diminished. "Well, I will soon disprove their assertions and show China Jim to be the liar he most certainly is."

"That's the spirit, Mendick." Mackay stood up. "Now, I want a full report of your activities by noon. And find some decent clothes." He glanced at Sturrock, "But if you could give me a quick overview? This young constable appears eager for enlightenment."

Mendick nodded. "I know how China Jim makes

his money sir, and I may know about the Rose tattoo as well."

Mackay sat down again and waved Sturrock to join them. "Carry on, Mendick."

"It's whisky, sir." Mendick gave a quick explanation of his kidnap and attempted drowning. "When I was in the hold of the sloop, one of the kegs was leaking, it was pure whisky. I probed about half a dozen of the others as well and each one was the same. There is no reason to suppose that the others were any different."

Sturrock whistled, "An entire ship-load of peat reek? China Jim works on a large scale then. What must that be worth?"

"Thousands of pounds," Mackay said softly. "Thirty years ago the Highlands were rife with illicit distilling. It was virtual war between the Excise and the smugglers." He stood up. "If China Jim has an entire shipload he must have a wide net. These illegal stills are small scale, capable of producing only a few dozen gallons. Well done, Mendick. I must consult with the Excise officers and get their opinion on this."

"There is more, sir," Mendick said. "Do you recall the riot the other day?"

"Of course," Mackay snapped at him, "we have not all been dead here, Mendick. Only you."

"Yes, sir. China Jim paid the rioters to start fires in the middle of Dundee, if you remember, and when the fire engines were in the High Street, there was a fire at the Scouringburn Distillery. Mr Fyffe, the Fire superintendent, suspected fire-raising but any evidence would have been destroyed." Mendick winced as the bump on his head began to throb.

"For what reason?" Sturrock asked, "Dundee has

hundreds of pubs and cheeping shops, surely there is enough for both the distillery and China?"

"Yes, constable," Mendick tried to be patient, "but China does not want a mere share of the market. He wants to control it." He rose and began to pace the room, weaving between the desks. "Imagine what he could do with a monopoly or even a near-monopoly of the whisky supply? He could charge what he liked. How much whisky is drunk in Dundee on a daily basis? And we know he is even exporting the stuff!"

"Good work, Mendick." Once again he almost smiled, "You should be killed more often, you uncover more that way."

"There's more, sir." Mendick said, "Listen. When Thoms was murdered, we found the tattoo Rose on his arm. We have been looking for a girl of that name, but it may be a ship."

Mackay raised his eyebrows, thought for a moment and finally nodded. "That is true only if Thoms was a seaman, and he was not. He was a shopkeeper and a resetter of stolen property."

"Maybe that's what he was this year, sir, but what was he in 1842? I'll wager he was a seaman seven years ago." Mendick said. "I think we've been looking at this all the wrong way, sir. We've been looking for a Chinese connection, but this case does not revolve around China, it revolves around the sea."

Mackay grunted. "I'm not convinced about that, Mendick. These ugly murders are Oriental, you mark my words." He stood erect and walked towards the door. "Now you are back in the land of the living, you may as well make yourself useful. Take some men to Fish Street. I want you to shake that house upside down and see what you can find, and Mendick," Mackay turned around, "find yourself some decent clothes for heaven's sake. You're a disgrace to the Dundee Police."

"Yes, sir," Mendick waited until Mackay left the room before adding. "While I'm organising Fish Street, Sturrock, I want you to look at the shipping list for Dundee and find every ship that has the name Rose. And consult the Lloyds lists as well. Check which companies own them and find out if Thoms was a seaman at one time. Do the same for Milne."

"Yes, Sergeant." Sturrock stood up.

"Deuchars, find me the name of every sloop in and around Dundee. I want to know who owns them, where they are now and what their cargo should be." Mendick grinned around the room. "Up until now we have played pat-a-cake with China Jim, now I am going to show him what a dead man can do."

The leading horse pawed the cobbles and whinnied softly, a call repeated by two of the other three horses. All stood in front of black hackney cabs while their drivers sat holding long whips with their hats tilted forward against the slow seeping drizzle that glistened momentarily in the yellow gas light. Mendick ordered his men inside.

They filed in quickly, tall men in tall hats and swallow tail coats, some still bearing the marks of battle from the late riot in the High Street. The cabs rocked under their weight as the drivers looked on sourly.

"Mind you keep together," Mendick ordered, and they glowered at him in silence. "I want us to arrive simultaneously, not in penny packets. Once I get inside, get moving." He checked his pockets for his pistol. "Step on!"

The hackney jerked and pulled into the road, the others following, their heavy wheels growling on the cobbled road.

"Ready?" Mendick nodded to the three policemen who shared the interior of the cab with him. They nodded, each man firmly grasping his staff. "This is the counter-attack, lads. Dundee has taken enough from China Jim. Now we will hound him and destroy his business. He made his first mistake leaving me alive. We will force a second, and then snatch him . . ." Mendick grabbed empty air, "just like that."

"Are you sure you are fit, Sergeant?" Sturrock pointed to the bruises disfiguring Mendick's face. "You took quite a beating there."

Mendick grinned, "Oh, I am fit for this, Sturrock." He tapped the comfortable weight inside his now much battered and repaired Chesterfield. "And I am more than ready. I bought myself another barker." He pulled back his coat to show the chequered black handle of the Harrison pepperpot revolver. "It has a self-cocking hammer and a rotating cylinder. I don't care if we meet dogs, men or that devil Beth, the Dundee Police will win this battle."

"That's a clumsy-looking thing," Sturrock said. He brandished his staff. "This will do me. Get me to close quarters and nobody will give me any trouble."

The constable opposite, a lugubrious man with carefully shaped sidewhiskers and a gap in his front teeth, grunted. "Criminals prefer a simple pistol with a large bore. They are easier to carry and one shot from them can tear your arm off or stop an elephant dead."

"And after one shot it is nothing better than a clumsy blackjack," Mendick told him.

"Where did you get the gun, Sergeant?" The fourth constable was pink-faced with eager eyes.

"I bought it from McGregor's of Union Street, youngster. You stick with Sturrock there and don't try to be a hero." Mendick raised his voice. "Now listen lads, I have no idea what is waiting for us. The place could be full of blackguards just waiting to slit our throats, and it could be empty. We will go in hard and fast, but for God's sake watch out for dogs."

The two cabs arrived in a jingle of harness and rumble of wheels. The drivers reined in simultaneously and a phalanx of blue-coated officers tumbled out. Holding his official staff in his left hand, Mendick raced up the steps and turned the handle of the front door. It held firm. He swore. His packet of lock-picking tools had gone the same way as his watch, so he had to resort to the more old-fashioned method of booting a door panel until it splintered, inserting an arm and unlocking the door from the inside. The noise alerted half the street and must have sounded like the knell of doom to anybody inside.

"Lanterns, lads!"

Three beams probed the darkness, highlighting patches of floor, the banister of a turnpike stair and the handle of an inner door. The policemen flicked their lanterns up and down. The hallway was empty. Mendick led the way inside. "Pair off and arrest everyone you find, we can work out the details later."

"Arrest them on what charge, Sergeant?" The young policeman asked.

"Suspicion!" Mendick shouted. He took the stairs two at a time.

"Where are we going?" Sturrock kept pace with him, staff held ready and his left hand holding his hat firm on his head.

"Either the room where I was captured or somewhere I can look down on the cellar," Mendick told him. "This way." He smashed through a flimsy door and they were in a labyrinth of corridors and doorways, each room leading to another, all divided or subdivided, with paper thin partition walls and floors of solid oak.

"Sergeant . . ." Sturrock pointed to a solid pair of shutters set in an internal wall. "That could be interesting."

Mendick pulled open the simple hook-and-eye catch and opened the shutters to reveal a wooden panel held between two horizontal slides. He remembered its grating sound very well.

"This is the place, Sturrock. China Jim and Beth watched me from here."

He looked down, seeing the cellar where he had fought the dogs from China Jim's viewpoint. The bleak, stone chamber was now lit by dancing lanterns. "We're going down there," he said.

There were three dead dogs, two of them ripped to ribbons and masked with congealed blood. Mendick stepped over the bodies without a glance.

"Careful boys, there may be more somewhere." He saw the broken shaft of his cane protruding from the eye of one dog and dragged it out. "That was a waste of a good cane," he said, and landed a vindictive kick in the ribcage of the dead dog.

"You had some fight, Sergeant," Deuchars arrived, panting.

"Where the devil have you been?" Mendick asked. "Get some light in here so we can inspect the place properly."

It was the work of moments to light the oil lamps

suspended from the ceiling above, and Mendick examined the chamber where he had nearly been torn apart. It was larger than he had thought, now empty of barrels or indeed, anything else. He looked at the chute through which he had escaped and pointed to a battered cover low down on the opposite wall.

"Kick that open," he ordered. "Be quick about it."

The opening behind was dark and wide; the chute led downwards at a slight angle.

"That will lead to a stable where the barrels were loaded onto carts." Mendick said. "I think we've found where China stored his whisky. We're central to a score of pubs so nobody would think twice if they saw a cart unloading here, and it's handy for the docks."

"The place is empty though, Sergeant," a constable reported to him. "There is nobody here."

Mendick hid his disappointment. "I want this building scoured. Collect anything that might be useful and bring it to me." He nodded to Sturrock. "That was a complete fudge, let's finish off and get back to the office."

A yell came from outside, followed by a harsh laugh and a scream of pain.

"Where's the back door?" Mendick pushed open a door, entered another room and swore as he saw another tiny room with three more doors. "This place is a blasted rabbit warren!"

Mendick cursed as he ran through the house. He entered rooms filled with the stench of mould and followed corridors leading nowhere before he crashed through a door which opened into the stable. There were four box stalls, bundles of straw on the floor and a bay for carts, with an arched doorway that opened into a narrow lane. A young policeman lay crumpled on the

199

ground, his hat and staff beside him, holding his hands to his face.

"Did you see who did this?" Mendick eased the man's hands away. Blood surged from a straight slash above his eyes.

"I'm blind," the man moaned. "I can't see anything!"

"You've got blood in your eyes," Mendick licked his thumb and passed it over the man's eyelids. "Open them slowly. It's an old trick, son. You'll be fine. Did you see who did it?"

"She came out of the straw, just like a ghost. One minute I was alone and the next she was there with her razor." The man rose, clutched his forehead and staggered. Mendick caught him and lowered him to the ground.

"Get him to the surgeon," he said. "Sturrock, you're with me. This sounds like Beth's work."

Mendick led the way into the cobbled lane curving gently downward towards Dock Street and Earl Grey Dock. He peered into the unlit street at the score of people who lounged around. Seamen with rolling gaits and sunbrowned faces, prostitutes in feathered hats and skirts that stopped shy of their ankles, the ubiquitous gaggle of ragged children who made crude comments, but Beth was not there.

"Keep going," Mendick said as he hurried past Sturrock. "She might be wearing a green cloak."

There was no green cloak to be seen and none of the people they questioned admitted to having seen any woman passing that way. The uniformity of their denials raised Mendick's suspicions as they either held his eyes in a flat stare or gave voluble explanations that told him nothing. The gaping doors of cheeping houses invited inspection, but by the time Deuchars had brought half a dozen reinforcements, most of the clientele had vanished into the morass of closes which made up what had once been Dundee's maritime quarter.

"We'll get nothing here," Sturrock said, pushing past the entrance of the lane and into Dock Street, "She's well away."

Mendick glared along the length of the street. As always it bustled with life but there was no sight of a swirling green cloak, and with so many pubs and closes into which Beth could disappear he had little chance of finding her. "You are right, Sturrock. We'll just give the building a thorough search and close it off."

"The search was worthwhile," Mendick reported to Mackay as they gathered back in the Police Office.

"We discovered where China Jim stored the whisky before he shipped it away and we will soon find the owner of the property as well. We have disrupted China's operation, flushed out one of his people, that woman, and let him and the criminal classes know that when the Dundee police come after him, he has to cut and run."

Mendick lifted a hessian sack. "This is what we found in the property, sir. An assortment of papers and other material." He looked inside. "It will take some time to sift through, but there might be something there."

"Let me know as soon as you can," Mackay said. "I was sorry to hear we had a good man injured. Constable McKee will be off for some time while his wound heals."

Mendick nodded. "It was a surface slash, sir. It's a trick the Baltic seamen use a lot, a cut across the forehead so the blood flows into the eyes. It will leave a scar but no lasting damage. Constable McKee will be back on duty before you know it."

"I hope you are right, Mendick," Mackay said.

"Now, sir," Mendick said. "We must push China Jim hard, flush him out and destroy him." He drew on his military experience. "We have effectively removed his place of storage in Dundee; we know what type of vessel he uses to transport the whisky . . ."

"We know more than that," Mackay said. "We have checked all the Dundee registered sloops and rejected those that were not black-hulled. Only three sailed within the last few days: *Elena Swan*, bound for Riga in the Baltic; *Our Mary*, for Lerwick; and *Rebecca,* for London."

"One of those vessels, then," Mendick said, "and if they are heading to their intended destinations we can have a stab at capturing them." He shifted in his seat as he recalled the conversation he had heard before he was thrown overboard. "The vessel I was in was heading south, they spoke of Fife Ness."

Mackay smiled. "*Rebecca*, then. We have her! I will contact the police in London and check if she has arrived yet. Confiscating her cargo will be a massive blow for China Jim."

"Do we know the owners of these crafts?" Mendick asked.

"We do," Mackay said. "*Elena Swan* and *Our Mary* are owned by the Robertson Brothers and your vessel, *Rebecca*, by Gilbride."

"Of course: Rebecca. She's a character in Walter Scott's *Ivanhoe*." Mendick said. "I should have caught that one. Gilbride again; maybe he names his men after Scott's characters as well."

"We have discussed this before, Mendick. Mr Gilbride is a respectable business man," Mackay said.

"Indeed, sir." Mendick kept his voice level. "As you know, the most unlikely people can turn to crime, members of the criminal class or not. Why, I only became sergeant when my predecessor, a Scotland Yard detective, turned traitor against the Queen." He stopped as Mackay stirred uncomfortably in his seat.

"That will do, Sergeant. Keep to the matter in hand, if you please."

"Sir." Mendick realised that Mackay did not want to face the unpleasant reality that money and position and smart clothes did not always equate with decency, respectability and honesty. "Mr Gilbride, sir, is a man who has no alibi for any of the murders, has a fixation with Walter Scott and his whale boiling yard is right next door to the Arctic Yard where Milne was found."

"These are merely circumstantial facts, Mendick; they prove nothing." Mackay's gaze did not falter for a second. "I would be obliged if you treat Mr Gilbride as a gentleman when you interview him."

"I will sir." Mendick hid his smile, Mackay had just sanctioned an investigation of Gilbride's business affairs and a personal visit. He lifted the bag. "I will speak to him once I have looked through this material, sir."

Mendick tipped out the bag and sifted through the resultant shower of scraps of paper, pieces of broken glass and fragments of cloth.

"Anything, Sergeant?" Sturrock asked.

"Not that I can see," Mendick said. He held up some papers, "although this may be something." He looked more closely at the fragment. "Someone has tried to burn this, Sturrock, and they would not do that unless they were hiding something." He read what remained of the words:

"Wap . . . ee . . . Dow . . . arf."

"It means nothing," Deuchars decided with a shrug.

"I agree, Sergeant. It might have been important if even one of the names had been intact, but those are just meaningless letters." Sturrock said.

Mendick shook his head, "That, gentlemen, is where you are both wrong. These letters say a great deal. You both have far more Dundee knowledge than I do but I know London. 'Wap' could be Wapping; the 'ee' means nothing I agree, but 'Dow' and 'arf' could be Downie's Wharf, which is in Wapping in London. Gentlemen," Mendick looked up, "I think we may now know where *Rebecca* will be docking. Sturrock, go to Mr Mackay with this information, if you please."

Mendick stood up. "We have just begun this campaign. We had a partial victory at Fish Street in closing off China's store room. Our next step will be to find out where this whisky originates." Mendick reached for his hat. Having used most of his spare money to buy the pepperpot revolver, he had clothed himself from the nearest pawnshop and his hat was a tall monstrosity with wax stains on the brim. "I think it is time for another visit to Mr Gilbride. When I return, we will concentrate on the source of the whisky."

The Waverley Whale Fishing Company operated from Whale Lane, at the east end of the Seagate and a seagull's call from the poisonous aroma of the boiling yards. The offices occupied a central site in the lane, a freestanding two storey building amidst a jumble of unpretentious architecture. The name was etched on a polished brass plaque and a brass railing protected a brass-faced clerk who eventually ushered Mendick up the stairs to Gilbride's office.

"Good God! Sergeant Mendick, I heard you were dead!" Gilbride stood up with his hand outstretched. "My dear fellow, it is good to see you, good indeed. Do sit down, Sergeant. I do hope you are making progress with your enquiries over that unfortunate affair at the boiling yard?"

"We are pursuing some definite ideas, sir," Mendick said. He looked around the room; oak-panelled and spacious, it contained ship-builder's half-models of the hull of *Rose Flammock* and *Evelyn Berenger.* "I see you have models of two of your vessels, sir."

"My whaling ships, Sergeant." Gilbride stepped around his desk as he spoke, one hand on Mendick's arm and the other pointing to the ships. "See how we have shaped the hulls, Sergeant? They are sharp, so when the ice nips them, they are lifted clear rather than crushed like eggshells."

"I do see, sir." Despite himself Mendick was captured by Gilbride's enthusiasm. "And did you have *Rebecca* designed the same way?" He watched Gilbride closely, hoping for a reaction.

"Good Lord, no, Sergeant. What a strange question to ask. *Rebecca* is a coasting sloop, not a whaling ship. Not a ship at all, really. Why do you enquire after her, pray?" Gilbride stood up; his eyes, wide and quizzical.

"You do own *Rebecca*, Mr Gilbride?" Mendick asked.

"I am one of her owners, yes," Gilbride confirmed at once.

"So you will know what type of cargo she carries?"

Gilbride shrugged. "I do not know that, Sergeant, she is chartered out." He sat down at the desk, opened a drawer and pulled out a file. "Here we are. She is chartered to Robert Marmion of the Overgate." He looked up. "A name after my own heart, Sergeant."

Mendick kept his face expressionless. "I am sure it is, sir. Do you have the full address?"

"Of course, Sergeant." Gilbride wrote it down and handed it over. "Would you stay for a cup of tea?"

"Thank you, sir, but no. I must pursue my enquiries." Mendick looked at the address: Doig's Close, Overgate.

Mendick stood up. "Thank you, Mr Gilbride. If you can be of any more help I will be in touch."

He took a deep breath. Another clue that just led in a circle. China Jim certainly knew how to cover his tracks in whatever he did, but at least he had ascertained a definite link between the mysterious Marmion and China Jim.

CHAPTER FIFTEEN

Mendick stood outside the Greenland Inn where Hitchins still begged in his ragged, once-scarlet jacket, and the same shifty clientele sidled in and out.

"Evening, Hitchins. Remember me?"

There were upwards of five hundred pubs, licensed grocers, shebeens and cheeping shops in Dundee and by the Tuesday of the following week Mendick and his team of officers had visited every one. Sometimes Mendick had taken Sturrock with him, sometimes Deuchars, and often he had gone alone, but always with the same objective in mind. Now he filled his pipe outside the Greenland Inn.

The beggar peered at him through narrowed eyes. "Why, no, sir, I can't say as I do. Are you the gentleman who gave me two shillings yesterday?"

"No, Hitchins, I am the police sergeant who gave you the sore head some weeks ago."

Hitchins cringed. "Oh! Sergeant Mendick! I didn't recognise you sir, it's my eyes, you see."

"You see as well as I do, and that's damnably near to perfect." Mendick pulled Hitchins close. "Robert was telling me I should be kind to you."

"Indeed sir, that is very kind of Robert. He is a good man, indeed." The beggar bowed and shuffled.

"You know Robert of course?" Mendick opened the flap of his Chesterfield and allowed the head of his staff to show, "or should I remind you? Robert Marmion?"

Hitchins looked around, but there was no pretence in his trembling. "For God's sake, Sergeant! You'll get me killed stone dead!"

"Who is he? Obviously you know full well." Mendick pulled his staff out to half its length, but Hitchins was looking in every direction save at him.

"Marmion's China Jim's man, Sergeant. Now go away, for God's own sake. China will skin me and feed me to the dogs if he knows I told you." Hitchins crouched against the wall as a group of seamen lurched past.

"I promise I will never tell him," Mendick said. "Now. You know this corner better than anybody, Hitchins. Who supplies the spirits for this establishment?"

Hitchins stared, "What sort of question is that? How the devil should I know who supplies the spirits?"

"Try," Mendick had no cane to aid him so he relied on a soft smile as he ground the heel of his boot into Hitchin's toes.

"I don't know!" Hitchins wailed, "I honestly don't know!" His voice dropped to a whisper as he realised he was attracting attention. "I don't know, Sergeant. Ask the landlord. It comes in a cart, that's all I know."

"Don't go away," Mendick said. "I might need you later." He pushed open the door of the pub and walked in.

The sounds and scents and scenes were utterly familiar to Mendick. Apart from the preponderance of Dundee accents he could be in any dockside pub in any town in Britain. There were the same raucous seamen, tanned, fit and three sheets to the wind. They spent weeks and months in unremitting hardship to earn their wages and now they wasted them in a careless debauch. In his time Mendick had done the same. He recognised the behaviour as well as he recognised the same over-dressed women clinging to the arms of the men, pretending undying love as they transformed the wages of their catch into something liquid to pour down their throats. There were the same clamouring children, the same false, good humour from the landlord and the same perfume of beer and whisky.

"Whisky," Mendick ordered. He spun a silver threepence onto the counter and looked around. The tables were crowded, but he squeezed onto a bench near the counter where a large man stared into a near-empty glass and a done old man clawed at his stomach and muttered to himself.

"He's coming out," the old man said, and looked up. "They do that you know, they come back to get you. He's got two so far and I'm next."

"I'm sure they do." Mendick looked closely, there was something vaguely familiar about the man's features. He grunted. He had been in the same place and intoned the same words on Mendick's last visit to this pub. Having no desire to share his time with a meandering drunkard, Mendick looked for another seat, but the pub was just about full.

"I'm Andy," the drunk slurred. He looked at Mendick with shadowed eyes. "I was Andrew Cleghorn once, but now everyone calls me Old Andy." He began to sing, his voice surprisingly melodious.

"The captain has gone to the topmast high,
with a spy-glass in his hand,
a whale, a whale, a whale, cries he,
and she blows at every span, brave boys,
And she blows at every span."

Mendick did not know the words but the tune was familiar, from where he could not say.

"Oh, for God's sake!" The large man nudged his neighbour with a ready elbow. "Shut your mouth, you drunken old bastard. You only did the one bloody voyage anyway."

"I did one more than you, you little dog, so shut your teeth." For a second Andy's voice altered and the benign old face altered to something intrinsically unpleasant.

"You little dog." It was the combination of that unique expression and the new, hard voice that Mendick recognised. The surge of fear was instinctive, a memory from long ago, and he fought the urge to cringe and raise his hands to protect himself.

"Get up there, you little dog, and get it swept."

The voice echoed in the choking darkness, distorted by the surrounding brickwork but still containing enough menace to make Jamie shiver. He looked upward to where the flue ascended forever, the sides black and slippery with soot and the exit a tiny circle of light diminished by distance.

"Move you bugger! Or it will be the worse for you!"

Mendick looked closer into the face of old Andy and rolled back the years. In place of the wrinkled, broken old man he saw the beery brutality of the man he had only known as Master; in place of the whines he heard the barked orders given in all their guttural obscenity.

"You used to be a Master Sweep," Mendick found it hard to control the tremor in his voice.

Old Andy glowered across the width of the table before lowering his eyes. "I might have been," he said.

"You don't remember me at all, do you?" Mendick asked. He reached across the table, grabbed Andy's chin and forced the man's head up. Andy's glare returned momentarily before fear replaced it.

"He's coming out," Andy said, and scratched at his stomach.

"I asked if you remember me." When Andy tried to pull his head away Mendick held him tight and ignored the protests from the large man. Andy closed his eyes. Mendick leaned forward, pinched one wrinkled old eyelid and pulled the eye open.

"Hey, there! Enough of that!" The large man said.

Mendick's look froze him into silence.

Andy pushed himself as far back into his seat as he could. "Why should I remember you?"

"I was your climbing boy once," Mendick said softly. He released Andy's eyelid and watched the old eyes open wide. For a long moment, Mendick was tempted. The desire to stand up and break this man almost overwhelmed him. The years of pain returned in all their horror; the frustration of being trapped in a never-ending cycle of misery; the constant fear; the pain; the hunger and cold.

He looked at Andy and slowly drew back his fist. But this was 1849, not 1827. He had been looking for a burly man in his thirties. Perhaps his Master had only been large when seen through the eyes of a child. Instead Mendick saw Old Andy as he was now: a shrivelled, broken old man with fear in his eyes and deep lines of poverty in his face. He saw a man ravaged by drink and time so that he trembled where he sat and the only thing left was a broken mind, the failing strength of middle-age and a liking for drink.

At that moment Mendick glimpsed his own reflection in the window of the pub. He saw a man in the prime of life, a man of position and authority, a man with twenty years of life experience over half the world and a man with a responsible duty to perform. He had walked a dark road from his childhood and if he followed his instincts and hammered this man to a pulp, all his efforts would have been in vain. The police would discard him, his reputation would be destroyed forever and he would be lucky to find any other work. Andrew Cleghorn would have destroyed his adult life as he had destroyed his childhood.

"No," Mendick shook his head as the gibbering black ghosts of the past dissipated. "No. I was mistaken, I don't know you. I thought you were someone important but now I see you are a . . ." He searched for a word to reveal his contempt for Old Andy but there was none. Instead, he shook his head. "You are nothing," he finished. He stood up. "You are nothing," he repeated. When he stalked to the counter, Old Andy was rubbing at his stomach and still mumbling to himself.

"He's coming out." Old Andy said and began his song once more.

"Excellent whisky." Mendick placed his glass on the counter. "Not like the usual rot-gut rubbish. In fact, I will buy you one myself." He passed over a silver three-penny piece, which the barman accepted without hesitation.

"Very kind of you, sir." He bit into the coin and put it in his fob pocket while pouring himself a generous measure of whisky. "It's always easy to recognise a genuine gentleman when one graces my establishment."

"Indeed, sir," Mendick sipped at his own glass, "a compliment like that deserves another dram any day of the week." He flipped a second threepence onto the counter and smiled. "You really must tell me the name of your supplier." He had followed the same routine in pub after pub throughout Dundee, sometimes rejected by laughter or threats of violence, often given the name of a perfectly legitimate distiller, but this time the barman looked at him shrewdly.

"Are you in the trade?" He asked, once the coin had been safely deposited beside its companion in his fob pocket.

"In a manner of speaking," Mendick leaned across the counter and lowered his voice. "I'm not in competition with you. I was getting peat reek from the Glens but my man withdrew his supply. He said he was advised to stop."

"Muscled out, was he?" The barman finished his drink in a single swallow. "There's some rough play going on up north just now. My supply comes regularly, though. The carrier never gives the name, but we all know who it is." He winked and withdrew.

Mendick slapped a crown piece on the counter but kept his hand on top of it with his fingers splayed open. "Perhaps he could supply me as well?"

The barman looked at the glint of the silver coin between Mendick's fingers. "I am due a delivery tomorrow night, a barrel of the finest." His hand hovered above Mendick's. "Give me your name and I can have a word with the boys."

Mendick slid the coin back into his pocket. "I will speak to them in person," he said. "It will be a local man, I expect?"

The barman looked pointedly at Mendick's pocket and shrugged. "Maybe so," he said.

Mendick replaced the crown piece where it was. It

shone bright against the scarred wood of the counter. The barman slammed his hand over it in case Mendick changed his mind. "The whisky comes from one of the towns in Strathmore." He hesitated, "It might be Blairgowrie."

"Thank you," Mendick placed his hand on top of the landlord's, "and the supplier's name?"

"China Jim," the barman whispered and looked up sharply in case he had been overheard, even in that noisy bar.

When Mendick left the pub Old Andy was still clawing at his stomach and warbling his song.

"Our mate stood on the quarter-deck,
And a quick little man was he.
Overhaul, overhaul, let the boat-tackle fall,
And we launched them into the sea, brave boys,
And we launched them into the sea."

Mendick did not look back. Old Andy was not important. His link to China Jim certainly was.

CHAPTER SIXTEEN

Mackay appeared even more ascetic than normal as he looked over his men. The hectic colouring of his face around high cheekbones was more pronounced under the hissing gas light, his nose even sharper and his full dress uniform, complete with the long curved sword in its scabbard, was faintly ridiculous. But any sense of ridicule ended as he began to speak.

"Settle down, lads, and take note! We have ascertained that China Jim is involved with the supply of whisky to Dundee and we think he operates a distillery, or a number of small stills, in the Blairgowrie area." Mackay smiled at the ripple of comments. "I have contacted the County force and they are looking into that situation."

Mendick shifted uncomfortably in his seat. "Can we not go after the distillery ourselves, sir?"

"We have enough to do in here, Sergeant," Mackay said. "Now, pay attention. We have spoken to every publican in Dundee, both respectable and unlicensed, and we know there is a shipment of whisky coming to Dundee tonight. We know of at least five different pubs who are expecting supplies, so that speaks of more than a couple of pack horses. I think we can fairly say there will be a wagon-load."

Mendick watched his colleagues stir restlessly at this intelligence. There was a slight murmur of approval, a stamping of booted feet and touching of hands on the shafts of staffs.

Mackay continued, speaking slowly. "Now, remember. Although we are hunting for whisky today, we are still on a murder hunt. This man we only know as China Jim has butchered and," he lowered his voice, "actually eaten parts of three men. He also tried to murder Sergeant Mendick here."

Some of the men turned around to stare at Mendick as if they had never seen him before until Mackay rapped his knuckles on the desk for attention. "We know the whisky wagon is coming from one of the towns in Strathmore, which means it must go through the Sidlaw Hills. And that is where we will stop it."

Mendick spoke again. "The Sidlaws are quite extensive, sir. How do we know which way they will come?"

Mackay held up a map and used a length of stick as a pointer.

"There are three main routes suitable for a wagon," he said. "The western route by the Coupar Angus Road that passes Tullybaccart, the central route through the Glack of Newtyle or the eastern route from Glamis." He paused, "We do not know which route China Jim will take so we will cover all three. I will take six men and an Excise officer to Tullybaccart and inspect all traffic there, Lieutenant Cameron will do the same on the Glamis route and Sergeant Mendick will guard the Glack of Newtyle." He folded the map. "I have arranged for a mounted man to call on every party in turn so as soon as we find the whisky, the others will be alerted. That will be all, gentlemen. Remember to do your duty; this man must be removed from Dundee."

Two of the groups stood and left the room but Mendick's men remained seated, waiting for him. He nodded to each officer individually. He had handpicked these men and they included Sturrock and the scarred, saturnine Deuchars.

"Right boys, you heard Mr Mackay. We all know what China Jim is capable of, and we know about Beth with her knuckle dusters and her razor so be careful. Watch each other's backs out there. Now, let's step out together and get these monsters behind bars."

They stood up, lifted their tall hats, checked their batons, fastened the leather neck stocks that were to protect them from strangulation and followed Mendick outside. They moved in disciplined silence that would have not been out of place at Horse Guards but Mendick wondered how they would cope if they met China Jim. They were mainly young men, some still with cheeks that hardly recognised the bite of a razor, and they were mostly from Dundee. They were experienced in dealing with pub brawlers and drunken rioters, but a murderer who dissected and ate his victims was something on a completely new level.

Used to the marching columns of redcoats that had fought in the China War, he was still impressed by the long convoy of hired hackney cabs that rolled out of Bell Street, each one carrying its cramped quota of blue-uniformed policemen. Faces turned to stare as they growled past, the great wheels grating over the cobblestones and then grinding over the roads as the convoy split into pairs and jolted out of Dundee.

"Here we go again," Sturrock grinned at Mendick in the stuffy interior of the cab. He shuffled his feet in the straw and tapped his fingers against his staff.

"Let's just hope China Jim is driving the whisky himself," Deuchars fingered his scar. "He might well be sitting in his den pulling strings and not becoming involved in anything at all."

Mendick nodded. He recognised the signs of nervousness; the desire to speak, the hectic eyes, the fidgeting. These men knew they could be heading into great danger.

"Once more into the breach . . ." Miller intoned. He was a young man with thin whiskers just forming around his mouth and obviously had some literary knowledge. He looked around, met Mendick's eye and looked away again.

"Now, you just do as you are ordered, Miller," Mendick said, "and if you get into difficulties, for God's sake, call for help. Don't look for glory, look for a successful arrest."

Miller nodded. "Yes, Sergeant." He glanced over to Deuchars, who winked at him and resumed his normal bulldog glower.

"This road seems devilishly long," Sturrock said. He glanced out of the window. "We are just leaving Dundee now."

Mendick nodded. They were sliding past the variegated fields of Forfarshire now. He cursed as they negotiated a corner and all four men slid together.

Sturrock grabbed hold of Mendick's sleeve for support, realised what he was doing and let go immediately. "Is this driver trying to tip us over?"

"I think he works for China Jim!" Miller said as they banged into a pothole that rattled their teeth.

Mendick grunted. Compared to marching day after day through the humidity of China, this was a life of ease and comfort but he allowed his men to assuage their nerves with complaints until the cab eased to a halt. For a second they sat still until Mendick opened the door, peered outside and stepped onto the hard surface of the road.

"Right, lads," Mendick said. "Out we come."

The constables stepped out of the cab and looked around. They stamped their feet and stretched their arms to straighten cramped limbs. Miller tapped the side of his coat to ensure his staff was securely in place.

"I've never been out of Dundee before," he admitted.

"This is the Glack of Newtyle," Deuchars said. He pulled out his pipe and examined it as if he had never seen it before. "Good place for an ambush."

Mendick looked around. Dark and narrow, the road twisted around the flank of a wooded hill. Dislodged by the passage of vehicles and the action of wind and weather, fallen twigs created an intermittent carpet while a number of rivulets trickled from the forest, across the road surface and descended to the wooded gorge on the opposite side. Overhanging trees gloomed above, with sunlight flicking and dancing between the spreading branches. To the right of the road and at the foot of the shallow gorge, the tracks of the Newtyle Railway shone in intermittent silver between the dark green of the trees, and beyond them cattle grazed in fields that rose to the slopes of the Sidlaw Hills. Mendick felt as if he was in a dark, shifting tunnel of green.

He shook his head. "This won't do," he said. "I want somewhere more open where I can see in both directions." He jerked a thumb to the north. "What lies that way, Deuchars?"

"The hills pull back right and left and there's the village of Newtyle," Deuchars said. "There's a crossroad there, and a church."

"And Mandarin House," Mendick remembered. He shook his head. "No good." He looked south towards Dundee but they had just travelled that road and it was equally unsuitable. "I don't fully like this but it will have to do." He pointed to Miller. "Go ahead and watch for vehicles. If you see a cart coming, signal to us: don't do anything on your own. Understand?"

Miller nodded. "Yes, Sergeant." He clasped a hand to his hat to hold it steady and walked long-strided down the road.

Mendick looked for the largest of the officers. "Menzies, you go further up towards Dundee. You are the cork in this bottle. If by chance one of China's boys gets past us, it is up to you to stop him, you are the most important man here." He watched as Menzies strode off. "The rest of us will get off the road and in among the trees," Mendick said. "Keep hidden and only move on my word."

Mendick knew the waiting was always the worst part of any engagement. He stepped into the fringe of trees and listened as the wind shifted the branches and the small sounds of nature sounded all around. He waited as the tension rose and every movement irritated. He waited as his heart thumped in his chest and he watched a small red spider crawl around his thumb.

He thought of all the other times he had waited, in all the other places, for all the other events. Waiting for the ice to break and free his ship in Riga, waiting for the typhoon to strike in the Indian Ocean, waiting for the order to be sent into battle in the sultry, heavy heat of China. Each event had seemed vital at the time, but now they were consigned to the past, done and forgotten, the days survived, added to the store of experiences that made him who and what he was now. He heard the subdued mumble of Sturrock's voice and smelled the perfume of Deuchars' pipe smoke. They were waiting too, living the span of their life temporarily parallel to his own but separate, with their own thoughts and hopes and fears.

A fly buzzed around him, exploring. He ignored it and looked up the length of the road. He touched the butt of his revolver, checked his staff was in place and hoped this day was successful so he could return to his real life in London.

And yet, within him there was a nagging ache that he could not deny. He thought of sunlight coming through those tall windows in Broughty and highlighting the rich dark red of Johanna's hair. He thought of that gurgling laugh and the changing glow of her eyes. He wanted her, not just for her body. He wanted her mind and her company and her presence to infiltrate every strand of him. He shook his head, still unable to admit this truth even to himself. It had seemed so clear in Unicorn Cottage, but now, with the passage of time, he was less sure of himself and his own feelings. What had been certain was now merely possible.

He focussed, placed Johanna square in the centre of his mind and knew that despite his intense loyalty to Emma, he had fallen in love. The old Dundee, the Dundee of nightmares and oppression, was gone. He had killed it in the Greenland Inn. The past was a closed book and he was already rewriting his future; it was based around a woman who was married to someone else.

"Sergeant!" The voice interrupted his reverie. Sturrock was looking directly at him. "Sergeant, it's the signal!"

221

Half an hour had passed deep in thought. The day had stretched on that much further and China Jim was still at large. Mendick nodded. "Right, Sturrock. I see him."

Miller had stepped into the middle of the road at the sharpest angle of the bend. He whistled, removed his hat and waved it back and forth three times.

When Sturrock responded in kind, Miller retreated into the trees. There was the sound of jingling harness, the heavy grinding of wheels and the sharp clap of a whip, and Mendick saw a team of six horses drag around the bend with the carter walking at the side. The carter's mixed shouts of abuse and encouragement were clear and loud but stopped as Mendick stepped in front of him, followed by two uniformed police.

"What the devil . . . what's this all about?" The carter held his whip in front of him.

"There is nothing for you to worry about," Mendick said, "provided you are not carrying anything illegal, of course." He nodded to the constables, "Right lads, take it apart."

"If you tell me what you are looking for . . ."

"We are looking for whisky," Mendick replied, "and China Jim."

The carter glowered as the officers engulfed his wagon. "I can save you a lot of bother then. I have no whisky in my wagon and I am not China Jim." He lifted his whip as Deuchars unfastened the canvas tarpaulin that protected his load. "You had better put everything back properly!"

There were bundles of flax and sacks of potatoes, new dug from their winter homes; bundles of linen from Forfar and carefully parcelled personal packets addressed to all quarters of Dundee. There were no kegs and no barrels. No whisky. And the carter watched, shaking his head critically as the policemen tried to repack the wagon and replace the tarpaulin on top.

"Who in creation taught you how to pack . . .?"

"Right, off you go." Mendick pointed towards Dundee. "If you meet China Jim, tell him that Mendick will put salt on his dragon tail."

The carter grunted. "I'll be making a complaint to Mr Mackay in person."

Mendick jerked his thumb to the rising woodland to his left. "You'll find him about three miles in that direction on the Couper Angus Road."

The carter spat on the ground, cracked his whip and trailed on towards Dundee.

"That was a waste of an hour," Sturrock said.

"We might waste the whole day," Mendick told him, "or meet China Jim in two minutes time."

Three more fruitless searches were undertaken within the next two hours, and then Miller whistled and waved both hands.

"He looks a bit excited," Mendick said, "Sturrock, go and see what's happening."

Sturrock ran down the road, spoke to Miller and returned, waving his tall hat in the air. "It's a whole convoy of carts," he shouted, "three of them!"

"Right, lads. This may be it." Mendick said: "Back into the trees with you so we don't alarm them. Come out on my signal."

The three wagons filled the road as they approached at a steady pace, the carters snapping their whips at the incline, and slowing when they came to the bend. The strings of horses plodded on, leather harnesses creaking.

Mendick waited until they were at their slowest and stepped in front of the leading cart.

He raised his hand. "Dundee Police! We want to search your wagons."

The carter swore loudly, looked at the uniformed men easing from the trees and swung his whip at Mendick's head. "Get out of my way!"

Mendick had expected this, he ducked and moved in close. The long lash whistled above his head as he swung his staff at the carter's upper arm.

"You blackguard!" The carter dropped the whip and clutched his injured arm. Bereft of guidance, the horses walked on. Mendick grabbed the harness and pulled. The following carts pulled up behind the stationary wagon amidst a confusion of yells and protests.

"This sounds promising," Mendick said. "Deuchars, call in Miller and Menzies; two men every wagon." Mendick gave quick orders and stepped back. "Sturrock, get this cover off! Deuchars, once Miller comes up, you and he take the third wagon."

The leading carter watched sullenly, holding his injured arm as Mendick untied the canvas cover from its ringbolts. The knots gave easily under his fingers and he tossed the opposite end of the cover to Sturrock. The officers dragged the canvas back and Mendick smiled.

"What have we here?" he smiled at the array of barrels. He raised his voice. "That's us lads!"

The sharp crack of a pistol took Mendick by surprise and he flinched, and dived behind the cover of the wagon. He smelled the powder smoke but could not see the origin of the shot although he thought it had come from trees on the opposite side the road. He waved the suddenly retreating policemen past to safety, saw

Menzies' hat tumble off. Menzies hesitated and turned back to retrieve it.

"Leave the blessed thing and get under cover!" Mendick roared. He leaped out, grabbed Menzies' arm and hauled him behind the wagon just as a second shot rang out. Splinters exploded around him and Mendick ducked underneath the wagon beside Menzies as the injured carter laughed openly.

"Not so tough now, bluebottle!"

Mendick pulled the pepperpot from inside his coat and peered between the back wheels of the cart. He glanced at the carter.

"You keep down as well, you stupid bugger! Whoever is shooting might well hit you!"

The spokes gave minimum protection, breaking Mendick's view into segments that were themselves shadowed by the trees. The leading two horses of the next wagon were in sight, the last hidden by the curve of the road. There was no sign of the gunman.

He could hear nothing save for the soft rustle of the trees, the occasional snort from the horses and the harsh breathing of the carter. The birds had been shocked into silence and the officers too. The carter leaned against the side of his cart, sniffing snuff from a whalebone box. His sneeze took them all by surprise.

"Sorry gents, I did not mean to startle you." His laugh proved the lie.

"Sturrock, take this bloody man in custody!" Mendick emerged from behind the wheel and swore as another shot barked. This time he saw the jet of white smoke among the fringes of the trees but did not see the fall of the ball.

"Dundee Police!" Mendick stood beside the wheel,

counted the seconds it took to reload and hoped there was only a single gunman. He aimed his pepperpot at the smoke and fired, feeling the kick of the recoil.

Three shots volleyed from the trees, one of which ripped close to Mendick's head and another slamming into one of the barrels behind him. Liquid spurted onto the road, formed an amber pool around the nearside rear wheel and trickled towards the gorge.

Mendick grunted and crouched low. He aimed and fired twice, each shot kicking the revolver back into his hand. There was no return fire from the trees and Mendick wondered if the remaining carters had just fired a defiant volley and then run. Perhaps there had been an escort who had been prepared to fight off a single highwayman but had fled when he realised they were facing the police. He raised his voice.

"Dundee Police! Give yourself up!" There was no reply. "I am coming for you!" He glanced over his shoulder. Sturrock had the injured carter in handcuffs while the other officers had left their places of shelter to advance on the wagons. He raised his voice.

"Menzies, you and Smith begin the search. Miller, you and Scrymgeour come with me. Spread out and walk steady, but if you see smoke or hear a shot, run for the trees. Don't let the bastards see you bob!"

With the pepperpot held low in his right hand, Mendick walked forward, very aware the unseen attackers would recognise him as being in charge and would single him out. Every step brought him nearer to danger. His smile was twisted. It would be bitterly ironic if he had survived the typhoons of the Indian Ocean and the nightmare of the Chinese War only to be murdered by an unseen criminal, a few miles outside Dundee. The always present thought returned. Death did not matter as Emma was waiting if he was killed.

Unexpectedly he felt the renewed hammer of his heart. There was another aspect to his life now, for Johanna was waiting if he lived. The thought of danger was suddenly much more alarming. Mendick moved faster, jinking right and left. There was no movement from the trees. He entered the outer thickets, pushed back the spring growth of bracken and fresh thorn and peered up the hill. There was no sign of movement except the slight sway of undergrowth in the breeze.

Deuchars pushed back a swinging bough with his staff. "I can't see a blessed thing."

"I think they've run." Mendick said. "No matter, we have the wagons."

The three carts stood in a row, the horses patient, heads down in harness, deserted by their drivers. They looked poorly cared for and forlorn. A whip lay abandoned, its lash stretched towards the trees as if pointing to its owner.

Mendick clapped his hands. "Right boys, get rummaging . . ."

"There's no need, Sergeant." Menzies grinned. "Look," he indicated the leading wagon, where liquid still gushed from the punctured barrels. They were ranged in neat rows, three deep by four across. Menzies hauled himself onto the back, found the wooden bung of the nearest barrel and wrestled it free. Even from the road, Mendick could smell the aroma.

"Whisky," he said. "Check the others."

He watched as the tarpaulins were dragged from the remaining two carts and Menzies checked a barrel on each.

227

"Yes, Sergeant, they're whisky barrels all right." He thrust a finger deep into the contents, took it out and licked it clean. "Not the best I have tasted and probably watered down but still, a drop of the real peat reek there."

"Three carts with twelve hogshead barrels on each. A hogshead holds sixty-three gallons so that's over two thousand gallons." Mendick allowed himself a smile. "That's a fair amount of money saved for the revenue, and a big dent in China Jim's business." He reloaded his pepperpot and secured it in its holster, "Let's get these carts off the road until we can get them to Dundee." He turned to the first cart just as the woman slipped off the side.

Mendick recognised the green cloak and the bitter twist of cruel lips just before she crashed into the trees. "Stop that woman! That's Beth!"

Menzies jumped down from the back of the cart, stumbled and held on to Deuchars for support as Sturrock tried to manoeuvre around them.

"She must have been hiding among the barrels." Sturrock gave up his attempt to follow. "She's gone now."

"I want that woman!" Mendick raised his voice: "Stop! Dundee Police!" He strode across the road and followed into the woodland. He saw the flick of a cloak ahead, heard a shrill curse and plunged on, feeling his feet sink deep into the soft ground beneath. A branch flicked against his hat, another whipped his face, briars and brambles hooked thorns into his coat and ripped at his hands; he plunged uphill with the breath rasping in his throat and his lungs already burning. Town life had many advantages but it was poor preparation for thundering up a wooded hillside in pursuit of a suspect.

He stopped to listen. Above the creaking of branches and the whisper of the undergrowth he heard the crash of Beth's progress, not far above him.

"Dundee Police!" He drew a deep breath and plunged on. The trees were densely packed now, rank upon rank stretching out gnarled branches to impede him and aid the fugitive. He registered green leaves budding, the old green of coniferous trees, the fresh green of grass and bracken underfoot mixed with the rustling brown of last year's dead leaves. He no longer shouted for Beth to stop and saved his breath for the climb, gasping, swearing as the hill became steeper and he had to support his progress using the boles of the trees.

Beth was in sight, her sparse figure flitting through the trees like a wraith. Mendick fixed his gaze on her cloak, rippling green among the green. He saw her stop and redoubled his efforts. Perhaps the hill had defeated her. As he drew closer he saw her cloak had been discarded and lay on top of a battered bramble bush.

Mendick swore, sucked in a hard breath and thrust on, step after step, the muscles in his legs screaming in protest and sweat blurring his vision. Then miraculously he was clear of the trees. The hillside opened up in front of him: wind-cropped grass and budding heather in a long rising ridge, undulating in folds of sunlight and shadow that rolled towards the west. Beth was about quarter of a mile ahead. Bereft of her cloak she looked even slighter as she lifted her skirts high and her bare legs powered her forward.

With his quarry in sight Mendick needed no encouragement. He ignored the burning of his throat and lungs and the ache in his leg and pushed on. He saw Beth stop, saw her face white against the green-brown hill, but she turned and ran again. The summit rose in a series of broad ridges, with the ground falling away in steep heather slopes either side, the sweet farmland of Strathmore on the right and the rippling blue water of a small loch to the left. In front of him the ground rose, dipped and rose again and still Beth ran on, legs white and stick-thin but seemingly tireless.

To his right, far below, Mendick saw a number of carriages pulled up in the driveway of Mandarin House. He heard high male laughter and the blare of a hunting trumpet and wondered how two different worlds could co-exist, so close but so far apart. While he tried to find a murderer, Gordon was holding a party. Unless the murderer and the party holder were one and the same person? He shook his head, he had no time for speculation. He had to concentrate on catching Beth.

"Stop!" Mendick shouted again, but the wind snatched the word and tossed it aside, unheeded and unheard. He had closed the gap on Beth, she was only a few hundred yards in front of him now. She held something in her right hand but he could not see what it was. He lengthened his stride and ran on, his boots thudding on the spongy peat underfoot.

A short, steep rise lay ahead, leading to a distinctly conical knoll. Beth stopped half way up and turned to watch him for a moment. A sudden shaft of sunlight probed the scudding clouds to highlight her face. She was sheet-white, her features set, and even from this distance Mendick could sense her malevolence. She turned and ran on. Mendick followed, cresting the hill, bracing his hands against his knees as the pain in his muscles increased. The ridge broadened slightly now although the slope on the left was steeper than ever. The path narrowed onto the top of a short rocky cliff easing to a near-vertical slope that descended forever to a tear-shaped loch.

Beth moved more slowly now as she felt her way between the top edge of the cliff and a tall drystone wall on the right. She was forced onto a very narrow path, broken in places, and she held onto the wall for support as she clambered along. Mendick followed. He clutched the coping stones of the wall and stumbled as one shifted under his hand and crashed onto the path, bounced once and tumbled over the cliff, down towards the loch. A small avalanche of soil and small pebbles accompanied it. Mendick watched for a second, saw the splash far beneath and continued. Beth had increased her lead now and seemed to glide along the track.

A few hundred yards more and the path deteriorated to only a few inches in width, the slope slithering down and the loch below, dark and chill. Mendick heard the hunting cry of an eagle and blinked as the shadow passed over him. The bird swooped from above, its wings so close he could hear the rustle, and then it was beneath him, gliding above the loch, a splendid vision of gold and brown, so beautiful, so deadly, and a reminder of the precariousness of his position up there.

Beth stopped at the narrowest section of the path. She turned to him, her face lined and set. "So, it is you and me again, Mendick." She was balanced on the finger-thin path. "How often do I have to kill you before you stay dead?"

"I think you have run yourself out," Mendick said. He heard the eagle call again and felt the drop suck at him as if in invitation to step over and join Emma. But Johanna was here, in the land of the living. "If you surrender now it will save us both a lot of trouble."

Beth laughed harshly. "Sergeant Mendick; pray tell me why should I give up when I have you exactly where I want you?" She lifted her hand and pointed a double-barrelled pistol at him. "Or did you think I was running away because I was scared of you?" She shook her head. "That's twice I've caught you with the same trick, Sergeant. I'm surprised at you."

Mendick realised he had been led into an ambush all of his own making. Beth had lured him up the hill and along the ridge. He wondered briefly why she had come so far when she might have stopped and shot at him at any time since leaving the wagons, but the answer was obvious. Up here she was far from any witness. Now she was breathing easier and on this narrow path he was unable to dodge a bullet. Trapped between the stone wall and the sheer drop, Mendick knew he had nowhere to run and nowhere to hide. He could only plead for his life, retreat, or pull out his revolver and attack.

He lunged forward, yelling, in an attempt to put Beth off her aim. She stood firm, extended her arm and pulled the trigger. Mendick had expected that. The second Beth committed herself to the shot, he dropped to the ground. He saw the flash and the jet of smoke, felt the burning zip of the ball passing just over his shoulder. He rolled towards the wall in the hope it might provide some shelter, tried to release his pepperpot and saw Beth take careful aim with the second barrel. He had not enough time to draw and fire.

Beth's grip on her pistol did not waver, "Before you die, Sergeant Mendick, I thought you should know that your men will also be dying in a very few seconds. If you hold on you may just about hear them . . ." She grinned and put pressure on the trigger.

The explosion was muffled by distance but quite distinct. The concussion was like distant thunder and Beth began to laugh. "That should be them now . . ." and in that instant, as her concentration wavered, Mendick flicked the stone.

It was no larger than his thumb and he had no time to throw it properly but the impact on Beth's sleeve was enough to cause her to pull the trigger. There was a spurt of white smoke from the pistol, a momentary flash, a whine and the ball ploughed a long furrow in the dirt near Mendick's head.

He threw himself forward, almost tripped over an uneven tussock of grass and smashed into Beth. They fell on to the stone wall together and slid to the ground, his arms around her as she snarled obscenities into his ear. She tried to thrust a thumb in his eye but he blocked, she reached for his groin with savage fingers and he blocked again. She twisted free, swearing.

"This way is better than any pistol," Beth dropped her razor from her sleeve and whipped it through the air. "How does it feel, Mendick? Your men all blown to shreds and you about to be sliced to ribbons? And you still don't know who China Jim is, or anything about him!" Her laugh was as harsh and cruel as anything Mendick had ever heard. "China knows all about you, Mendick but you will never know about . . ." She stopped in mid sentence and slashed sideways at his face.

Mendick ducked and withdrew step by step as Beth followed, slashing with the glittering silver blade that made such pretty patterns in the air. He gasped as his left foot slipped on the very edge of the path and a small shower of dirt and pebbles cascaded to the loch below. They seemed to hang in the air for agonisingly long moments before landing with a barely audible splash.

Beth laughed again, her pinched, white face convulsed. "I'm going to rip you to pieces, Mendick! And then spit on you as you lie bleeding on the ground!"

"And then cut slices of me and eat them? Is that what you do, Beth? Is that what you and China Jim do to people who cross you?" Mendick feinted forward with his left hand, but Beth did not fall for it. Instead she slashed upwards with her razor, an evil stroke aimed at Mendick's groin.

Her laugh was as ugly as her weapon. "You really have no idea, do you?" She flicked her wrist, sending the razor into a figure of eight movement that was impossible for Mendick to pass. She stepped forward slowly and he retreated step by step along the crumbling path. "You will die as ignorant as you lived, you bluebottle bastard!"

Darting forward, she sliced at his face. Mendick raised a protective arm; his world exploded in white hot agony as the blade slashed through his jacket and up the length of his forearm, still he pushed forward, smacking his elbow into Beth's jaw. The impact momentarily stopped her, leaving just enough opportunity for Mendick to snatch at her wrist and snap it behind her back. The razor clattered to the ground and Mendick toed it over the edge.

"You bastard Mendick! You dirty bastard!"

"That's me all the way." Mendick agreed. "Now. You and I are going back to the police office, and we are going to have a nice long chat about China Jim and whisky and dead people being cut to pieces. Then a nice judge will send you to the gallows or to Australia for the remainder of your natural life."

Beth said nothing as she crashed her boot into Mendick's shin. The pain was sudden and unexpected. He swore and fractionally relaxed his grip on her wrist. She wriggled free and stepped back.

"You'll never send me to Van Diemen's Land, and you'll never find out about China Jim, bluebottle!"

As Mendick reached for his revolver, Beth spat at him, swivelled and jumped over the edge. For a second she seemed to hang, suspended parallel to the path, her skirt ballooning around her thighs and her legs shockingly white and exposed, then she plunged down, voiceless, her arms flapping.

"Beth!" Mendick reached out too late and he watched her fall for a second that felt like an hour. She landed with an audible crunch on the bank of the loch and lay still. Even from his position far above, Mendick could see the slow stain of blood seeping from her head into the dark waters, but he had no time to spare on sentiment for a dead criminal. He had to check on his men.

He ran with trembling legs, ignoring the rasp of breath in his lungs. He ran back along the ridge with the memory of the explosion uppermost in his mind and the thought that his men lay screaming and in pieces. He ran, aware that the party at Mandarin House was in full swing, hearing snatches of music and the sound of male laughter. As he ran Mendick could smell the drift of gunpowder in the wind. He saw a column of dark smoke smudge the sky and he cursed and threw himself down the wooded slope. Brambles ripped at his face and clothes, branches whipped at him but he ran, sliding, slithering and staggering towards the road where he had left his men. There was a rustle and a muttered curse from a patch of bracken. A ginger head appeared.

"Sergeant!" Sturrock gave his characteristic grin. He carried his official staff held over his shoulder, rather like a recruit with a musket. "Are you all right, Sergeant? We heard gunfire, I was coming to help."

"I'm fine, Sturrock. Beth is dead. The explosion?" Mendick gasped for breath and spoke in short, staccato phrases.

"Oh, aye," Sturrock shrugged. "The convoy was a trap. China Jim hid a barrel of gunpowder in the middle of the first wagon. Between that and the whisky there would have been a hell of a mess."

"So what happened?" Mendick whooped oxygen into his lungs.

"We saw the fuse spluttering so we rolled the thing down the slope." Sturrock shrugged, "There was a bit of a bang but no harm done. Beth is dead, then? Oh well, we still have a carter to question."

There was so much left unsaid that Mendick merely nodded. He pictured the scene. The realisation there was a barrel of gunpowder about to be detonated, the brave man who climbed onto the wagon to see what could be done; the scrambled search for the fuse, the seconds of effort to lift the barrel and roll it down the hill. Mendick's respect for the Dundee police increased.

"You are brave men," he said. The words were inadequate but all he could manage.

The three wagons were just as he had left them, the police lounging against them or sitting on top, chatting or puffing on their pipes as if they had never heard of gunpowder.

"Who rolled the barrel away?" Mendick asked.

Menzies removed the pipe from his mouth and pointed with the stem. "Sturrock. Him and Deuchars jumped on the wagon and threw it down the hill." He replaced his pipe then pointed along the Dundee road. "Horseman coming."

Mendick loosened his revolver and stepped into the road while the others watched with varying degrees of interest as the horseman galloped in. He reined up so abruptly that his horse reared. Lieutenant Cameron slapped the surface dust from his riding cloak and surveyed the cynically watching policemen.

"Where's Mendick?"

Mendick took a step forward. "I am Sergeant Mendick."

Cameron nodded. "There are three cabs coming behind me, Mendick. Get your men back to Dundee. While you have been playing in the country, China Jim's been at it again. There's been another murder."

CHAPTER SEVENTEEN

The man lay spread-eagled on his back with his insides removed and slices of flesh cut from his thighs. A linen bag lay in the bleeding hole where his intestines had been. There were thirty coins, all dated 1842. Mendick looked down at the bearded face. The eyes were open, glazed in death.

"Good evening to you, Iain Grant," he said. "You have harpooned your last whale, then."

"Do you know this man?" Sturrock asked.

"Constable Sturrock, meet Iain Grant, harpooner from the *Rose Flammock*." Mendick knelt at Grant's side. As well as the kindly wisdom, he recalled the the man's hidden strength and menace. "Now, Sturrock, Grant was a handy, capable and strong man. As a harpooner he had a position of authority in the ship, he would make good money. I can't imagine why he would have dealings with the criminal class or why China Jim would want to butcher him like this." Mendick indicated the surrounding carnage. "It's frightening to think there is someone capable of incapacitating a man as physically powerful as Grant."

"There doesn't seem to have been a struggle," Sturrock said. "Look, the room is undamaged."

Mendick glanced around. "There isn't much to damage." They were in a one room flat in a tenement in Trade's Lane, with a box bed in one corner, a deal table in the other and a shuttered window. There was nothing else.

In common with the previous murders, Grant's clothes were neatly folded and placed at his side, but this time the pockets were empty of all possessions.

"That's not like our man," Mendick observed. "He doesn't normally rob his victims, and look here." He bent closer and pointed to Grant's fob pocket. "See how this is ripped? The killer has just torn it straight out. He's even left a couple of links of the gold chain there. He's getting greedy." Mendick stood up. "Let's hope that's his downfall."

Sturrock nodded. "Yes, Sergeant. But once again, why would anyone do this? What on earth could this man have done?"

"As we agreed," Mendick said softly, "we have to discover the reason. If we find that, we find our murderer." He stepped to the table where a pewter plate lay with a selection of cuts of meat on it. He wrinkled his nose. "This will be human flesh, I presume. And probably pretty tough if it's from a whaling seaman. Whoever the cannibal is, he's not doing it for the taste."

Mendick tapped the table. "Sturrock, we've been looking in all the wrong places. There is no Chinese connection here at all. Grant was a professional whaler: I doubt he sailed anywhere else in his life."

"We still have not discounted Gordon," Sturrock said, "he even lives in Forfarshire. Very handy for the whisky distilling. I wonder where he was when we were searching that convoy?"

"He was at home," Mendick remembered the coaches ranked in front of Mandarin House. "So we can remove him from our list. That leaves one man. Gilbride, with the limp."

"Gilbride who owns *Rose Flammock*, and who loves Walter Scott," Sturrock said quietly.

"And there is our connection," Mendick pulled out his pipe. "Grant was a harpooner on *Rose Flammock* and Thoms had the name Rose tattooed on his arm." He pushed tobacco into the bowl of his pipe. "All right. We'll get the surgeon's report tomorrow. In the meantime, I want the crew lists of *Rose Flammock* for the last few years and particularly for 1842. Something happened that year and perhaps on that ship. I want to know if all our murdered men were in her crew that year."

Mendick knelt at the front door of the house. "This lock has not been forced. Like the whaling yard and Candle Lane a key was used." He looked up. "I want you to find the flat's owner, Sturrock, and who has access," Mendick glanced once more at the broken watch chain. "And order every pawnbroker and jeweller in Dundee to look out for a gold watch being handed in. It may be a long shot, but I'll wager our murderer doesn't keep Grant's watch for long."

He opened the shutters and checked the catch. "This is perfectly sound, Sturrock, and the window is intact." He looked down Trade's Lane to Dock Street where the nightly crowds were beginning to gather outside the pubs. "Before we do anything else, we'll ask the good people of the lane if they saw anything last night. You take the right side and I'll take the left."

"Did I see anything unusual?" The woman repeated. She stood outside her tenement flat and closed the door, too late to hide the smell of stale alcohol that followed her. "Not really." She looked up the lane to the flat where Grant was found "Have they got rid of that body yet?"

"They will do, did you see anything?"

"There was a dark coach," the woman looked around her as if she expected the coach to come rattling down the stair. She lowered her voice. "It was the ghost."

"The ghost?" Mendick remembered that Hitchins had used the same term. "Which ghost?"

"The ghost." The woman opened the door behind her and retreated into her house. "I saw him."

Mendick put his foot behind the jamb to prevent the woman from closing the door. "Describe him to me. What was he like?"

"No." the woman shook her head. "I can't. He'll get me."

Mendick pushed the door. He stepped inside the room with its basic furniture and minimum comfort. There was half a loaf on the table, a chair, an open bottle of whisky on the mantelpiece, a shakedown bed and nothing else. He removed his hat and opened the shutters at the window.

"Was this where you stood?" He could see the entire lane, with a good view of the stair where the dead man had been found. "Tell me what you saw."

"It was the ghost, it was the devil himself in his own coach, driven by a demon." The woman was trembling. She took the bottle from the mantelpiece and gulped down a few swallows. The level dropped noticeably. "He'll get me next!"

Mendick ushered her to the chair. "All right, now take your time. I am Sergeant Mendick of the Dundee Police." He showed the crown on his staff. "No devil, man or ghost can hurt you when I am here. That I promise you. Now tell me your name and what you saw."

The woman looked towards the window as if she

expected some horned monster to burst through, but Mendick tapped his staff on the table. "It's all right. You are safe when I am here."

"I'm Elizabeth Elder." The woman clung to her bottle as if it contained holy water. "I saw the ghost. He came in a black, black coach drawn by six black horses and his face was all black and his head was all black and huge and folded down."

"Folded down?" Mendick asked; "What do you mean, folded down?"

"I mean just folded down!" Elder's voice rose in a scream. "It was like his horns had been flattened and folded over his face and it was black as all hell itself!"

"Were you drinking last night?" Mendick looked around the room. There was another empty bottle under the table. "Tell me more about the ghost."

Elder reinforced herself with more whisky and held the bottle tight, presumably in case Mendick should want to share. "The demon stopped the coach and the ghost and another demon came out. The three of them carried the dead man into the shop and killed him again. They drove away with the coach swaying from side to side and when they turned the corner the horses struck fire from the ground."

"I see. Thank you, Elizabeth. Can you tell me what the demons looked like? Were they from Dundee? Did you recognise them?"

Elder shook her head. "No, they were from hell, I'm telling you! Horrible demons from hell, with black faces and imp bodies."

"Imp bodies?" Mendick repeated. "Pray tell me about these imp bodies?"

"The bodies of imps!" Elder pointed a long, taloned

finger at Mendick as she spoke while specks of spittle sprayed from her mouth and her left hand clamped around the bottle. "Horrible, horrible imps they were; small and with great long cloaks that swept the ground!"

"I see, thank you, Elizabeth." Mendick replaced his staff in its pocket and lifted his hat. "You have been a great help to me."

Sturrock knelt on the pavement at the corner of Trade's Lane and Dock Street. "Sergeant, this might be of interest." He pointed to the angle of the building, about two feet from the ground. "I think the driver left the road and damaged one of his wheels here. Look, you can see a smear of paint, quite distinctly."

Mendick hurried over, "That ties in with what I was told. The body was dumped by three small men in a coach. One of my witnesses claimed she saw sparks, that could have been when the coach hit the wall." He knelt beside Sturrock. "Yellow paint. How many broughams have yellow wheels?"

Sturrock stood up. "I've never checked, Sergeant, but it is easy enough to paint over a scrape."

"We'll be pulling over any brougham with yellow wheels as of today," Mendick said. "Well spotted, Sturrock. This case is finally beginning to unravel. We have a lot of work to do, so let's get on with it. Step out, my lad!"

Simpson, the young clerk at the Waverley Whale Fishing Company, peered through the ornate brass latticework that bisected the counter behind which he worked and nodded eagerly. "You want crew lists, Sergeant? Anything to help the police." He brought out advance wage lists, records of oil money and fast-boat money paid, slops issued and crew lists for every ship in the company, and then explained the relevance of each list.

"You see, Sergeant Mendick, the Merchant Shipping Act of 1835 obliged us to make up Agreements and Crew Lists and file them with the Registrar General of Shipping and Seamen." He looked up, "Some companies do not keep their records but Mr Gilbride insists the Waverley Company hold ours. That way we know whether we have a good man or not. We even keep duplicates, ever since that unfortunate robbery attempt a few years ago . . . ."

"I'm sure you do it very well." Mendick stopped him in mid-flow. "I would like you to copy me out the crew lists of *Rose Flammock* for every year from 1842 to the present. Do you hold a copy of the ship's log as well?"

"Good Lord, no, sir!" Simpson said. "We send them immediately to . . ."

"No matter then. Write out the crew lists for me." Mendick ordered.

"Of course, sir," Simpson bowed low, "if you could come back tomorrow say, or perhaps the next day?"

"I will wait for them." Mendick placed his official staff on the counter and allowed the light from the whale oil lamp to reflect on the golden VR. It was a trick he employed to remind petty officials and potential witnesses he was on the Queen's business.

There were nine crew lists of fifty names each; the clerk pored over each one, his pen scraping at the smooth paper, dipping into the pewter inkwell and scraping again. Eventually he handed over the earliest.

"There we are sir, 1842. I have written them according to rank, as we do on the log books."

Mendick scanned the page. From the fifty names, four jumped out at him at once:

Iain Grant
David Thoms
David Torrie
Robert Milne

"These men here," Mendick asked the clerk, "was there anything specific about them? Did they stand out in any way?"

Simpson glanced at the names and shook his head. "Nothing that springs to mind, sir. They were just crewmen, the usual blackguards that fill every ship."

"Blackguards?" Mendick leaned across the counter as his anger rose. "These are men, Simpson. These are the men who risk their lives day after day to make the money that keeps this company running and keeps you in a position." He looked around at the neatly-panelled room with the brass railing that separated Simpson from the outside world. "I suggest you take one trip with these blackguards and see what the world is like outside your gilded cage." He rapped his staff down on the counter and Simpson flinched. "I have changed my mind. I want crew lists from 1840 onward for both your whaling ships. Now!"

"That will take some time, sir," Simpson looked at his watch.

"In that case you had better get started," Mendick told him. "I am in a hurry."

Sturrock peered at the names set out on the desk before him. "There are hundreds of different seamen here," he said.

"Ships do not have the same crews year after year,"

Mendick told him. "Seamen sign articles for only one voyage, and if they are dissatisfied or fancy a change of ship they are free to go elsewhere once the ship docks. But whaling seaman can be specialists, so they have more chance of remaining in the same trade, or even with the same ship, for years."

"Why would anyone want to sail to the Arctic?" Sturrock wondered. "It's a terrible place, ships are always sinking and men die in a hundred different ways."

"It pays well." Mendick replied. "The boys can double their wages with their share of the money from whale oil, and if they are out on the boats they pick up bonuses for getting fast to a whale as well. As a harpooner, Grant was one of the highest paid men on the ship."

Sturrock was matching names from one list to the next. "But that also raises a question, Sergeant. If he was well paid, why would he get involved with China Jim at all, unless he was providing whisky for him to smuggle. Do they have duty-free whisky on whaling ships?"

Mendick shook his head, "No, they don't. They have rum and tobacco but not whisky. There must be another reason." He continued to study the lists. "I don't know what we're looking for here, Sturrock, but I am convinced that this ship is the answer. Something happened in 1842 and *Rose Flammock* is the key."

"Here's something interesting," Sturrock crossed to Mendick's desk. "Look. In 1840, '41 and '42 the *Rose* had less than 10 changes in the crew. Then in 1843 there were 25 changes. Twenty five men chose not to go back to sea in that ship again."

"That's a lot of changes for a whaling ship, right enough. Half the crew." Mendick looked at the lists,

"There are two of our boys right away: David Thoms and Robert Milne sailed in *Rose* in 1842 but not in 1843. Iain Grant and David Torrie went back to sea the next year though. Do any of the others appear in a later list?"

Sturrock scanned the lists. "Some do, Sergeant. Thoms and Milne do not and Torrie only sailed again in 1843 and then stopped. Grant sailed every year."

"Write me two lists: those that appear again and those that don't." Mendick said. "I think we are finally making some progress, Sturrock." Mendick pulled out his pipe. "Thoms and Milne were single men. Torrie's wife died of fever but Grant had a family. I will speak to his wife."

"That is not decent, Sergeant," Sturrock said. "She has just been widowed. Surely it's best we leave her in peace."

Mendick slipped on his tattered Chesterfield. "We have our duty to do, Sturrock. Sometimes that means we have to upset innocent people in order to achieve justice."

Mrs Grant lived in a quiet, impeccably neat house in the Nethergate. She sat straight-backed opposite Mendick, her eyes red-rimmed but her face composed.

"No, Sergeant Mendick. I know of no reason why my husband was murdered." Her hands twisted a handkerchief in her lap, writhing it into a warped snake of white linen.

Mendick sipped the tea Mrs Grant had offered him. "This may sound a strange question, Mrs Grant, but did your husband know anybody from China or with a connection to China?"

"You are referring to China Jim, of course." She

247

might have been recently widowed but Mrs Grant's mind was as sharp as any Criminal Officer's. "No, Sergeant Mendick. My husband had no connection with China or with this China Jim." She curled the handkerchief into a ball and straightened it out again, her face as immobile as ever. "Iain was a Greenlandman, Sergeant. He was no angel − he could drink and roar with the best of them, but he was never a friend of this China Jim or anyone like him. He was a good man, a good father and a good husband."

Mendick nodded. "I have never heard anybody say anything against him, Mrs Grant. However, you do understand that I do have to ask these questions."

Mrs Grant gave a brief nod. "Pray continue."

Mendick took a deep breath. "Did Mr Grant have any enemies at sea? In particular, did he have any from *Rose Flammock*?"

"No, Sergeant." Mrs Grant was emphatic. "My husband was a hard worker and a fair man."

"I have just one more question to ask and then I'll leave you in peace." Mendick waited for a second as the street sounds drifted in from the open window. Mrs Grant held her steady gaze on him. "Are you aware of any event in 1842 that Mr Grant might have been involved in?"

The noise from outside seemed to increase as Mrs Grant carefully placed the handkerchief on the table and smoothed it flat before folding it into a neat square. "Of course I am, Sergeant. That was the year two whaleboats were lost in the fog. One was never found again and all six men died up there."

For a moment Mendick pictured the small open boat drifting in the biting cold of the Arctic, surrounded by icebergs gaunt and wicked, and the insidious creep of frostbite gradually killing the crew. He held Mrs Grant's eye. "Was Mr Grant involved in that incident?"

"Mr Grant was the harpooner of the other whaleboat," there was pride in Mrs Grant's voice. "He kept them alive, except one who died of the frost. Mr Grant brought the rest back safely."

Mendick remembered the knowledge in Grant's eyes. "He looked a capable man when I met him," he said.

"You knew him?" Mrs Grant looked pleased.

"He rescued me from a sandbank in the Tay," Mendick said frankly. "He helped save my life as well as the men in that whaleboat." He placed his cup on the table. "Thank you for the tea, Mrs Grant. I assure you I will do all I can to hunt down his killer."

"Thank you, Sergeant." Mrs Grant stood up. "That is a comfort." For a second her mask fell and her terrible grief took over. She looked old and broken and utterly forlorn.

"Here. Come here." Mendick held out his arms to comfort her but she recovered herself and drew back.

"No, Sergeant Mendick." Mrs Grant held herself as erect as any soldier on sentry duty. "I appreciate your offer but I was married to Iain for thirty-three years." She controlled the catch in her voice. "No other arms will do."

"Of course, Mrs Grant." Mendick lifted his hat from the top of the table. "Thank you for your time. Do you wish the Dundee Police to keep you informed on the progress of this investigation?"

"No, Sergeant." Mrs Grant shook her head. "But please catch this brute." She hesitated for a moment. "You must be very careful, Sergeant. This Chinaman must be terribly powerful to be able to overpower Iain, he was strong as an ox."

Mendick gave a short bow. "Thank you Mrs Grant. You have been most helpful." He tried to protest as she insisted on showing him to the door, but he knew it was in vain. Mrs Grant would never forget her impeccable manners no matter what the circumstances.

Mendick did not look back as he left the close. He knew Mrs Grant would stand in her doorway until his footsteps ceased and he was safely out of her close; she would cling to his presence as a link to her husband. Then she would close the door quietly and firmly, wash up his cup and replace it in the cupboard. She would close that door as well then sit upright on her hard chair, fold her hands neatly in her lap, close her eyes and cry inwardly.

Without her husband, what had she to look forward to? A bleak, lonely old age of increasing poverty, or a hurried re-marriage to a man who would never compare to her Iain. She was the true victim here. She, and the decent, suffering people like her, they were the reason the country had a police force. Mrs Grant was a reminder that he was dealing with people with hopes and feelings, not just with criminals and victims. Mendick stepped into the Nethergate and looked upward to the window of Mrs Grant's house. He saw the shutters closing. Mrs Grant was alone with her grief.

Mendick could hear a blackbird singing as he walked back to the police office, the sound a contrast to the sordid images that pervaded his mind. He recalled the muscular figure of Grant as he had been in life and wondered what sort of man could overpower and kill him. Hitchins had spoken of four men. Mrs Elder had spoken of three small men in a dark carriage, possibly a brougham, driven by a fourth. They were cannibals, possibly with a connection to *Rose Flammock* in 1842.

So why did the leader call himself China Jim? And where did Grant or Thoms or Milne or Torrie fit in with the whisky smuggling? Mendick shook his head. Something here did not make sense. There were too many threads that led nowhere, but his instincts were tingling now. Despite the apparent confusion, he knew he was close to a solution and he would soon return home to London. But that would mean leaving Johanna behind and that thought ripped a huge hole in his heart.

CHAPTER EIGHTEEN

The man waiting at the public counter was round-shouldered, grey-haired and nervous. He looked up as Mendick appeared, smiled briefly and returned to his scrutiny of the floor.

"Yes, sir?" Mendick said. "You asked to see me?"

The man looked over his shoulder to where a policeman was arbitrating between two brass-tongued harpies in dispute over a hat. "I own a jewellery business, sir. Constable Scrymgeour said I was to alert you if there was any gold watches handed in."

Mendick nodded. Ever since he had asked the beat policemen to alert pawnbrokers and jewellers about his stolen watch he had been inundated with enquiries. They had all proved fruitless. "That is correct, pray come away from prying eyes." He ushered the man up the stairway to his office.

"My name is Edmund Anderson, of Anderson's the Jewellers of Reform Street. You may have heard of us? We advertise quite widely." Anderson looked up hopefully and Mendick nodded.

"Indeed, Mr Anderson, your firm is well known. Your premises are opposite Mr Leslie's crockery business." Mendick dragged Sturrock's chair across the room and waited until Anderson was settled before sitting down himself. "Now, what can we do for each other?"

"I had a gold watch handed in to me, Sergeant Mendick, but there was something not right about it, you see."

Anderson plunged his hand deep into his pocket and pulled out a paper-wrapped packet which he placed on the desk. "Here it is." Very slowly he removed the wrapping and placed the watch in front of him. "It's a splendid watch, Sergeant. Craftsman made by Marshall of Edinburgh."

Mendick picked it up and turned it around. The name Marshall was prominent on the watch plate alongside some evident scrapes. "Do you know who handed this watch in, Mr Anderson?"

"I have his name as Robert Roy Durward, Sergeant," Anderson looked up warily, as if expecting Mendick to blame him for the name of his client.

Mendick looked more closely at the watch. "I see, Mr Anderson. And do you have any reason to believe that is not his real name? In my experience criminals tend to choose aliases that are more common, such as Smith or Jones, so they can merge with the crowd." He looked up, frowning. "Robert Roy Durward, you say?"

"Indeed, Sergeant," Anderson produced a small slip of paper, "we give our clients a receipt for their property. They hold half and we hold half and when they return they bring their half and the numbers match . . ."

"I understand. Thank you Mr Anderson." Mendick pointed at the scrapes on the watch plate. "Are these significant?"

"That is the crux of the matter, Sergeant, you have it exactly!" Anderson beamed. "You see, it is quite common for clients to bring in second-hand watches they have purchased from pawn shops and require us to remove the old owner's name and replace it with a new one. Sometimes they file off the old name themselves, gold is a soft metal, you see, and they believe they are saving themselves money although it takes me as much time and expense to clean up the mess they have made." Anderson reclaimed the watch in tender hands and pointed at the scrapes.

"As you said, Sergeant Mendick, the name of the previous owner has been filed off the watch plate. But so has the watch number. You do know that all quality watches have their own number?" Anderson looked up to ensure Mendick was paying attention.

"I was aware of that," Mendick confirmed.

"Well, my customer asked me to engrave his name, Robert Roy Durward, on the plate. I had hardly begun when I noticed the number was also missing. Marshall watches are unusual, because as well as engraving his number on the upper surface, he also engraves it on the underside." He unfastened the watch plate and showed it to Mendick: "You see?"

"I see," Mendick read the watch number. "Now, Mr Anderson, is there any way we can ascertain the previous owner of that watch?"

"Mr Marshall keeps a list," Anderson said. "I took the liberty of writing to him as soon as I became suspicious and he informed me he sold it to a Mrs Charlotte Grant."

"Thank you, Mr Anderson." Mendick pushed the watch across the desk. He controlled his surge of triumph. "You keep hold of this just now. When is Mr Durward coming to pick his watch up?"

"Ten on Thursday morning," Anderson stared at the watch as if it would explode. "Should you not keep it, Sergeant?"

"No, Mr Anderson." Mendick pressed the watch into Anderson's hand. "When Mr Durward arrives, you hand the watch over and leave the rest to us." He rose from his seat. "That will be all just now Mr Anderson, we will be in touch."

"That's it then!" Sturrock slapped a hand on his thigh as soon as Anderson left the room. "That's China Jim's big mistake! He's got greedy and now we've got him."

"This is Tuesday and the collection is on Thursday. I will ask Mr Mackay to have the shop watched from this hour, in case this Durward fellow arrives before his time. We will be waiting, Sturrock, and we will follow him to wherever he lives." Mendick leaned back in his chair and smiled. "I think you are right, he has made a mistake and we have him."

"Durward: that's Walter Scott again." Sturrock shrugged, "he seems to be getting everywhere nowadays."

"Walter Scott?" Mendick looked up, "What do you mean, Sturrock?"

Sturrock shrugged. "Those are two of Scott's novels, Sergeant. *Quentin Durward* and *Rob Roy*; China has combined both into one name."

Mendick grunted. "I can guess that Durward is another alias of Marmion and Oldbuck. And who do we know who likes Walter Scott?" Mendick answered his own question. "James Gilbride likes Walter Scott. The man with the damaged leg, the man who owns the ship on which the murdered men served, the man Marmion robbed." He stood up slowly. "We have had him watched for weeks and he has not put a foot wrong but mark my words, Sturrock, he is connected to this in some way." He hauled his pipe from his pocket and furiously began to thumb tobacco into the bowl. "I don't think he is China Jim, but I think somebody is trying to make us believe he is. China is laying a false trail to Gilbride, and it is all to do with something that happened on *Rose Flammock* in 1842."

"Do we remove the man watching Gilbride's office?" Sturrock asked but Mendick shook his head.

"No, we leave him there to guard Gilbride rather than to watch him. He may be China Jim's next victim." Mendick scratched a Lucifer. "Things are unravelling Sturrock; let's step out, man."

Mendick pulled up the collar of his coat, jammed his hat further down his head and huddled deeper into the corner of the close mouth. The brief spell of warm weather had broken and an easterly wind threw a torrent of rain against the mud-coloured tenements of Reform Street. He had watched a slow trickle of people come in and out of the jewellery shop for the past two hours without any signal or message from Anderson. Disguised as an artisan, Sturrock worked on the broken door of a close opposite. Judging by the less-than-muttered curses that Mendick heard, the door would be all the worse for his attentions.

A young girl skipped past Anderson's window, paused to peer in, pulled a face at Sturrock and ran away, giggling. Mendick watched her for a second and returned his attention to the shop. There had been a trickle of customers this morning. Of the three lone females, one had been an obvious prostitute in cheap finery and bouncing feathers, the others were probably wives who had sold their jewellery to raise money for household bills or drink. There had been a respectable-looking gentleman who checked both ways before sliding into the shop, so was probably buying something for his sweetheart and not his wife, and a courting couple, all glowing eyes and touching hands.

The man who walked down the street was so nondescript that Mendick barely noticed him. He would have merged into any crowd with ease. He was of average height and build, with clothes that could have belonged to a respectable servant or tradesman. Only his walk gave his profession away, the slightly rolling, swaying gait of a seaman that Mendick knew so well.

When he saw the seaman glance over his shoulder and slide into the shop, Mendick knew he was watching his quarry. His low whistle alerted Sturrock, who lifted a screwdriver in acknowledgement. Within five minutes Anderson appeared at the window of his flat, immediately above the shop and waved frantically.

"For God's sake, control yourself," Mendick muttered, "else you'll be taking off like a bird. You'll have half the street watching!" He lifted a hand in acknowledgement: the insignificant man must be Durward or Marmion or whatever alias suited him this time.

It was another ten minutes before Durward emerged and slouched towards the High Street. Mendick followed a short distance behind on the opposite side of the road. He did not see Sturrock but knew he would be there. Mendick took the usual precautions of not looking at his quarry directly, of matching his footsteps so their feet hit the ground simultaneously and there was no distinctive click-clack of heels against paving stones for Durward to notice, and of looking around so he was aware of every side street and close mouth.

Durward walked quickly and did not look behind him but still Mendick remained at a distance and well out of his line of sight. When the seaman lingered to look in the Hammermen Tavern at the corner of the Overgate, Mendick hurried in front, stopped at a shop to buy a newspaper and only re-emerged when he saw Sturrock saunter past, whistling tunelessly.

"Step out, Sturrock, I will follow you." Mendick said and lagged behind, keeping Sturrock in sight as they headed west to where the High Street merged with Nethergate and then onto the more open prosperity and fine villas of the Perth Road.

Durward became more cautious when they reached these more spacious and quieter surroundings. He paused twice to look behind him, and Mendick signalled for Sturrock to disappear up one of the side streets while he again took over the lead position. They passed the splendid Airlie Place and the seaman turned left and hurried down Roseangle with its detached villas and on to the open space of Magdalen Green. He stopped much more often to turn and peer around, now stopping every ten or twenty steps. Mendick swore softly, either Durward was becoming nervous because he was getting close to his destination or he suspected he was being followed.

Spotting a small thicket on his left, Mendick stopped and pretended to light his pipe. He signalled for Sturrock to take over his position and then hurried on. He overtook Durward on the opposite side of the road, paused to check the time on the cheap metal watch that had replaced his own and lengthened his stride as if he had just realised he was late for an appointment.

A hundred yards past the entrance to Magdalen Place, Mendick stopped again and looked back. The street was empty: Durward had cut off somewhere. He cursed and doubled back, to see Sturrock striding down Magdalen Place.

"I've lost him," Mendick admitted. "I thought he saw me so I overtook him, but I think he took fright and ran."

Sturrock shook his head. "He went into the servant's entrance of one of the houses at the top of Magdalen Place."

"Well done, Sturrock. Which house?" Mendick stood in the shadow of a tall tree, looking up the short cul-de-sac.

"Juniper Lea," Sturrock pointed it out, "that's the one . . ."

"I know Juniper Lea," Mendick said. He remembered the bumbling, slightly nervous Adam Leslie with his dominant wife and the two daughters. "I know it very well indeed." Was Durward China Jim? Was Durward using the Leslie's house as a base for his murders?

"Should we go in and arrest him?" Sturrock reached inside his coat for his staff.

Mendick shook his head. "Not yet. We know where he is. You keep guard over the house just now, but don't be seen."

"If he leaves, should I follow him?" Sturrock asked.

"Most assuredly, but if he does not leave, then I will call in person by-and-by, and I won't be seen either. I think Mr Durward may have more than just a watch for us." Mendick produced his pipe, turned his back against the rain and stuffed tobacco into the bowl. "That is Adam Leslie's house, Sturrock, and a more charming gentleman never drew breath."

"Is he China Jim?" Sturrock asked

Mendick applied a Lucifer to his tobacco and puffed it to a red glow. "I do not know," he said truthfully, "but I will admit to being surprised if he is. At present my money is on some third party who Durward works for. Durward is a seaman who appears to have some grudge against Gilbride."

259

Sturrock examined the street of beautiful classical villas. "Maybe Leslie doesn't know that his servant works for China Jim? This is hardly the environment I would expect to find a murderer, Sergeant. It is most eminently respectable."

"Wickedness can hide under the most benign front," Mendick retorted, "and the smile of the devil deceives all who are unaware." He puffed out aromatic smoke that merged with the rain. "I would not be at all surprised if China Jim is preparing to rob Mr Leslie and our good Durward is his method of access into the house." He pointed the stem of his pipe at Juniper Lea. "But I do not want the servant, Sturrock. I want China Jim and tarry-jack here will be the key that locks him securely in the condemned cell."

The afternoon rain gave way to an evening of cloud that drifted in from the Tay and wrapped grey tendrils around the gardens and houses of Magdalen Place. Mendick walked in the shadows of the garden walls, his rubber-soled shoes making no sound and his grey jacket and trousers making him indistinguishable in the gloom. He stopped opposite and slightly short of Juniper Lea and saw that the windows appeared unlit. Either the family were early bedders or they had already secured the internal shutters for security.

Rather than attempt the squeaking gate, Mendick climbed up onto the wall, swore as he cut a hand on the broken glass protecting the top and dropped into the Leslie's garden. He lay amidst a clump of fuchsia, listened to the immediate silence and the distant rumbling of the city and then crept closer to the front door. The haar thickened, blown in by a soft wind, and when he heard the jingle of harness and the clip of a horse's hooves he slipped close to the front door and hid around the corner of the house. He watched the gig lamps throw their beam of light onto the street and highlight the intertwined initials on the gate.

"Halloa!" A bulky man jumped down from the driver's perch and shouted at the house. "I said halloa there!"

One of the shutters behind an upstairs window opened and the light from the room glowed yellow. Voices sounded faintly from inside with only Mrs Leslie's sharp tones discernible. "See who that is, James. Take the gun."

The door opened and James the driver stood, a lantern in his left hand and a large pistol in his right. He peered at the cab parked at the bottom of the garden, but rather than shout and further disturb the respectable neighbourhood, he walked down the drive in his black coat, with his seaman's gait telling its own story and the pistol held ready. Mendick nodded. James and Durward were one and the same person. Durward was the faceless man who could merge with a crowd: a human chameleon.

"Halloa!" Sturrock bellowed for the third time as James gestured with the gun to keep him quiet. "Is this where Isiah MacPherson lives?"

"No, it is not! Be off with you, you scoundrel!"

Under cover of this diversion Mendick slipped inside the open door. He remembered the layout of the house from his previous visit and headed downstairs, unlocked a broom cupboard at the foot of the stairs, stepped into the darkest corner and waited for the house to quieten down.

He heard the murmur of voices, footsteps passing and re-passing his hiding place, heard the impatient tut of Mrs Leslie, a muttered "I must speak to Mary about locking doors," and the faint snick of the key turning in the cupboard lock and then the drum of feet on the stairs. There was the rattle of a door opening, a click as it shut and Mendick remained still; w,iting. A few moments later he heard the sound of a horse and the grind of wheels on gravel; the family had left the house. He was alone inside a locked cupboard in Juniper Lea and all the night was before him.

Mendick reached for his outsider, a pair of thin-jawed pliers which he inserted into the keyhole and used to grasp the butt of the key and turn it until the lock clicked. He pushed the door open. He was at the beginning of a short corridor with three closed doors, two had keys still in their locks. The first door opened to an unused bedroom. Mendick checked quickly: a box bed with a straw mattress and a pitcher and ewer on top of a cheap wooden chest. The chest was empty, the floorboards screwed in place and there were no hidden corners in the room; this room held no interest for him. The second door had no key visible, Mendick guessed the maidservant was inside and moved on. The last door opened to James' room.

Mendick took the key and entered the room. It was a mirror image of the first room with a similar box bed and chest, this one obviously inhabited, with covers on the bed and the chest decorated and carved with the initials A. C. Mendick frowned. Who was A.C? Was that another alias for Durward or perhaps even the man's real initials?

He lifted the lid. The chest contained the usual knick-knacks and souvenirs collected over years at sea. There was an assortment of clothes, a seaman's knife and a leather belt. A carved whale puzzled Mendick for a moment before he realised its possible significance. He held the whale in his hand, closed his fist and breathed out slowly.

It was a piece of scrimshaw: baleen from the whale's jaw, carefully shaped with a knife into the likeness of a whale. Durward had been a Greenlandman like Iain Grant, yet his name had not been on any of the crew lists; at least not under any of the aliases that Mendick knew. Mendick shrugged. Every year hundreds of Dundee men went whaling in many different ships. Durward may never have sailed on *Rose Flammock* in his life, but somehow, he suspected that he had, and in 1842.

There was nothing else of interest in the room. Mendick looked in the bed, under the bed and felt the straw mattress. He checked the floorboards for signs of tampering; he checked the walls for hidden compartments but found nothing. There were no housebreaking tools, no store of stolen watches, nothing to incriminate Durward. In a fit of frustration, Mendick lifted the chest and turned it upside down, hoping for a false bottom, but once more he found nothing. The chest was simply a chest.

Adam Leslie employed Durward as a driver but the question was: did he know anything? Was Durward working for China Jim without Leslie's knowledge? Or were there more secrets in this house?

Room by room, Mendick checked Juniper Lea, aware he was trespassing in a place where he had been shown nothing but hospitality and openness. He carefully closed each door behind him before lighting the gas and inspecting every corner. There was nothing to suggest any criminality, nothing except the usual family belongings. He felt like a traitor to kindness but that was part of his job. He examined the family portraits once more: the image of the immature young man stared solemnly at him from within the black frame, drowned on his first voyage, a tragedy for his family.

The stables stood apart from the house, slightly larger than Mendick would have expected, with the usual small door set within a large entrance. The lock was simple to pick and he stepped inside, to be greeted by the usual familiar smell of horses and straw, and the low dark shape of the family gig. Mendick touched the woodwork, if the gig was here, what was the family riding in? Did they own two coaches? Mendick glanced around the spacious interior of the stables, was their second coach a brougham?

There was a battered oil lantern on a small shelf amongst a litter of tools and equipment. Mendick scraped a Lucifer and set it to life. The soft glow illuminated the interior; a horse whinnied softly at this disruption to her rest, but Mendick was more interested in the pot of yellow paint set under a shelf and a collection of lengths of wood in the corner. He lifted the first. It matched the wood from the rope ladder found at the scene of the first murder. The coils of old rope told their own story: Durward had made the ladder here. But was Durward, the man of many aliases, also China Jim?

There was only one room remaining and Mendick hesitated at the door. This was the chapel, the sanctuary, a place obviously sacred to the Leslie family. The door was securely fastened. Mendick extracted a lock pick from his pocket, worked the lock and stepped inside.

He stopped immediately and allowed his eyes to become accustomed to the Cimmerian dark. The room was larger than he had expected, with a collection of candlesticks on a long low table. Mendick scratched a Lucifer and lit the nearest candle, shielding the flame with his hand as he looked around.

Here were all the trappings of a chapel: an altar and pews, windows of stained glass and an atmosphere of reverence, a shelf of books and a cross. But that was where the resemblance ended.

"Dear God in heaven! What is this place?" Shielding the light with his hand, Mendick stared at the pictures covering the walls and the objects displayed in a score of glass cases beneath them. The pictures were of one person, but rather than any religious deity, they showed the life of the Leslie's son from a swaddled baby lying in a crib to a handsome young man in seaman's clothes.

"It's a mausoleum," Mendick said quietly. He allowed the candlelight to pool on the pictures. "It's a memorial to the boy who was lost at sea."

He shook his head. After the death of his wife Emma in childbirth he understood the terrible grief this family must feel for the loss of one of their own. He shuddered with sympathy and wished he had not entered what was obviously a place of very private mourning.

"I'm sorry," he said quietly. "I really don't like to betray your trust, but I must do my duty."

He knew Durward had worked with this family for some time and he must investigate thoroughly while he had the opportunity. Lifting his candlestick high, he walked around the chapel, probing every corner and tapping the wall for secret compartments.

He found the list of names on top of the altar, sewn

in red thread beneath an embroidered background of an open boat on a waste of sea. The artist had caught the atmosphere of the Arctic perfectly, with each of the six men depicted individually. One with a grey beard and stern eyes, one with a drawn, haggard face, a third had red whiskers peppered with white frost, a fourth: an open mouth as if shouting or singing, a fifth holding the steering oar and a sixth who lay across the thwarts. The artist had ensured that the sixth crewman was central to the picture. He was the youngest of them all and the most handsome. It did not take a great leap of imagination for Mendick to recognise young Jonathan Leslie.

The inference was obvious. The boy had drowned at sea. Jonathan Leslie had been on a whaleboat and had drowned. Mendick turned his attention from the picture to the list so neatly sewn below. There was one blank space and four names in alphabetical order:

Iain Grant
Robert Milne
David Torrie
David Thoms

Beneath the names in bold black thread was the single word: Justice.

Mendick stepped back as enlightenment dawned. Mrs Grant had told him her husband had been in charge of one of *Rose Flammock's* whaleboats when it had been lost in a fog. One man had died; Jonathan Leslie. And now Mr Leslie was taking a terrible revenge on those who had survived. Mendick had to discover the last person who had been in that whaleboat — Jonathan and four others were dead. But what was the significance of China Jim and where did the whisky fit in?

Mendick had been aware of the sound for some time

before it entered his consciousness. It was the sound of sobbing, not that of a child; deeper, as if someone was tearing himself apart in grief.

"Who's there?" Mendick looked around again, the lantern danced flickering shadows. The sobbing died away as he strode forward with the lantern held high. The man was crouched in the far corner, hiding beneath a table with both hands folded over his head. "Come on out of that!" Mendick said, "Come on, nobody is going to hurt you."

Mendick did not immediately recognise Adam Leslie in the human wreck who crouched in front of him. His clothes were rumpled and stained and his eyes haunted.

"Mr Leslie?" Mendick tried to keep his voice gentle.

Leslie nodded vigorously. He began to speak, slowly at first and then faster as though to ease himself of some burden. "I love her you see, but I can't keep her in the comfort she deserves. Her first husband, Grandison, was a wealthy man with the whisky, but my shop just does not make enough money, so I had to do something else." He crouched back on the floor and began to play with the hem of his jacket.

Mendick joined him. "What did you do, Mr Leslie?"

Leslie buried his head in his folded arms. "Whisky," he said. "Crockery is a luxury people only buy when they have money to spare and in these times of dull trade no-one has money to spare but they always have money for drink. So I moved into Grandison's whisky trade." He looked up, his face streaked with tears and his mouth working loosely, "Then they caught my boat and my wagons and closed down my distillery! I have lost the house too. She will be a pauper in the poorhouse!"

"And China Jim?" Mendick asked. "Are you China Jim? Why did China Jim kill these men?"

Leslie shook his head. "I'm China Jim, but I have never killed anyone. When you started asking questions I had to get rid of you in case you caught her."

A chill hand clutched around Mendick's heart. "Who killed these men, Mr Leslie?"

Leslie buried his face in his hands and began to cry.

"Who is next, Leslie? Who is next to be killed?"

Leslie said nothing, the deep sobbing continued.

Mendick closed his eyes. He knew exactly where he would discover the name of the final member of the boat's crew. He looked down at Leslie. China Jim was a broken man and no threat to anybody.

Sturrock was waiting in the hired gig. He looked up as Mendick appeared clutching his hat to his head.

"You're in a hurry, Sergeant," Sturrock lifted the reins. "Did you find anything?"

Mendick threw himself into the carriage. "I found nearly everything, Sturrock. I'll fill you in as we go. Whip up, man!"

"Where to?" Sturrock was grinning, enjoying the excitement; "Back to the office?"

"No, Unicorn Cottage."

"Johanna Lednock's house?" Sturrock flicked the reins and the horse moved off at a brisk trot. "Don't tell me she is China Jim?"

"No, she's not, Sturrock, but she is the key to the next murder. Come on, man! Hurry!"

Sturrock cracked the reins and the gig lurched forward, its wheels growling over the road as it sped past the villas of Magdalen Yard Road and up the incline to the Perth Road, heading eastward to Dundee. "Is she in danger, Sergeant?"

"Not her, but someone else is and the faster we get

to her the more chance we have of saving his life." Mendick held on to his hat as Sturrock turned the gig into the High Street. He saw Deuchars stepping towards them, one hand in the air as he tried to stop them for furious driving, but Sturrock whipped on, rattling into the Seagate and towards the Arbroath Road.

It was fully dark now, night-time revellers were roaring in the road, prostitutes plying their trade and respectable families sheltered behind secure shutters as the gig rattled along. Broughty Ferry was quiet as they entered, most of the men would be out at the fishing and the sea hushed deceptively soft at the beach.

Johanna answered her own door, her dressing gown wrapped around her and a candlestick held high. "Why, Sergeant Mendick!, Whatever is the matter?" She looked so very vulnerable with her hair in a cap and a few loose strands across her face that Mendick wanted to hug her in reassurance.

Instead he removed his hat, very aware that Sturrock was watching. "I am very sorry to disturb you Mrs Gordon, but I would like access to your portraits."

Johanna stepped aside at once. She glanced towards Sturrock and understood. "Of course, Sergeant, pray step inside. Would you and your companion like a cup of tea? I can make it myself rather than ringing for the maid . . ."

About to push past, Mendick collected himself and smiled. "Thank you for your kindness, Johanna, but I fear we do not have the time. I must just look at one of your paintings, if I may?"

Johanna ushered him inside and closed the door on the outside world. "All this hurry for a painting, and at this time of night?" Her hand lingered on his arm as her eyes searched his face. "Of course you may. You know the way, James. Which picture interests you?"

"I would like to see the boat's crew with Iain Grant in it." Mendick was already heading for the stairs and Johanna followed, holding the candle high so the yellow light pooled in front of him.

"Has there been another murder, James?"

"Not yet, Johanna, but I may be in a position to prevent one."

The picture was as he remembered it; bearded Iain Grant and six other men, the boat's crew of *Rose Flammock* and one other man, all staring at the artist. The youngest man was smiling, the others staring with expressions of morose patience. He could name four of them and guess at the identity of the fifth but it was the sixth and seventh that interested him – the older man who sat on the left and the nondescript fellow with his face shielded by a fur hat who sat on the extreme right.

"Could you name these men, Johanna?" Mendick asked.

"Not all of them," She was at his side and he could feel her body heat and smell the freshness of her. "That one is Iain Grant, of course, and that is David Thoms and . . ." She stopped as the realisation hit her. "These are the men who were murdered!"

"Yes." Mendick pointed to the boy. "Can you remind me of his name?"

"Jonathan Grandison," Johanna said at once.

Mendick nodded. Grandison, not Leslie. The boy had kept his father's name. That was why he had not recognised the name on a crew list., "That's who I thought it was. He died on that voyage didn't he?"

Johanna nodded, "Yes, I remember that picture well.

I sketched it first and then painted from the sketch. He was a nice young lad."

"And this man here?" Mendick pointed to the older man.

"Andrew Cleghorn," Johanna replied at once. "Everybody knows him as Old Andy. That voyage was his first and last, his mind could not take the strain . . ."

Mendick took a deep breath.

"Get up there, you little dog, and get it swept!"

The voice echoed in the choking darkness, distorted by the surrounding brickwork but still containing enough menace to make Jamie shiver. He looked upward to where the flue ascended forever, the sides black and slippery with soot and the exit a tiny circle of light diminished by distance.

"Move, you bugger! Or it will be the worse for you!"

Mendick remembered the misery of his childhood and Cleghorn's constant bullying. He remembered Old Andy in the Greenland Inn warbling his whaling song and clutching at his stomach. They were one and the same person. If he did nothing now, the monster who had tormented him so badly would die. The past would be cleansed forever.

"James?" Johanna was watching him, her eyes concerned. "Are you all right?"

Mendick nodded. What would Johanna think of him if he left a man to such a terrible death, even such a man as Andrew Cleghorn. He had to rescue him. Cleghorn would be hard to prise from the Greenland Inn but an easy victim compared to Alex Grant.

"And this one?" Mendick pointed to the nondescript man on the far right. "Do you remember him?"

Johanna shook her head. "Honestly, James, I can't

even remember painting him. He could be Robert or Thomas."

"Or Oldbuck, perhaps? Could he have been Oldbuck, or Marmion or Durward?" Mendick looked closely. Each man in the painting had some character: experience, youth, cheerfulness; Johanna had caught something that set them apart, but the final man was merely a face. Even although he had met Durward and followed him just that afternoon, Mendick was not sure he recognised him.

"He could be Durward," Johanna said. "I am so sorry, Sergeant, but I truly cannot recall."

"You have nothing to be sorry about," Mendick said. "Indeed, you have been far more helpful than you realise, particularly since I came to your house at this ungodly hour of the night."

"You are always welcome, James." Her hand was on his arm again. "Do you have time . . . no, of course, you have a man waiting." Johanna followed as Mendick strode outside. When he looked over his shoulder she was still watching as the gig clattered back towards Dundee.

CHAPTER NINETEEN

"Did you find what you wanted?" asked Sturrock.

Mendick explained about the crew of the whaleboat being murdered one by one, with only two left: Old Andy and the man who might be Durward. "It appears he is murdering the others," he said, "together with the three masked men."

"Do you know where Old Andy lives?" Sturrock took a corner on three wheels, winced as the gig clattered back down, bounced on a prominent stone and righted itself.

"No, but I would wager the publican does." Mendick held on to the edge of the gig as they jolted over a succession of potholes. "Can't you drive this thing?"

"The horse is tired, Sergeant!" Sturrock said. "And the oil in the lamps is getting low so we can't see the potholes in the road."

Although there were gas lamps in the principal streets of Dundee, the approaches were dark and the gig banged and rattled its way into the town. A sliver of moon reflected from the Firth of Tay and glinted on the twin tracks of the Arbroath Railway, pointing the way to Dundee. It was three in the morning when they rattled along Dock Street, wind whining through the rigging of the ships only a few yards away and the last of the night's drunks weaving their way home.

"Pull up in front of the pub," Mendick ordered. He jumped out of the gig as Sturrock patted the horse.

"Open up in there!"

There was no answer. The Greenland Inn remained in darkness. Mendick hammered his fist against the door. "Halloa! Dundee Police!"

Sturrock joined him; "Let me, Sergeant." He reached into the gig and pulled out his staff. "They'll hear this, unless they're deaf." He hammered the staff against the door and roared out, "Hello in there! Open up for the Dundee Police!"

Lights came on in neighbouring houses, some the slender flicker of single candles, others the more diffused glow of a lantern. Voices floated through the dark.

"What the devil is all the noise out there?"

"Answer your bloody door, why can't you?"

At last the window above the pub scraped open and a bald man peered out. "What is it?"

"Dundee Police!" Mendick displayed the crown on Sturrock's staff. "Let us in."

"Oh, Christ! What now? What time of night do you call this? Go away and come back in the morning." He reached to close the window.

"We'll stay here until you let us in," Mendick yelled, "think what that will do to your custom!"

The man muttered a few curses. "Wait," he said, "I'll come down."

Mendick heard the bolts creak back.

"Come in if you must." The room was empty, the atmosphere flat, rancid with stale tobacco smoke. He placed the lantern on the table. "Well, what is it?"

"We're looking for Old Andy," Mendick said.

"He drinks here, he doesn't live here," the bald man breathed whisky fumes over Mendick. "What's Old Andy done that's so important? Everybody wants to see him now."

"What do you mean everybody?" Sturrock tapped his staff on the counter. "Who else wants to see him?"

The man shrugged. "Blessed if I know their names, there were a couple of shipmates of his asking for him. The three of them left arm in arm, friendly as you please." He lifted a greasy cloth from the bar and smeared it over a ring-marked table. "Mind you, Andy was three sheets in the wind by then. The old bugger was so far gone they near had to carry him out."

Mendick glanced at Sturrock. "What were these friends of his like? Describe them!"

Cleaning duties completed, the bald man shrugged. "One was a little fellow, slight, like. He never said a word. He had a big hat on . . ."

"A wide-awake hat?" Mendick asked.

"Aye, one of them. A stupid thing to wear in the evening, I thought." The man slumped on to a seat and glared at Mendick. "Anyway, does it matter? Andy's a useless wretch anyway. He just scrounges drink off everybody, scratches his belly and moans that song of his."

"And the other man? What was he like?" Sturrock took over the questioning.

The bald man scratched his head. "Do you know, I cannot recall, he was a nothing. I can't think of a single feature of him that stands out."

Mendick nodded. "That's our man," he said. "Now, in which direction did they go, and how long ago was it?"

"Oh, it was a fair time back now," the bald man said. "Before midnight anyway, maybe quarter of an hour before. They left in a dark coach. It was covered though, not an open gig like yours. Stupid things, gigs, in this climate . . ."

"Did you see which direction they travelled?" Mendick asked. "Hurry now, a man's life could be at stake here."

"That way. Upriver," the bald man jerked a thumb towards the west. "Which man's life might be at stake?"

The horse responded without enthusiasm as Sturrock cracked the reins, and they pulled off along Dock Street, heading west.

"Three hours ago?" Sturrock shook his head. "Old Andy will be long dead and cut into collops."

"We have to try. Whip up."

The horse was drooping but Sturrock applied the whip and it gained a little life, pulling the gig past the railway station and onto the Nethergate. Constable Deuchars stared when Mendick hailed him.

"Deuchars! Have you seen a dark coach pass by during your beat? It may be a brougham."

Deuchars pushed his hat up with his staff. "Aye, Sergeant, I've seen two tonight. One headed north, up Tay Street, the other went west."

"When was this? What hour?"

Deuchars checked the time on the Steeple clock. "The Tay Street coach was maybe an hour past, Sergeant. The other was long before that, maybe ten after midnight."

"That's our man." Mendick said. "Whip up, Sturrock! Perth Road, man!"

The mist thickened, great swathes rolling in from the sea to writhe around the villas of Perth Road and send clammy grey tentacles along the narrow streets on either side.

"Which way?" Sturrock asked.

"I have no idea, keep on the main road and look for a brougham."

They moved on, wheels grinding on the packed stones of the road and the lamps now throwing a mere glimmer of light in front of them. They passed the Sinderins: the Y junction that sent a road back to Dundee along the Hawkhill, and pushed on into thicker mist and with hope fading at every turn of the wheels. They passed the Western Cemetery and the mansions of Farrington Hall and Hazel Hall with the slopes of Balgay Hill steep but hidden to their right.

"Sergeant!" Sturrock spoke in a hoarse whisper. "What's that ahead?"

Mendick looked: there, dead ahead, was a square, bulky coach on the road, almost invisible in the mist. "Slow down and pull up beside it."

The brougham lay at a drunken angle: the spokes of its back nearside wheel splintered, the end of the axle almost touching the ground. The horse was head down in its harness and the nearside door swung lazily open. Mendick examined the coach. "That's our man," he said. "Look, this wheel has been damaged before. The iron rim is buckled and there's fresh paint on the spokes. Remember the killer crashed his coach after Grant's murder? He must have weakened the wheel then."

"Yes, Sergeant." Sturrock said. "But where is he now?"

"I think the murderer is a woman," Mendick said. He looked ahead; the road disappeared into the mist, empty as far as they could see. "They have left the carriage and gone on foot. Where does this road lead?"

Sturrock shrugged. "Perth, eventually" he said. "A woman? For God's sake, man . . ."

Mendick ignored the outburst. "What's before Perth? They will want somewhere quiet and isolated to murder

Cleghorn. Think man! You have the local knowledge here!" Mendick rapped the side of the coach with his knuckles. "Come on, think!"

"There's a quarry at Kingoodie, or the old Church of St Peter's at Invergowrie. That's long deserted now, nobody ever goes there." Sturrock nodded towards the unseen coast. "It's down that way."

Mendick lifted a scrap of cloth that lay amidst the clean straw on the floor of the coach. "What's this?"

"A handkerchief?" Sturrock hazarded. "It smells strange, if it is."

Mendick sniffed carefully and pulled away quickly. "There's something not right with this, Sturrock. My head is spinning." He tucked the cloth in his pocket. "We'll investigate further when we get back to the office. Now, take us to this church of yours."

"There's not much left in the horse," Sturrock warned.

"She can have a rest the minute I do! Get her moving!"

Another ten minutes and they were well outside Dundee with dark fields and rustling orchards on either side. Already there was the faintest glim of dawn in the east, a preliminary of a bright day to come, but the mist remained, shading everything in thin white moisture, altering the shapes of trees and houses, distorting sound and vision. They heard running water and Mendick ordered Sturrock to halt the gig at one end of a wooden bridge.

"If we cross that in the coach we will alert everyone," he said. A chance slant of wind brought the crash of waves and he shivered. To him, breaking surf always seemed sinister at night. He looked over the river, to where the ground rose in a wooded mound and on top, set amongst a yard of tumbled gravestones, hunched the remains of the church of St Peter.

"What a perfect spot for a murder." Mendick reached for his staff and swore when he remembered he had neither staff, cane nor revolver. He was completely unarmed, about to confront the most savage murderer he had ever known.

They guided the gig off the road and left the horse grazing beside the churning burn.

They headed through the tangle of bracken and weeds guarding the churchyard wall. Mendick swore as he tripped over a trailing branch of bramble and halted as a wail rose, high and shocking in the air. The sound raised the small hairs on the back of his neck and Sturrock stopped and lifted his staff.

"What in God's name was that?"

"I don't think God has anything to do with it, Sturrock. Elizabeth Elder was right, there were demons in that coach." The sound had been unlike anything he had heard before but he knew it was Andrew Cleghorn screaming in agony. "Come on man! Step out!" Wishing he had at least his staff, he plunged on through the grasping vegetation of the graveyard and towards the ruin that rose dark and forlorn in the mist. Even as he watched, a slight glow appeared, followed by two more. Yellow light reflected from the mist, highlighting the clutching branches of snarled trees.

The four walls of the church were intact but the roof was missing and the gables crumbling, drooping under the assault of wind and weather. The moan crawled through the graveyard like something dragged from the deepest pit and Mendick lifted a length of fallen wood from the ground. He tested it. About two feet long and as thick as his wrist, it was not much.

He paced the final few steps, feeling the sickness of tension mount inside him and Sturrock crashing beside him with as much finesse as the Brigade of Guards on field exercises. He could hear a man singing, the words obviously forced, there were frequent breaks punctuated by intense gasps of pain and obvious fear. Between the words, Mendick heard a woman's voice, sharp with menace. For a moment he thought he recognised the voice, but the idea was so ludicrous he dismissed it.

The song continued and he shuddered. It was Old Andy's voice and Old Andy's words, but rather than a rollicking song of the High Arctic, it now sounded like a funeral dirge.

"The whale was struck and away she went,
With a flourish of her tail
Alas, alas! And we lost four men,
But we did not catch the whale, brave boys,
But we did not catch the whale."

The tune was familiar – he had last heard it played in a comfortable drawing room – Sarah Leslie at the piano and her mother sitting embroidering at her side. Mendick shuddered. Were these respectable women involved in this horror? Or had China Jim – Adam Leslie – merely used them as an excuse for his slaughters. The next verse began:

"And when the news to the captain was brought,
He down his colours drew,
Crying, alas, alas, for my four pretty men,
The darlings of our crew, brave boys,
The darlings of our crew."

A hideous scream interrupted the song and was immediately cut short. Mendick glanced at Sturrock now even whiter than usual in the deep dark of the pre-dawn, and then he intoned the mantra Sergeant Restiaux had taught him in the teeming slum of the Holy Land.

Lord, I shall be very busy this day; I may forget thee, but do not forget me. Lord, I shall be very busy this day; I may forget thee, but do not forget me. Lord I shall . . .

Mendick spotted a doorway in the west gable, protected by a devil's web of semi-rotting vegetation and thorn-edged branches of bramble. Using his stick to push his way through, Mendick peered inside and immediately felt the nausea rising hot from his stomach.

The interior of the church no longer resembled sacred ground. Bright spring grass battled rampant nettles and leafless brambles, while tumbled stones protruded like lost souls bewailing their lack of redemption. Oil lamps sat on three of the four interior corners to create a devil's triangle of light.

"Oh, sweet God in Heaven."

Within the walls was an image he could never have imagined in his most tormented nightmare and in a moment that stretched to an eternity, and which he knew would always remain with him, he attempted to make sense of what he saw.

Old Andy was spread-eagled and tied upright between two vertical poles, his eyes bulging in pain and horror. He was stark naked and gagged with a filthy rag. Behind him were four men, all masked. While one sliced carefully at Andy's buttocks and thighs with a broad-bladed knife the others watched, their faces taut with concentration.

Sturrock touched his arm. "Oh, dear God! Oh, sweet

God in Heaven! This is a nightmare. No-one can be that cruel."

They could. Old Andy writhed in hideous agony as the knife-wielder eased the blade into his left buttock, sliced slowly downwards and handed a strip of bloody flesh to the man on his left, before repeating the procedure twice more. Holding their trophies, all three men walked around to face their victim.

Sturrock made to step forward but Mendick held him back. "Get round the other side. Hurry man! Signal once you are there."

The three men stood abreast and on a sign from the smallest they removed their masks.

"Oh, sweet Jesus!" Mendick tried to shake away the truth he had been trying to deny. Mrs Leslie stood in the centre, Louise on her left and Sarah on her right, all three chewing on raw human flesh, warm blood trickling from the sides of their mouths. For a long second, Mendick stared, and then Mrs Leslie began to speak, putting an intensity of emotion in her words.

"You were one of the boat's crew, Andrew. You were one of the men who swore to me you would look after my boy, and you were one of the men who chopped him up and ate him. You betrayed his trust, Andrew. How does it feel, Andrew? How does it feel to be eaten? How does it feel to have people cut slices off your haunches?"

His eyes bulging in horror and small mewling sounds escaping from behind the gag, Old Andy shivered and tried to pull back from the three women. Mrs Leslie displayed the strip of raw flesh to him and then delicately placed it in her mouth and began to chew. Warm blood ran down her face and dripped onto the already sodden ground below.

The veins in Old Andy's forehead were prominent as he strained backwards, his mouth working in a scream that his makeshift gag only partially stifled.

Mrs Leslie politely swallowed her raw meat before speaking. "If we leave you like this, Andrew, you'll bleed to death, but we won't allow that to happen. We want you to suffer as much as my son suffered. We will castrate and eviscerate you before you die. Justice must be done."

"Justice must be done," the other two women echoed, as if the words were a sacred mantra.

"Stop!" Without waiting for Sturrock's signal, Mendick stepped out from the shelter of the undergrowth. He held his length of wood and hoped he appeared more dangerous than he felt.

All three women spun round. Rather than fear, there was anger and surprise in their faces. Mrs Leslie pointed her knife at him in accusation.

"This is no affair of yours!"

Louise pointed to Mendick. "Mother is right! This is a family affair." Blood ran down the sides of her mouth and she held a chunk of thigh in her right hand.

"This is murder!" Mendick saw Sturrock make a belated appearance on the opposite side of the church. "This is not justice!"

Mrs Leslie pointed at him, blood dripping from her finger. "My son was murdered, Sergeant Mendick. Justice must be done."

Her scream took Mendick by surprise and he lifted his staff defensively as she pulled back her hand and lunged, not at him, but at Old Andy's wrinkled belly.

"No!" Mendick thrust his staff between the knife and its intended target. The force of the blow shocked him, but the blade thudded into the heavy wood and stuck, leaving Mrs Leslie screaming.

"He murdered my son! He killed my Jonathan!"

Beside her, Old Andy gyrated and squirmed, his eyes wide in terror as Mrs Leslie released her hold on the knife and advanced on him, still yelling her hatred.

"You murdered my son!" She slapped at him, raking her nails down the length of his face and his writhing body. "You killed my boy!"

"No!" Mendick grabbed her wrist to haul her back. "Stand back! Leave him be!"

Mrs Leslie's arm felt taut and as hard as a steel bar. She screamed, breaking free from his grip as easily as if he was a child, and attacked again, Louise and Sarah joining her. Together they punched, clawed and kicked at Old Andy's writhing body, all the while, horrible choking noises escaping from behind the gag. Mendick threw himself forward as Durward appeared, holding what appeared to be a metal ball on a chain. As Mendick lifted his length of wood, Durward smashed the ball against Mendick's forehead. Mendick staggered back and Durward followed, coiling the chain to bring the iron ball back to the palm of his hand.

"I've nothing against you, Mendick, but you can't interfere." Durward held his hand poised to unleash the ball again. "If you back off now, this will be over soon and you won't be hurt."

"We both know I can't do that," Mendick blinked as the pain in his head intensified. He lifted his stick, just as Sturrock appeared.

Without any hesitation Sturrock smashed his staff against the side of Durward's head. Durward staggered and Sturrock followed through, cracking the man's knuckles and knocking the iron ball from his hand.

Mendick left Sturrock to subdue Durward and ran to help Old Andy. He hauled Mrs Leslie from the writhing man and threw her onto the grass. She fell, shrieking, her knife flying behind her. Mendick knelt, pulled the handcuffs from his pocket and snapped them around her right wrist and left ankle. She screamed at him, blood frothing around her mouth as she urged her daughters on.

"Kill him! Justice must be done!"

Sarah and Louise slapped and scratched at Andy, working with a concentrated intensity that was terrifying to see. Yet beneath his disgust and horror, Mendick felt a twist of sympathy. Mrs Leslie had lost her only son on that whaleboat and she blamed the other members of the crew. He knew what it was like to lose a loved one. The death of her son had clearly unhinged Mrs Leslie's mind.

"Enough!" As Old Andy cringed under the attack, Mendick hauled Louise back. "End it, now!" He staggered at a sudden weight on his back, twisted his head around and saw Sarah, snarling into his ear. She pressed a pad to his mouth and held it there as he tried to wrestle free. Mendick felt strangely weak. He tried to shake Sarah off but instead saw the ground rising to meet him. The smell was strangely comforting as he slumped down. He saw Louise watch him fall with a twisted smile on her face. She lifted her mother's knife from the ground and stepped towards Old Andy. Mendick heard her speak but when he tried to move he felt as if he was swimming in treacle.

"Just you and me, Andrew," Louise said, softly. "Just you and me and justice."

"Louise!" Mendick tried to speak but his words were

slurred and slow. He tried to rise but had no control over his limbs. He half-rose and fell again. He could only watch as Louise stepped towards Old Andy. She held the knife underhand, ready for a groin thrust. Andy watched, wide-eyed in anticipation of unbearable agony.

"No, Miss Leslie. That won't do at all!" Sturrock appeared, bleeding heavily from an ugly wound in his forehead and Louise turned. She screamed something incomprehensible and slashed sideways but Sturrock blocked with his staff, twisted and smashed it against her arm. The knife fell, bounced once, stuck in the ground, and remained there, quivering.

"All right miss, enough of this." As Louise held her injured arm Sturrock held her in an armlock. "You keep silent like a good little cannibal, it's over now."

Left alone, Sarah lost all her defiance. She crumpled to the ground, shoulders heaving and sobs tearing her apart. Sturrock glanced at her and strode over to Mendick.

"Sergeant! Are you all right?" He lifted the pad, sniffed it and threw it away. "Filthy thing! That will be some oriental drug, no doubt." He held out a massive hand and hauled Mendick to his feet. "Up you get, Sergeant. Take deep breaths to clear your head."

The mist was beginning to clear, wafting across the ruins of the church and retreating to the Gowrie Burn. Already there was a sliver of silver above the Tay as the sun crept up, and the darkness of the sky was changing to grey; the song of a solitary blackbird pierced the morning.

"Now Jonathan will never be avenged!" Mrs Leslie writhed on the ground as she attempted to get closer to Old Andy. "Release me! Release me so I can finish the job!"

"Justice has not yet been done!" Louise spoke through her anguish, and clutched her injured arm. Sarah nodded, chewing fervently on a piece of Old Andy's flesh.

"It shall be, soon." Mendick controlled the shaking of his hand as he lifted Sturrock's official staff. "Mrs Adam Leslie, Sarah Leslie and Louise Leslie, I arrest you all on the charge of murder." He looked at Old Andy, bleeding within the confines of his bonds and added softly, "And cannibalism, God help us all."

CHAPTER TWENTY

"So, tell me what it was all about." Johanna stood with her feet sinking into the soft sand and tiny waves breaking around her ankles.

"It is not a pleasant story," Mendick said, "perhaps not for delicate ears."

Johanna lifted a stone and skimmed it across the water, counting the splashes, "Seven, eight, nine . . . if it is not for delicate ears, James, I suggest you do not mention it to any such. Now, tell me what it was all about, please."

Mendick saw the challenge in those green eyes and smiled. Here was no milk-and-water girl but a grown woman with a mind of her own. "As you wish, Johanna. You will remember that young Jonathan Grandison was a Greenman, a first voyager on Mr Gilbride's whaling ship *Rose Flammock*. You painted his picture, together with the whaleboat crew. Iain Grant was the harpooner, and there was Robert Milne, David Thoms, Andrew Souter and David Torrie."

"I remember," Johanna waved to John, who was running knee-deep in the water and laughing at the high, splashing spray. "I love it when he's happy," she said. "And I hate to think he will be going to school soon. Childhood is so short and so precious. We don't make enough of it as parents, don't you think?"

"I never had the chance to find out," Mendick said.

"No, no, of course not." Johanna placed her hand on

his arm. "I'm sorry, James. I did not mean to open old hurts. Pray continue."

"Before they left Dundee, Mrs Leslie, the mother of Jonathan Grandison by her first marriage, made the five members of the boat's crew swear to look after her son. They all swore a solemn oath and she rewarded them with five sovereigns each. That's good money for a sea labourer."

"I know, James." Johanna gave her quiet smile. "I was not always married to a wealthy man."

They began to walk along the edge of the sea, hands touching slightly, and Johanna turning constantly to watch the antics of her son.

"They sailed in *Rose Flammock*, in early spring of 1842, bound for the Davis Straits whale fishery. They were off Cape Farewell at the southern tip of Greenland when the master sighted a whale and sent out the whaleboats. As you know, Jonathan Grandison was in Iain Grant's boat. All was fine for a while and then a fog closed in, as happens in those latitudes. All the whaleboats were lost in the fog."

Johanna stopped to lift an intricate shell and show it to John who looked for a moment then returned to his private world in the waves.

"All of them were lost?" She asked. "But I know Alex Grant brought his back safely. He was a hero in Dundee."

"One boat was lost with all hands, one was picked up by another whaling ship and Grant brought his back to *Rose Flammock* after two weeks in the Arctic. He brought all the men back alive except Jonathan Grandison who had died of exposure." Mendick darted into the waves and caught John as he stumbled. He held the small, warm body for a moment and then put the boy down, aware that Johanna was watching him very closely.

"One minor detail was omitted, Johanna. Jonathan Grandison did not die of exposure, he was murdered and eaten by the other men in the boat." Mendick waited for the words to sink in as he watched John splash away into the long surf.

"There were rumours," Johanna said at last, "but I did not want to believe them." She was quiet for a while as they continued to walk along the beach. "That poor boy." She looked towards John and Mendick knew she was vowing never to let her son go to sea. "Do you know how it happened?"

"I do now," Mendick said. "The boat was completely cut off from the ship, the men could see only the fog, and when that cleared they were surrounded by brash ice with some bergy bits – like small ice floes – and no sign of the ship anywhere."

Johanna watched as John ran after a small flock of oyster-catchers, clapping his hands. The birds lifted, piping at him, flew a few yards and returned to the beach. "They are so innocent at that age, aren't they? How old was Jonathan?"

"He was fourteen," Mendick said. "Just a boy."

"Just a boy." Johanna watched her son and Mendick knew she was picturing him in an open boat out in the Arctic, surrounded by icebergs.

"I asked Old Andy and Durward, or Andrew Couper as his real name may be, what had happened and they both gave me their versions of the story. They were not quite the same, but close enough. After a few days the men were losing hope, they were suffering from frostbite and hunger. They decided they should kill and eat one of their number in order to save the lives of the others."

"And Jonathan was chosen?" Johanna asked.

"They drew lots," Mendick said, "but it was fixed and Jonathan lost. According to both men he cried and pleaded for his life, but they held him down. They stripped Jonathan and ate the flesh from his thighs and . . ." Mendick looked at Johanna. "Well, they murdered and ate him."

"So my friend Iain Grant was not a hero then." Johanna looked sad. "He was such a gentleman, too."

"Perhaps we all have some measure of darkness within us," Mendick said. "But we do not realise it until we face real danger. When *Rose* came back to Dundee most of that boat's crew left the sea. Only Iain Grant continued, but the secret remained until Durward found a job as Leslie's coachman and handyman. He had not known Jonathan was Mrs Leslie's son of course, she had changed her name after her second marriage."

Johanna waded into the sea and picked up John. She carried him onto the beach and held him as they walked. "That must have come as a huge shock to them both."

"I expect so, but Durward got drunk one night and told what was really a shipboard secret. Mrs Leslie sent him into Gilbride's to find the addresses of the boat's crew and . . . " Mendick shrugged, "once she discovered the truth, she planned her revenge on the men who had, in her mind, betrayed and murdered her son." Mendick watched as Johanna held John even closer and kissed him on his forehead.

"And Durward helped?" Johanna walked on, her feet in the sea and her arms wrapped closely around her son.

"He did. He found the men, Sarah Leslie rendered them senseless with chloroform and all three Leslie women butchered them." Mendick pulled out his pipe and stuffed tobacco into the bowl. He watched a brig batter its way past the sandbars with half a dozen hands struggling along the yards and wondered how best to ask Johanna his question.

"So where did China Jim come into it?" Johanna put John back on the sand and watched him scamper away towards the oyster-catchers.

"China Jim was Mr Leslie: Adam James Leslie. He was not involved in the murders at all." Mendick said. "When he married Mrs Leslie, he moved into her house. He was a small crockery merchant and he could not make enough money to keep her and her family in the style they were used to, so he turned to crime. In his case crime meant whisky smuggling."

"It's sad," Johanna said. "A sad story."

"All murders are sad," agreed Mendick. "They are always sordid, horrible affairs, usually involving people who just can't cope with their lives or who have too much to drink."

They turned around and headed back to Unicorn Cottage, the sun glinting silver from the sea and highlighting the fields of Fife. Johanna reached out and took hold of his hand. Her grip was strong. They did not look at each other but he was aware of every movement she made, every slightly-emphasised swing of her hips, every turn of her head and every loose strand of her hair. He measured every step of their journey, sick with the bittersweet, agonised pleasure of her company yet knowing it might be the last time he ever saw her.

They reached the gates of Unicorn Cottage and he had to speak.

"Johanna," the words were stilted in his own ears. "I have something to ask you."

Her smile was as beautiful as ever, with that little dimple forming at the left side of her mouth. She raised her eyebrows. "I know. You've been thinking about how to say it," she allowed her eyelids to dip, "whatever *it* may be."

Mendick closed his mind to the memory of Emma lying in her deathbed. "When I go back to London," he said. "I'd like you to come with me." He held up his hand as Johanna began to speak. "Now, hear me out please, before you say anything."

"Carry on," Johanna looked out to sea. She kept her hand tight in his.

"You are in a loveless marriage, Johanna, married to a man you hardly ever see, yet alone speak to. He ignores young John here. I would be with you every evening unless I was on duty, and I would be as good a father to John as I could be." He saw her slowly shaking her head, her smile more wistful than he liked. "It would not be perfect, Johanna; I do not make as much money as Gordon, and I never will, but I do love you . . ." he stopped as she placed two fingers on his lips.

"Hush, James. Please. You are only hurting us both." She was shaking her head, "I will make this short, James. I cannot go back to London with you."

"Johanna," Mendick saw the deep sadness in her eyes reflecting his own. Pain tore horizontally across his chest. "I will take good care of you and I am growing fond of the boy."

"No, James." Johanna said again. "You are correct in a lot of what you say. Gordon and I do not love one another. I do believe you love me. I truly do, James, and I know you would be a good husband."

"But?" Mendick said, "you are about to say, 'but,'" he forced a smile.

"I am," she said, "and it is a large 'but'." She placed her hands on his arms and swivelled him around to face John. "There it is. John. My son."

"John?" Mendick frowned, "I will look after John. I like the little tyke. There's no 'but' there, Johanna."

She was shaking her head again, with that soft, twisted smile he had learned meant bad news. "Yes, there is, James. What you propose is beautiful, but it is not practical. Please, please, James, think about the practicalities here . . ." For an instant her face fell and he saw deep pain in her eyes, "Oh, God. I hate being practical sometimes," then the smile masked her sadness once more. "James, as a police sergeant, how much will you earn . . . no. Don't tell me you might make lieutenant some time. I know you have the capability, but how long would that take? Five years? Ten?"

"Perhaps five," Mendick agreed cautiously.

"In five years John will be ten. Gordon will send him to school in two years time. That will be hard for John and hard for me, but it will prepare him for the best possible start in life. That's what money does, James." Johanna watched her son. "I will do anything for him James, anything to make his life secure, and that takes money. With Gordon he will go to the best schools, get the best education and inherit a great deal of wealth, property and position."

Mendick felt the tear in his chest deepen. "I see." He looked away.

"James . . ." she put a soft hand on his chin and turned his face towards her. "Please try to understand. Don't hate me, James."

"I could never hate you," Mendick tried to smile. "Of course I understand, your son means everything to you."

Johanna nodded slowly. "When you told me about Jonathan I pictured John in that situation . . ." she sighed. "With Gordon's money behind him he will never know danger, or real fear."

"And us?" Mendick said, "What about us?"

She gripped his hand again, squeezed it hard and slowly withdrew, allowing her fingers to drift away from his. "There can never be an 'us', James."

The pain twisted inside him. A broad band that compressed his chest and tore him apart from the inside. He did not want a life without Johanna: he could not face the world without hearing her gurgling laugh or seeing the flick of her hair across her face, or the sway and roll of her hips or the steel wisdom of her eyes. And yet, even as he fought the agony, he knew that same practical wisdom had gone right to the heart of the matter and found the truth. John was central to her life and Gordon could give him a better future than he ever could.

Johanna was right, and in that moment Mendick realised he was more like China Jim or Mrs Leslie than he had realised. While Adam Leslie hid his criminal activities behind the façade of a respectable businessman, and Mrs Leslie concealed her abominations by playing the mother and wife, he was guilty of courting another man's wife whilst acting as a guardian of law, order and justice. Many people pretended to be something they were not and in each case the motive for deception was similar. Adam Leslie turned to crime out of love for his wife and family. Mrs Leslie murdered and cannibalised out of a warped love for her son, and he – James Mendick – loved and would always love a woman he could never have.

He watched as she walked away from him, straight-backed and proud. She entered Unicorn House and did not look back and Mendick held the dream as long as he was able. Johanna would always be with him, locked inside his memories, but his life was one of duty, not tenderness. Life, he knew, could never be that kind. If he held onto that dream he would only hurt himself.

With her pennant sagging in the July heat, the Dundee Perth and London steamer slogged to her berth in the Thames. Sergeant James Mendick of Scotland Yard jerked his handcuffs so that his prisoner walked beside him. "Back home, Thatcher; say hello to London. You'll soon be on your way to somewhere even sunnier."

"Bugger you, Mendick." Thatcher rattled the handcuffs. "There's not a jail in Van Diemen's Land that can hold me."

They stepped onto the quay and pushed through the crowds. It was good to be back in London. Although his memories of Dundee no longer festered, Mendick thought of Johanna and tried to ignore the new tearing ache within him.

"Mendick?" The man was in civilian clothes and his large nose betrayed French ancestry. "You managed to get back then."

"Restiaux," Mendick shook his hand. "Good to see you again."

"I have something of yours," Sergeant Restiaux fished in his pocket and produced a silver watch. "I took it from a seaman on a smuggling sloop."

Mendick held the watch secure. "Thank you, Restiaux, I value this. Emma gave me it." He fell into step beside Restiaux with Thatcher stumbling between them. The steamer would be returning to Dundee soon, back to Johanna.

Malcolm Archibald was born in Edinburgh and holds a history degree from Dundee University and a Masters in Urban History from Dundee University. Malcolm has worked as a lecturer and in historical research as well as in a variety of other jobs.

He writes mainly historical fiction with the occasional venture into folklore and believes that history should be accessible to everyone. A winner of The Dundee Book Prize 2005, he has published several novels with us. Among the most notable are Powerstone, Mother Law and The Darkest Walk. Malcolm lives in Moray with his wife Cathy.

Books by Malcolm Archibald

www.malcolmarchibald.com

Bridges, Islands and Villages of the Forth: Lang Syne Press, 1990

Scottish Battles: Chambers, 1990

Scottish Myths and Legends: Chambers, 1992

Scottish Animal and Bird Folklore: St Andrew Press, 1996

Across the Pond: Chapters from the Atlantic: Whittles, 2001

Soldier of the Queen: Fledgling Press, 2003

Whalehunters, Dundee and the Arctic Whalers: Mercat, 2004

Whales for the Wizard:Polygon Press, 2005, Dundee Book Prize 2005

Horseman of the Veldt: Fledgling Press, 2005

Selkirk of the Fethan: Fledgling Press, 2005

Aspects of the Boer War: Fledgling Press, 2005

Mother Law: A Parchment for Dundee: Fledgling Press, 2006

Pryde's Rock: Severn House, 2007

Powerstone: Fledgling Press, 2008

The Darkest Walk: Fledgling Press, 2011

A Sink of Atrocity: Crime of 19th Century Dundee: Black and White Publishing, 2012

Glasgow: The Real Mean City: True Crime and Punishment in the Second City of Empire: Black and White Publishing, 2013